SHADOW ME

IMMORTAL VICES AND VIRTUES: SHADOW SHIFTER BONDS

BOOK TWO

ANNIE ANDERSON

For every black cat girlie.
I found your golden retriever.
He's a little grumpy and absolutely filthy, but I don't
think you'll mind.

She is water. Soft enough to offer life. Tough enough to drown it away.

—RUPI KAUR

PROLOGUE

"Answer me, girl. What have you done to my father?"

Dried blood crusted my knuckles as I clenched my fists and teeth, refusing to give the goddess the satisfaction of hearing my answer. I'd already tried explaining myself. Hell, I'd tried everything, but she just wasn't listening. I would be damned if she heard me beg.

Her father had heard enough of that already, and it had done me no good.

It had done him no good, either.

His shriveled corpse was lying on the banks of the river right next to us, but she refused to believe the truth. I'd killed him, plain and simple. Not on purpose, of course, but I'd done it all the same, and there was no bringing him back.

Her brother planted his foot on my neck, cutting off my air, his face just as cold and cruel as his father's had been.

The power I'd stolen coursed through my veins as I tried to suck in a breath. Chains made of light tethered me to the shore as I surveyed their wrath. My parents' bloodied bodies were nothing but pieces of burnt flesh next to the rushing river. My sister and her children were nothing but ashes on the wind. An entire herd gone in their rage.

Thunder rumbled in the distance as lightning streaked across the sky, and the siblings ducked as if the heavens would open up and punish them. If there was justice, it would. Someone would make them pay.

Near death and hurtling closer to the end, I refused to break. Not for her, not for her brother, and not for the god that had invaded my home and had stolen... *everything*.

"You heard my sister, wretch," he demanded, pointing his golden arrow at my face. "Answer her."

I wasn't sure how I was supposed to answer her with his foot on my windpipe, but it didn't matter. I couldn't convince them of the facts right in front of their faces.

I'd killed a god and stolen his power.

And now I was paying the price.

"Banishment," the goddess crooned, a wicked smile curling her lip as she twirled her golden trident. "An eternity in Hell for your crimes should be sufficient. That is if you even survive the trip."

Her brother's smile was worse, reminding me of their father's brutality. His foot lifted from my neck as he joined hands with his sister, their whispered word opening a dark swirl of a portal. The visage beyond was no worse than this bloody beach, and it was as good a place to die as any.

I would have felt fear had I been smart, but all that was left was numbness. Their family had taken everything from me. What was banishment in the face of that? How could Hell be any worse than my family dead on this shore?

The goddess waved her arm, and instantly, I was airborne, my chains breaking as I hurtled toward that swirling vortex. The darkness swallowed me up and spat me out on another beach in another realm on another world.

She was right. The trip nearly did kill me.

But I would soon learn the meaning of an eternity.

Tartarus wasn't Hell.

No, the Hell lived in me.

CHAPTER 1

STYX

In the eons of dreaming up this plan, I had been under the impression there would be a hell of a lot more killing involved.

For the first hundred years of my sentence, Tartarus seemed like the prison it was always meant to be. With no sun and only twin moons, the climate was harsh and the landscape no better. Missing were the forests and softness of my homeland. Gone was the oasis of my river.

Until Caius arrived, I'd had no purpose other than to be the murderer they'd said I was.

Killer.

Traitor.

Thief.

Only two of those were right. By definition,

kelpies were born to be killers, and without a doubt, I was one. We were a cautionary tale told to wandering men.

Don't go by that river.

Don't step a toe in that lake.

And whatever you do, don't try to steal a ride from any horse.

But I didn't kill indiscriminately, and I wasn't a thief on purpose. That was just the luck of the draw. Had a god not tried to kill me, I would have never been a thief at all.

A traitor, though? Not while I had breath in my lungs.

As the years continued to scream by, I forgot about my home. I forgot the scent of flowers in bloom, forgot the color of the lilies that were always at the banks of my river, forgot the way the sun used to kiss my skin.

Forgot the faces of my family.

Their deaths, though, I remembered those well enough.

After thousands of years, I barely felt anything at all except for the mounting hatred that had been with me since the day I'd landed here—a hatred that kept me breathing.

I had devoted thousands of years to my king. I

was an adviser, an assassin, a shadow. Someone who could slip in and out undetected and handle what needed finesse. As a member of his inner circle, I knew more about him than most, which was why I had been watching him more closely as of late.

Caius deserved his revenge and so did I.

Betrayed by those he loved the most, his soul had been split in two. The primordial god had been stripped of most of his power, and we'd been on our way to retrieve what had been taken from him. Granted, that meant we'd be killing the guardian of his soul, but really, what was that in the face of thousands of years in prison?

I'd certainly killed for less.

The ward had broken on our prison, allowing some of the power he'd been denied to flow back to him. It had been just enough to open a portal—just enough to find our way back. And as our feet hit the other side, a pull had dragged him—and by extension us—to the universe's ultimate cock block to revenge.

Caius had a mate.

Primordial gods weren't supposed to have mates, which was why Caius, Oberon, and I had gotten on so well for so long. None of us wanted an attachment like that. But that was before the Fates decided to fuck with my king in the worst way possible. He'd fallen head over heels like a chump, and now I was stuck guarding the very portal that I had been waiting thousands of years for, all so he could try and woo the mate who didn't want him.

Who had rejected him.

Who held the other half of his soul.

My brain was slowly catching up to all that had transpired in just the last few hours.

It had started like any other day. Except... I'd known something was up. Caius had been having visions of the guardian more and more in the last few weeks. It was enough for me to worry. So while he stared at the dark waves near my river, naturally, I watched his back. And then the ward broke, and we'd traveled here—this hodgepodge of a place with no discernible leader and no rules.

The guardian had been dying, Caius' soul—his freedom—so close and he'd just... healed her, saved her, claimed she was his mate. And now I didn't know what we were going to do.

You've waited this long, girl. You can wait just a little bit longer.

But the thought of another day so close to freedom and not tasting it? That was pure torture.

I wanted revenge... justice... *something* to show

for the years I'd been trapped. I wanted the war to start. It had been the only thing I'd had to look forward to, the only bright spot in a sea of nothingness.

And now that hope, that drive was all gone.

And an extra slap in the face? Oberon and I were relegated to guard duty.

Don't kill anyone. Caius said to keep them safe.

Didn't Caius know that *I* was the danger to them?

Didn't he know that keeping people safe had never been in my job description?

After all the years he'd been my friend, didn't he know I had never been able to protect *anyone*, even when it mattered the most?

Grinding my teeth, I swept my gaze over the empty park, the single moon so much darker than Tartarus ever was. I didn't need the moon to see, but it was the principle of the thing. This foreign realm looked nothing like the Earth I'd left and nothing at all like the place I'd called home. The waning moon hung high in the sky, casting a paltry glow over the ruined city.

I could tell something awful had happened here not too far in the past and what this place might have been at the height of civilization. There had been much repair, but some places had been left to their ruin, moldering until there would soon be nothing left. It was an incomplete patchwork of new and old, ruined and restored, and I hated every inch of it.

The portal cleaved through a giant fountain, the water calming me slightly as I stared at the giant broken arch that seemed to watch our every move. And there was this itch—to move, to run, to... I wasn't quite sure, but the pull wrenched at my insides like the hand of an enemy.

A growl worked its way up my throat as my fingers itched to unsheathe the metal rods I used to keep my hair pinned up. Those rods were weapons hidden in plain sight, a way to channel the power I'd stolen far too many years ago to count. I didn't *need* them, but they helped harness some of the wildness of it.

"That is the third growl in the last hour," Oberon grumped, his black eyes scanning the darkness for threats. "Either say what's on your mind or zip it so I can listen."

Thunder rumbled in the distance, and he rolled his eyes. "Now don't throw a hissy fit. It doesn't suit you. Where's the stoic assassin I know and love? I think we left her back on Tartarus."

Yes, I was the cause of said thunder, and if he didn't quit being a dickhead, he'd have a real problem on his hands. Though, considering we'd been friends for longer than I could remember, I highly doubted I would strike him with lightning anytime soon.

Especially, since the fucker could probably harness it and use it against me—not that we tried before. The last thing I needed was to accidentally steal power again.

Especially power like his.

No, Oberon knew to use only real swords on me. And while I *could* steal those, at least I wouldn't be saddled with them for the rest of eternity.

"There's not going to be a war. You know that, right?" I hissed, crossing my arms over my chest just so I wouldn't punch something. "No great battle, no revenge, thousands of years in prison, and it's all down the drain because he has a fucking mate. I was supposed to be killing people by now."

Uncharitable, sure, but that didn't make my words any less true. After Caius kidnapped her cousin—a twist even I didn't understand—his *mate* had no other option but to follow him into our world. Said mate had passed through the portal no more than an hour ago, and I had been spiraling ever since.

Did I want Caius happy? Yes, but shadow shifters were a different breed. And Caius? He was the king of us all.

"Tell me how you really feel," he muttered, sliding a smirk my way. How he could be so chipper about this, I didn't know. Out of all of us, Oberon had been betrayed in the worst way by the person he'd loved the most.

Mates were for other people.

Not. Us.

And yes, I might have been throwing a tantrum, but if he wanted to know, I'd tell him exactly how I felt.

"Primordial gods don't get mates for a reason. You and I both know there's no way to kill Caius. So what's going to happen when his mate dies? And she will eventually. Is he going to go mad? Is he going to try to follow her into the abyss? And that *is* the best-case scenario."

Because the worst-case scenario involved collapsing entire worlds and praying that he didn't take the entire universe down with him. And that was *if* she accepted him.

We were fucked.

So.

Fucked.

Then again, if he did take the universe down with him, I knew a god or two that I wouldn't mind getting the axe.

That said nothing about the way the darkness of Tartarus followed Caius into this world. Inky fingers reached out from the portal, turning the grass itself black—the entire reason we were guarding the damn thing in the first fucking place. No one could touch it, no one could cross it—not without changing forever.

Our world did something to people.

It changed them.

Every single person who went to Tartarus—no matter what they were before—became something else once they crossed the barrier. Something darker. Something more.

If we didn't want this realm filled with shadow shifters, death magic users, or a little bit of both, we had to keep everyone away.

Fucking guard duty.

"You saw how the portal was reaching for him. We're supposed to keep the portal safe, keep people from crossing, but we've already failed once with that dipshit of a dog and now…"

And now I didn't know what I was supposed to do.

A family member of Caius' mate had touched the portal, and now he was a yappy little *yakima* of an animal that wouldn't feed a *warzog*. *Mmmm, yakimas.* They were a black potato-like plant that was exceptional pared with Tartarean beer.

It did not help that I was starving.

Yes, for the first century, Tartarus was a prison, but it had never been Hell. Despite the climate, we had made a society for ourselves. And while the worst of the worst still resided there, the rest of the poor souls stuck on our little world were regular people just trying to live their lives.

And I had been so eager to get to this stupid little world that I hadn't even considered us not sticking to the plan, hadn't even thought of what could happen if Caius didn't recover his soul.

I'd been stupid and short-sighted, which wasn't like me. Plus, I'd skipped breakfast.

"Any more bad news swimming around that brain of yours, or is there a ray of moonlight in there somewhere?"

For the moment, I was tapped out on the negative—other than zero revenge, zero killing, and the possible decimation of life as we knew it while I was stuck on guard duty.

Thunder cracked in the sky, his patronizing tone piling on the irritation. "No, that about sums it up."

Oberon sliced his gaze to me. "There is a perfectly good body of water right there," he chided, pointing at the river just up ahead. "Go for a swim, clear your head. Eat something—or someone—I don't give a shit. You know how you are when you don't eat. I'm not dealing with a cranky super-charged kelpie just because you've missed a meal. Shoo."

He waved me away, practically shoving me toward the river. "I've got this."

There were few people in this world—or any other, for that matter—that I trusted. Luckily, Oberon was one of them.

Still didn't mean I would bring him back any food, the ass.

And even as I headed toward the water, that pull, that awareness had me on edge.

Something—or someone—was out there, and they were just as dangerous to me as a predator.

I just hoped they didn't find me first.

CHAPTER 2

CORVIN

If I heard one more word about the portal opening up in the middle of Crossroads, I was going to set fire to something.

All I'd heard over the last two weeks was my pack's rumblings about the damn thing. It was "The new portal this" and "The new portal that" and "Are the Houses coming?" and "What's going to happen?"

All questions I didn't have an answer for.

All questions I needed the answer for.

It was enough to drive me insane.

Not being able to answer them reminded me of New York all over again. I'd thought I could work my way up the Syndicate ranks, that I could be the big man there, that I could protect the people under me. All I'd managed to do was fail so spectacularly that the city as a whole didn't want me. I had unceremoniously gotten the boot from the brand-new queen and her mates—one of which included my half-brother Ronan.

And I couldn't even blame them.

I had chosen the wrong side, believed the wrong person, trusted the wrong parent. Just thinking of my mother made me gnash my teeth. Laena had always looked out for herself and herself alone, not even bothering to raise me at all. As a child, I'd thought it was because my father could teach me more than she could about being what I was. As an adolescent, she was the ethereal being of fire and light, mysterious in a way that made me wish she wanted to know me. After my father died, I'd sought her out, trusted her without question, and now I was paying the price.

Now I knew that she'd used my father to make her longtime love jealous. And that man had betrayed my trust and had broken every deal he'd ever made. Luckily, Taron Rose was dead, but I had no doubt that my mother would find another poor sucker to leech from.

At least it wasn't me.

Fixing my mistakes had nearly killed me, the last thing I needed was a reminder of my own failures.

After my exile, I'd made my way down to Crossroads, the last true No Man's Land on the continent. Sure, Portland had one, but there were so many Houses surrounding it, that it was barely the Wild West it claimed itself to be.

Crossroads was everything I'd wanted in a new home.

There was no House to answer to, no rules, and more outcasts like me that wanted to make it a real home. I was just getting my feet under me, just carving out a place for myself. Hell, my new pack was barely six months old. The last thing I needed was all the Houses coming to Crossroads and causing a problem.

And they would, too.

Uncertainty weighed heavily on my shoulders as my claws dug into the stone outcropping of what used to be the old courthouse. No one used it anymore, the portal opening in Portland changing the landscape of this country faster than any world war ever could.

Half a century ago, humans were the dominant

species of this realm. Once the supernatural was exposed, that quickly went by the wayside, their kind dying out faster than the dodo. Lines were drawn, territories claimed, and soon our world divided into Houses. Nine Houses ran the majority of the land and sea, the last one created just a year ago after the Syndicates of New York were dismantled, making something better than it was before. And while there were plenty of portals around the world, a new one brought changes, brought unrest, and I'd had about enough of that to last a lifetime.

Which was probably why I was staring at said portal, contemplating our new future, glad my shifted form could blend in on a building such as this.

It was bad enough that I had been drawn to this very spot every single day since it had opened, but worse?

I wanted—no I *needed*—to get closer.

It wasn't just the uncertainty and unrest that a portal such as this brought, it was a scratching in my brain, a needling that prodded me closer and closer to the river. It was as if I needed to touch the portal with my very own hands, see it up close, know it for what it was. And even though I could see it from here, my legs ached to pull me closer.

A pair of booted feet landed nearby, their thuds against the stone heralding the arrival of my second. Knox and I had beaten each other bloody in a bar on my first night in Crossroads—the bastard more formidable in a fight than I'd given him credit for. Granted, I had stolen his beer, but it had been an honest mistake.

We'd been friends ever since, and he'd been the first person to join my fledgling pack.

Now we had ten members with new ones scouted every day. It wasn't what I'd had but it was a start.

"I knew I'd find you here," Knox grumbled, taking a seat near my perch on the ledge. Heights didn't bother him, and neither did my precarious position.

Like me, he could fly.

Unlike me, his shifted form did not blend, and his rarity had left him without a family until I came along. Typically, I blended in with the masonry, my stony skin taking on a chameleonlike camouflage with my surroundings. But this wasn't the first time this week he'd found me here, nor would it be the last if this pull in my gut didn't let up.

My thick serpent tail thrashed, his words annoying me far more than they should. We were in the middle of taking over the train lines of the city, and he needed me. Of course he would seek me out.

But this place was nothing like New York. There were no lines drawn, no territories, no order. It was spread out and complete chaos.

And the people who thought of themselves as the ruling class were nothing more than a hodge-podge of cells with such little influence from their "leader" it wasn't even funny.

All we needed was enough force, and the lines would be ours.

It helped that the fuckers who "ran" them were a bunch of vamps with barely half a century under their belts and less sense than the gods gave a rock. Why else would they be attacking shifters like there wouldn't be consequences? Why else would they be terrorizing whole communities, shaking them down for currency?

I'd fucked people up for a lot less back home, and I wasn't afraid of a fight.

What I was afraid of was bisecting the broken fountain, the swirling vortex heralding another change, another trial, another thing to overcome.

What else is new?

I wasn't a big talker in my shifted form, the lion-like jowls ill-suited for the English language, and it wasn't like gargoyles were known for their eloquence, anyway. But if Knox needed me, I wouldn't abandon him. Still, the thought of shifting back didn't sit well, so I settled in to wait. Knox would tell me what was on his mind eventually.

"Penny and Jude have been scoping out the stations near the portal. It seems like there's been an uptick in not good activity there. If we want to oust those fuckwads, we need to do it soon. Otherwise, some poor shmuck is going to get killed. Jude already had to take an arm off one of them 'cause they were hassling some poor pixie youngling. You know it's only going to get worse."

If the pixies in Crossroads were anything like the ones in New York, I seriously doubted Jude had needed to lift a finger. Pixies traveled in packs—vicious, bloodthirsty, violent ones that would fuck you up in a heartbeat if you so much as looked at them wrong.

Then again, a lot of things were not like home.

I needed to get off my ass and do something. Watching the portal do fuck all wouldn't make my pack any safer. It wouldn't get me more members. It wouldn't change a damn thing unless I made sure my people were insulated when the Houses came calling.

Wings ruffling, I nodded in the direction of the Gateway Station, the one closest to the portal and the one with the biggest problems. The Crimson Roses were a massive thorn in my side, and if they were harming children, it was past time to do something about it. And if they had just gotten shown up by members of my pack, they would come in droves to pick a fight.

A fight I would be all too happy to give them.

Shoving from the ledge, I let the wind carry me for as long as it could before I picked up speed. The sheer weight of gargoyles meant we shouldn't be able to fly. As big as I was, I should be hurtling to the ground like the stone my shifted form was made of. But the magic in my very being flipped off gravity and every other law of physics, allowing me to soar through the night sky.

The beauty of gargoyles?

We were rare.

I'd only known of one other and that was my own father. Like me, his shifted form was a chimera, complete with ram's horns, a lion's head and body, eagle wings, and a serpent's tail. We were strong and fast, protected from harm while shifted, and full of venom for our enemies.

And yet, all of that hadn't saved my father from betrayal.

It hadn't saved me, either.

But this place was different. I wasn't trying to take over an entire syndicate. No, I was just carving out a small place for shifters like me—with no home, no pack. A place that meant we had support, a family—even if it was not of blood, but one we made.

A gaping hole in the roof of the station meant my arrival was unencumbered by trying to fit through the paltry doorways. Penny and Jude paced the length of the platform, her large black wolf form and his giant grizzly bear both seemed too big for the space. And that scant remainder was quickly taken up by my shifted form.

It seemed I'd arrived before shit could go sideways.

A loose grouping of men stood on the other platform across the tracks, their leather jackets displaying their patches like the motorcycle clubs of old. They were younger than I'd thought they'd be, but that didn't make my apprehension ease one bit. If anything, their lack of years only made them dumber, less predictable, less calculated.

A young vampire might be weaker, but I knew better than to underestimate one.

As soon as Knox's feet hit the platform, the first vampire sprang into action, flying across the tracks in a single leap. I wouldn't say I was proud of what I did next, but in the interest of efficiency, I took to the air, catching the young vamp before he could ever touch the ground. My jaws locked around his skull, his pitiful squeak short-lived before my head shook, ripping his skull from his body in one single bite.

Everyone froze—the vamps and my pack alike. Everyone except for me. Thrashing my tail, I spat the head back at the dwindling group, the squelch of it hitting the chest of his frozen friend. Those same friends who hadn't so much as followed him into battle. The same ones that were blending into the shadows as they ran for their lives. The few who remained watched in horror as their friend's body still twitched, his nerve endings slowly realizing that death had already come and gone.

The shift back was quick, the blood remaining in my mouth, falling down my chest. I'd learned long ago that when it came to shows of strength, the bloodier the better. My crimson smile made the remaining vamps flinch, the swiftness of their leader's death making them hesitate.

"You and yours aren't welcome here anymore," I growled, wiping at the blood on my lips. "The lines don't belong to you—they never did. Find another mode of transportation, or the next time, it'll be your head in my jaws."

I didn't necessarily think that this was the last time we would clash. The Crimson Roses weren't known for their strategy, but I had hoped that it would buy us enough time to increase our numbers just enough to keep people safe.

Pale and shaking, the last vamp backed away, his eyes never leaving me.

Yeah, he'd be a problem.

"Stay here. Make sure none of them come back. Give me a call should it go sideways," I ordered my second, holding out my hand for the travel bag he usually kept for me.

Knox gave me a hesitant nod as he handed the bag over. Neither of us wanted to start a war, but it would quickly turn into one if we weren't careful.

Grumbling, I tore the bag open, finding a thin pair of joggers and ripping them up my legs. I didn't like being underground, and the sooner I could get out of here, the better. I soon found the broken escalator, taking the steps two at a time, the air filling my lungs as the pull of the portal drew me in.

I ached to see it, to know why it called to me so, and soon my feet cut through the park, taking me closer to exactly where I wanted to be.

It was the sound of panicked barking that had me picking up speed, and before I knew it, I was running, the fountain and portal quickly coming into view as I cleared the tree line.

A woman stood in between the portal and a yapping mutt of a dog, accompanied by a man who kept trying to edge around her toward the swirling vortex. Her dark tresses fell down her back in silky waves, a pair of thin metal rods in her fists.

But it wasn't just the hair that had me freezing in my tracks.

No, it was the way she commanded the crackling air around her, the way she stood tall and straight as an arrow, her feet planted wide as if she had been, and would always be, ready for battle.

Thunder rumbled in the sky as inky clouds swirled over the coming dawn, but none of that took away from the way her golden skin almost glowed with power, the way her eyes lit with it, the way her body screamed it.

"Shut *up*, Nog," she commanded, her voice just

as formidable as the thunder, her eyes sparking with lightning as the dog finally zipped his trap. "I don't care why you want to cross. It's not going to happen. Don't make me ask you twice."

Funny, I didn't recall her asking them a first time, but who was I to argue? It wasn't even my fight—even though I'd gladly make it so. Still, the man tried to sneak around her while her attention was diverted to the black corgi at her front.

Before I could even move, a bolt of lightning cracked through the air, reaching the rod in her hand before arching out, exploding at the man's feet, her body not even turning as the man at her left fell backward, scrambling away from her power.

Still as a statue, I was in awe—absolutely stunned at the beauty guarding the portal from would-be crossers. The breath froze in my lungs as I watched her, not caring when the rain started, not even batting an eye when thunder churned in the sky.

Then her gaze hit mine, and I knew several things at once.

First, this formidable being was the most beautiful woman I had ever seen in my life.

Sharp cheekbones set off her regal features, her full lips parted as she sucked in a gasp. Her dark eyes flashed with lightning, the traces of it flickered down her neck, to her arms, to her fingers, dancing to the ground in a shower of white-hot sparks. A tight black tank top hugged her torso as did her jeans, showing off her lithe frame and gorgeous curves. But it was the set to her shoulders that did me in. This woman hadn't backed down a day in her life.

And second?

I was one thousand percent certain she was my mate.

It was as if Fate herself had reached inside my chest and tied a string around my heart. The organ squeezed, and the air left my lungs in a sharp gust. My blood burned in my veins, lighting every inch of me on fire. The wind shifted, carrying her scent to me. She smelled of jasmine and moonflowers mixed with the wildness of the sea.

I took a staggering step toward her, the string tying her to me yanking at the pitiful organ of my heart, pulling me to her. She backed up three paces to my one, her eyes tightening, her lips pinching, the makings of real fear clouding her confident expression.

Fear.

Of me?

My gaze fell to my bloody chest, my scarlet hands, my blackened claws sprouting from my fingertips.

Oh, shit.

There was no way to explain that I wasn't a threat—not to her. Never to her. My hands rose in surrender, hoping to ease her worry, but she took another step back, her jaw clenching as that fear turned into terror. Lightning slammed into the ground between us, scorching the very earth as if she were drawing a clear line I should not cross.

Message received.

And in her distraction, the two trespassers took their shot, sneaking around her and jumping through the portal while her back was turned. Her chin shifted, irritation clouding those expressive eyes, but still they never left me. Not once.

"*Styx*," a large Fae roared, his voice carrying over the thunder, "wake the fuck up. Caius will have our asses if—"

She blinked, the tie between us fraying as her attention left me, flying to the Fae and swinging back to me. Her gaze shot to the swirling vortex, and something like relief hit her then. I didn't hear the rest of what the Fae said because she—*Styx*—turned, her hair fanning out behind her as she threw the metal rods in her hands to the ground and raced for the portal herself.

"*Wait*," I called, moving to follow her before stopping short not two steps later when a force of *something* knocked me back.

Scrambling to my feet, I ran bodily into a blond High Fae, the faint tang of blood in my mouth as his barely concealed power had me falling to my knees.

Wait.

But she didn't.

One second, I'd had everything within my reach, and the next, she was gone, leaving me behind for the darkness beyond. At my knees were the metal rods, and I grabbed for them, stealing them off the ground before the Fae could stop me. They hummed in my hands as the thunderclouds rolled back, and the dawn broke across the sky.

Styx.

As a boy, I'd read stories about a river death and the wild woman who inhabited it—a woman named Styx. I'd always loved those stories and wished for a woman like her as my mate.

Wild. Strong. Hard as iron and made of danger and death. Never to be tamed.

Styx.

"Move back. I won't tell you twice."

Not even looking at him, my gaze remained on the portal, the pull of it—of her—almost too much to bear. I had to grit my teeth against it.

"But she... she's..." I couldn't get the words out, my throat clogging with them.

Styx.

Yes, she was my mate, but it hadn't seemed to matter to her. She'd left without so much as a "Fuck you" for my trouble. An ache settled deep in my chest as her rejection washed over me. It was New York all over again, the brand-new lash of pain ripping through everything I'd built for myself here.

She'd run away without so much as a backward glance.

Just like my mother.

Just like Ronan.

Just like the Syndicates.

That pull I'd been feeling toward this place—to this portal—had been for her. The mating call so fierce I'd been almost blinded by it.

But I couldn't afford being blinded by anything —especially not a woman that didn't want me. I'd learned that lesson a long time ago. She couldn't be the woman from a stupid fairytale I'd read so long ago—a being long dead and likely a figment of fiction.

Mate or not, I had a pack to look after, and distractions would get me killed.

Finding my feet, I gave the Fae and the portal my back. I was done chasing after people who didn't want me.

Done.

I just hoped I could convince my heart.

10 WEEKS LATER

"Can't you just kill me?" I asked, rubbing my temple. "That would be way more efficient."

Staring at my king with his bride on his lap, I wondered just what I'd done to deserve this level of punishment. I did not need a mate—hadn't in thousands of years—and yet, I'd been bombarded with mate business since I'd returned to Tartarus. Caius had *somehow* found out about the man from the portal, and now I was being hounded to go back.

To find *him*.

And as soon as I found out *who* had spilled my

secret, I would eviscerate them until there was nothing left.

Caius stared up at Reagan, a softness to his expression easing my bitterness a bit. He'd fallen head over heels for that woman, convinced her to be his queen, and they were on their way to their happily ever after. My friends were damn near blissful—so much it almost hurt to look at them, and yet, I could not fathom wanting that for myself.

Mates made you vulnerable.

All it would take was one twist of Fate, and everything would be gone.

Dead.

Lost.

And yet... I was still here, letting one of my oldest friends try to convince me to return to a world that had the one thing I didn't want in it. *Him.*

"Sorry," he said, not taking his eyes off his bride, "can't. Would love to help you and all but..."

He wasn't sorry. He'd never been less sorry in his life, while *I* was fighting bile racing up my throat. They were so perfect for each other it made my heart squeeze and stomach churn all at the same time. Mostly because there hadn't been a moment of peace in the weeks since I'd come back.

Assassination attempts, power grabs, betrayal.

There had been more bullshit in the last ten weeks than in the last thousand years combined.

Hell, this morning there had already been a bombing of the castle wall to try and get to the portal. I'd been stretched thin, and yet, through it all, steel-blue eyes haunted me. It didn't matter that I was busy or working or anything else. Every single night I dreamed of them—the way they were so open, so trusting, so...

A flicker of blue sparks flared from my fingertips as thunder rumbled outside, betraying my unease. I had spent two weeks on Earth feeling eyes on me, and as soon as I met his, I'd finally understood why.

It had been *him*.

Now that they were gone, I missed them, which unnerved me enough to make me want to put my head through a wall.

Piercing.

Soul-stealing.

Even with the mother of all hangovers needling my brain after a night of too much Tartarean alcohol, I still couldn't get those damn eyes out of my head.

But the man they were attached to always followed suit. Covered in blood, bare-chested, he'd strode toward me like he wasn't a walking nightmare. Not even deterred by my lightning, he'd still tried to reach me, the single rough word he'd spoken like a brand.

Wait.

I'd done just the opposite. I'd taken Nog and Ben's trespassing—and my failure—as a gift, an escape, a way to flee to the safety of Tartarus like a coward. I'd always seen it as a prison, and yet, when it came to realizing I had a mate, it was the safest place I could be.

"But nothing," I grumped, rubbing at my temple, praying that the hangover from hell would just go away. This was what I got when I asked Legion to help me drown my sorrows. I should have known it would turn into hangovers and bar brawls. "You just want me to be happy and loved up like you are. No offense, but... *gross.* I think I'd prefer death. Or a stint in the dungeons. Or shoving *lombass* skewers under my fingernails."

Reagan's laugh mingled with Caius' as he squeezed her thigh possessively. He'd laughed more in ten weeks than he had in all the time I'd known him. I couldn't begrudge him that, but... *gag.*

Yes, death would be preferable to this... *guilt.* I'd left *him* behind, ran at the first chance, but I hadn't missed the way his eyes tightened at my rejection. I couldn't escape the way his shoulders bunched, the way his lips thinned. I didn't even know the man, and yet, it tore me up that I'd dismissed him.

That was the real kicker. I'd taken something pure into my hands and crushed it like I'd done so many times before, but this time...

"I was like you, you know," Reagan said, climbing from Caius' lap. "I swore I'd never have a mate. Promised myself that that kind of life wasn't for me. You see where that got me, right?"

Five thousand years old and you're getting schooled by an infant. How does that feel?

Like shit. Like absolute shit.

"Where are you going?" Caius asked, his gaze not leaving Reagan for a second, his shadows reaching for her, even though she was only a few feet away.

A secret smile crossed her lips, and I wondered if I'd ever looked at anyone like that. If I ever would. "You two need to talk about this, and if I'm around, Styx won't get that disgusted look off her face. Don't worry. I won't go far."

I used to be so hard to read, and now literal children could call me out. *Fantastic.* Honestly, killing me would be so much easier. I'd lived long enough, right?

As soon as she slipped from the room, Caius' black gaze fell on me, and I fought the urge to squirm.

"Did you know that it has rained more in the last ten weeks than it has in the last hundred years?" Caius asked, steepling his fingers as he practically stared into my soul. "And it's been reported that the lightning strikes on the grounds have jumped so much, people are afraid to go outside."

So I had been a little emotional. Was that a crime?

"I also know what happened during *Februlune*."

If I could have melted into the floor, I would have.

"It's fine. I locked myself up—"

Caius emitted the deadliest growl, one that had even me straightening in my seat. "No, you had Legion lock you up because I was occupied, and he was the only one strong enough to do it. You suffered for days because you were proving a point to yourself. How do you think that will end?"

Struggling to swallow, I remembered the agony of the last double new moon—or "*Februlune*," as we called it—and the shame of asking one of my oldest friends to lock me away, the mindlessness as I threw myself against the walls of my cell, trying to get back to the portal.

In Tartarus, *Februlune* was basically a holiday and for good reason. With a world filled with shadow shifters, nearly all of us went into heat on the new moon once our mate was found. When you had two new moons at the same time? It was days of hedonistic sex and pleasure, mating and bed play. But only for those with mates, and only for those who didn't mind tying their lives to someone forever.

Thousands of years I'd managed to go unscathed.

Thousands of years not feeling that searing ache that would not go away.

Thousands of years, and it was all ruined as soon as I met that steely-blue gaze.

"I've made it this far, haven't I?" It was a shitty comeback, but it was all I could come up with.

"You are holding yourself together with twine and obstinance, and even that is fraying. I know what you went through bef—"

That carefully culled rage I'd been banking flared to life. "No, you don't," I hissed, sparks from my fingers showering to the stone floor. "Even after all this time, you still only know the sanitized version.

And even if I gave you every detail, you would still not understand."

He couldn't possibly.

Something like pity flashed across Caius' expression before he hid it away. And that's why I never spoke about my past—not ever. The last thing I needed was Caius' pity.

Swallowing past the lump in my throat, I let my gaze trail to the window, the whole of Tartarus beyond. "If I go back, it won't be for him. It will be for me. To get my revenge, to take back what was stolen, to..." My voice left me, as reality crashed in. What was stolen could never be returned to me. The only thing I had to look forward to was revenge, and even that was a long shot.

"It can't be for him."

Because going back to find him would require me to trust, to drop my guard, to open myself up like a *monigra* pod, exposing the pale flesh below. I didn't know how to do that, and the last time I'd tried, I'd lost everything.

And then there was the rest of it. Why had he been bloody? Who was he? Why had he been there? How could I be sure he was a good man? How could I be sure he wouldn't use me for power, wouldn't enslave me?

"Why can't it be both? Why can't you go back for you and for him?"

I didn't have an answer—not a good one, anyway. "How can you so blindly believe that Fate would be kind to me?"

She'd never been before.

"If Fate can smile upon the darkest of souls, she can smile upon you, too," he murmured, halting the very breath in my lungs.

There was no argument for that, no retort. Just acceptance.

"Fine," I hissed, crossing my arms over my chest as rain lashed the window. "But when this all goes to shit, I reserve the right to tell you I told you so."

What I didn't tell him was that I would avoid my ma—*him*—like he was the plague and pray we didn't cross paths again.

"I would expect nothing less."

Pausing just outside the portal, I surveyed the swirling vortex and the world beyond from the shadows. I'd been there for an hour, watching, waiting, trying to gather the courage to take the first step.

"And how did I know I'd find you here?" Reagan whispered, her tone soft, caring.

I fucking hated it.

The best she got was a grunt, but even that got me a smile. *Dammit.* I'd grown to like her in the past few weeks, and a part of me even trusted her. Just a little.

She'd grown on me.

Like a fungus.

"I know—"

"Nothing," I growled, cutting her off. "You know nothing. You don't know how I feel, you don't know what's going on inside my head. You don't, okay?" I swallowed, trying to stuff that rage I kept carefully honed back inside its cage. "We are not the same, Reagan."

She was born to protect. I was born to destroy. She was tied to Caius—I was tied to no one. She had fallen in love, and I didn't know what that was. She had a loving family, and I...

"I can't put myself in your shoes, but I can say that I have been tied to someone I didn't choose. Someone I thought was worse than the devil himself. I don't regret it now, but then? It felt like I was dying a little every day."

Her words were meant to be a balm, but they just made it worse. Because in that scenario, I was the devil, wasn't I?

"We might not be in the same boat, but it's the same ocean at least. So at the risk of sounding like a know-it-all child to you, can I give you some advice?"

Unwaveringly kind, she'd give that advice whether I wanted it or not, so I simply shrugged.

"Keep an open mind. I wasted a lot of time here fighting the bond, fighting Caius, just *fighting*. Sometimes Fate has better plans for us, yes?"

I didn't know about that, but Reagan had wanted to be helpful, and so the least I could do was let her believe she had.

"I will."

She snorted, shaking her head. "No, you won't. You'll fight Fate at every turn until you can't anymore. But when you finally find what you're looking for and the dust settles, just let yourself be happy, okay? You deserve it."

I didn't know about that either, so I said nothing. Reagan bumped my shoulder with her own before turning to leave me to gather my courage in peace.

And when I finally crossed that barrier, I promised myself three things.

I would never accept my mate. No poor soul deserved to get saddled with a killer with no remorse.

Somehow, some way, I'd get rid of the power that had poisoned me every single day for five thousand years.

And last? My family deserved to be avenged. If there was a way to punish the gods who banished me, I would do it. I would end them—even if I had to die to do it.

Because Reagan had been wrong.

I hadn't earned my happiness.

And I never would.

CHAPTER 4
CORVIN

I was a liar.

I hadn't made it a single day before I was back at the portal begging for news, for information, for anything that would tell me who she was and why she had been there. I'd also wanted to know why she went back, but that question I didn't ask.

Not that it mattered.

I'd been stonewalled at every turn, the man in front of me just as resolute as he had been ten weeks ago. So far, I knew two things and two things only. The man in front of me was called Oberon, and just like the stories I'd read as a boy, my intended favored the water. Two and a half months, and that was all I had. Every day I came back to this very spot at dawn to get bupkis before returning to my pack just to do it all over again the next day.

I was starting to lose hope.

"Come on, give me something. I know her name is Styx, and evidently, she can control lightning. That's it. That is my mate over there, man. Can't you give me anything? Or at the very least let me through?"

He let out an exasperated sigh. "You know, what you're doing is called 'stalking' and generally it's frowned upon—even here, I'm told."

I rolled my eyes, thinking of every other mated pair I'd seen in the last two hundred years. Every single one of them had been mindless, focused, unnervingly resolute in finding and keeping their mate. Even in the Syndicates where laws were less than suggestions, mates were still treated like royalty, revered. Not everyone got one, and I'd been waiting a long fucking time to get mine.

"You obviously know her. Tell me something, anything. *Please.*"

And this was exactly what I didn't want to do. I didn't want to be this person. But here I was once again, showing my belly for a woman that likely didn't—*couldn't*—want me.

"You want to know something? Fine. I'll tell you what I know. I know you've got your work cut out for you because the likelihood that she will accept a mate is slim to never going to fucking happen. I know you'd be better off trying to drain that river over there with a straw than attempting to bend her to your will. I know that even though you probably aren't even half good enough for her, she's still going to think that she's the lesser one of the two of you."

His smile was part proud big brother and part attack dog. "But it's not going to matter because she's not coming back. She'd rather throw herself into an active volcano than accept a mate."

That was the most I'd ever gotten out of him, and it essentially told me everything I needed and nothing at all. Because how could I convince her I was good enough when I wasn't? I couldn't convince my own mother to stay. Convincing Styx that I was worth it wouldn't be an achievable task.

"I see. Any other words of advice?"

"Don't take it personally," he offered, his smile almost sad. "I can assure you mates aren't all they're cracked up to be."

"Only someone without a mate would say something like that."

And even though I had never had a mate myself, I knew his words couldn't possibly be true. I'd witnessed it—watched the way my brother stared at his mate, the way he would move mountains, destroy cities, bend worlds to his will to save her. Hell, he'd essentially dismantled the Syndicates and helped make her Queen of New York. Or what was it called now? *Destiny and Dragomir.* He helped create a whole House just for her.

I didn't care how old this Fae was, I knew the power mates held. Loving someone like that made you ruthless, unyielding, unbreakable. You'd do anything—be anything—for them.

But it didn't matter if she didn't return, now, did it?

Without another word, I turned, heading back to the pack house like I had every other time.

"Same time tomorrow?" the bastard taunted, and I flipped him off, not bothering to look at the swirling vortex of a portal that kept me from my mate.

Yes, I'd likely be there at the same time tomorrow.

And the next day.

And the fucking next.

Twelve hours later, I was shifted, silent, and in the middle of a sting operation. In the year since I'd moved here, there had been an influx of problems at the docks. Piracy wasn't as common as one would think in New York. With Sea and Serpentine so close, the likelihood of problems on the water was slim.

But there wasn't a sea for miles in the Crossroads, only a giant river with no one to police it.

Which was likely why the pirates had seemed to spring up from thin air, robbing river boats and trains and running back to the safety of the water. In all likelihood, they were either water Fae, aquatic shifters, or witches, stealing from the west side and shacking up in the east.

They had robbed three trains yesterday before disappearing on the water like a damn mirage. Normally, I wouldn't even bat an eye, considering where I'd come from, but in the last few weeks, we'd secured not just the subway lines but the freight as well. They were getting bolder, moving from the river boat passengers farther inland.

In the last robbery, a young shifter had been killed protecting his little sister, and I realized I couldn't be a good Alpha to my pack if I let other shifters get hurt under my watch. And robbing children? I wouldn't stand for that.

We wouldn't stand for that.

Nearly every member of the pack was out here tonight, watching, waiting, each dock covered on the west side from Victor Street up to past the old Eads Bridge. All we were waiting on was one of those cloaked boats to dock and then we would end this threat.

There wouldn't be a robbery tonight.

Not from a river pirate.

Not ever again.

But sitting there shifted as I was, the changes to my animal were difficult to hide, and I was starting to suspect the portal was the cause. Just like the ground surrounding it, the stone of my shifted form was darkening, becoming one with the shadows, blending into the night itself. The chameleonlike effect of my skin had changed, making me more like an absence of light rather than just blending in. Often, people's eyes just skated over me, not seeing the giant predator in their midst.

Even my own pack, even mid-fight.

The only person it didn't work on was the damn Fae at the portal, his black eyes seeing me before I could even get close enough to cross.

Considering the changes were working to my advantage otherwise, I hadn't complained, but it was difficult for even Knox to find me sometimes.

The winter sun had long since fallen, the biting wind picking up, but it didn't bother me in this form. Once I shifted back, though, I'd feel it cut through me like a knife. I was used to New York winters, but the wind here on the plains was something else.

And that rippling wind was the only reason I noticed them when I did. It crossed the gentle wake, rocking up to the shore, making frosty whitecaps on the water. The vessel that made it was invisible until it stopped at the dock, the night falling away from it as soon as it was tethered to the cleat. With a gentle measured shift of my foot, I engaged the signal.

This was the dock. This was the place. And my pack was coming to me.

The boat was a mid-sized vessel, and three vampires and a witch waltzed off the deck as if they didn't have a care in the world.

As if they hadn't just murdered a child the night before.

As if they had no remorse.

As if they would do it again.

The burning rage in my gut had a calming effect, loosening my limbs as I watched them saunter down the pier toward the passenger train lines. And as the wind whipped their scent in my direction, I knew we had the right people.

That scent would be in my brain until the day I died. As would his mother's screams when she'd found out her baby was dead. And her daughter's cries as she clung to me, begging me to help her brother who was already cold, his soul gone before I ever stepped foot on the train.

The one on the left was taller than the other three, his bulk making him the muscle of the group. The other two vamps were thinner, shorter, but just as formidable, and they all circled the witch as if they were her muscle and not the other way around.

She was the boss, likely a crone, and it wouldn't be easy to take them down without magic.

Luckily, we had some.

Unlike the Shifter Syndicate of New York, I didn't care about bloodlines. I didn't give a shit if people were mixed with witches or demons or Fae. Considering I was a half-breed myself, it didn't make much sense to put too much stock in purity. Even if I wasn't, the Fae and shifters had long been intermingled throughout the centuries, our magic amplifying each other's.

Penny and Jude both were mixed with other species, and I considered it a boon that they wanted to be in my pack. Penny was part-witch, her cloaking spells a bit rocky but her healing ones were top-notch. Jude was half earth Fae, and often helped Penny with growing her herbs. Knox was a rare male harpy, and Aster was part death Fae and part-panther, her black coat blending into the night as if she were made of it.

Most of my lieutenants converged on the dock behind me, taking flanking positions as we tightened the noose around them, the rest making escape impossible. I had no doubt that there were more than four people in that operation, but I wouldn't worry about that right then.

Aster emerged from the shadows in front of the pirates right as they hit the parking lot, her inky coat hiding just how close she was. All at once the quartet froze, Aster's eyes finally catching the streetlight as she prowled toward them, her scent reaching their noses. Then other members of my pack edged into the light—wolves and big cats, bears and equines—creating a wall of shifters unwilling to let them pass.

It was almost comical when they tried to turn back to the safety of the pier, their way blocked by the most formidable fighters I had.

I could understand thievery. Extortion. Blackmail. I understood making sure you had enough on your plate and some comfort besides. What I would never understand was murdering kids, butchering those weaker than you over a bit of currency.

If I were letting them go, I would have taught them a lesson. Made a speech coupled with a bit of pain so it sunk in. But they had gone too far already, and the only option was death. There had been a time when the thought of killing turned my stomach.

Now it was just a part of life.

I went for the big vamp first, my tail lashing out and wrapping around his leg, ripping him off his feet. Aster went for the witch, her giant paws taking her to the ground before she had a chance to fire off a spell. Penny and Jude went for the other two vamps, launching themselves at their chests as they attempted to flee. The rest of the pack moved as one, tearing, ripping, stomping them out in a melee of fur, fangs, and blood.

The big vamp managed to latch onto my tail, his fangs attempting to rip at the scaled flesh as a sizzle of magic raked across my muzzle, skating off the stone. Somehow the witch had gotten free of Aster, her frame covered in blood as she tried to crawl toward her moored boat, but her arms were cut to ribbons and refused to support her once Aster jumped onto her back, her fangs ripping into the back of the witch's neck and snapping the bone with a sickening crunch.

That just left the big vamp who had given up on my tail and desperately tried to flee.

Scrabbling against the cement, his gaze went to his dead friends, then back to me.

"Wh-what do you want? A cut of the profits? Territory?"

He thought he could negotiate. After what they'd done? There wasn't a bargain in the world that could be struck that could pay for that transgression.

No, I wanted my pound of flesh.

A frisson of heat hit my chest for a second—a tug, a pull—yanking my focus from the large vamp.

My head whipped south in the direction of the portal, a faint *knowing* filling my very bones.

Styx had crossed the portal.

She's back. She's here. She's—

Claws ripped into my shoulder, bringing me back to the task at hand. It wasn't exactly a good time to be distracted, and that was no more evident than the vamp trying to claw his way through stone.

Losing my patience, I let all the pain, the fury, the rejection fuel me as I tore into him as if he were tissue paper. Without a second thought, I bit into his shoulder, shredding the skin and pumping him full of venom. And then I let him go, enjoying the show of him slowly suffocating as his organs began to liquefy. Even vamp healing wouldn't save him from his fate, his punishment a bitter agony until I showed him mercy by ripping off his head.

Disgust bloomed in my gut as I stared at the bloody scene. The blow-back from this could be severe, but until we knew who we were dealing with, that was just speculation.

Shifting back, I took stock of the damage.

"Sound off. Any injuries?"

"No casualties, boss, but Aster is going to need Penny. That witch got her good." Knox passed me a pair of jeans as his brow furrowed, his wings slowly tucking back into his body. "Want to tell me why you froze there for a second? I thought that vamp worked some mojo on you or something."

Shaking my head, I gave him an easy smile. "Nothing. Thought I heard something is all."

Because telling him that the mate who didn't want me was back in this realm was a tough sell—even for me.

"Make sure this is cleaned up and check out the boat. See if you can find anything about who they were or why they were killing kids to make a buck." I thought about it for a second. "I'm going to go see someone about getting more info on the witch. Anyone who can go toe to toe with a death Fae and make a dent needs some investigating."

Knox pursed his lips, doubt clearly tightening his gold eyes. No one in my pack knew about Styx—not even Knox—but I had a feeling the harpy was far more astute than I gave him credit for.

"I see. And does this 'someone' happen to live near a certain portal?" he asked as he passed over the keys to my car.

See? Astute.

I twirled the keys on my finger before giving him a grin.

"As a matter of fact, they do."

Whistling, I turned my bare feet in the direction of my parked car, glad I'd had the forethought to pack a jacket and some boots. This time when I saw her again, I wouldn't be barefoot and bloody. I wouldn't be caught off guard.

And maybe, just maybe I'd get the chance to change her mind.

CHAPTER 5
STYX

Hunting gods without a game plan didn't seem like the healthiest way to stay breathing in a world like this. And considering even five thousand years later, I still didn't know the names of the gods who had banished me, simply crossing the portal to find them and them alone seemed daunting to say the least.

You could find him instead. Maybe ask for help. He might know something—

The voice in my head was an asshole, taunting me with impossibilities and futile imaginings. There was no way I would be looking for *him.*

Even though there was a distinct pull in my chest that ached to go north instead of west.

Even though guilt still coursed through my veins like acid.

Even though those steel-blue eyes haunted my every waking second.

I needed information and a lot of it if I wanted to have a chance in hell of killing those assholes. Information didn't often come cheap, but I had plenty to barter with, and if that didn't work, violence was always an option.

What I did not need were distractions. Those could get me killed...

In theory.

Pointing my feet toward the city center, I quickly found the shop I'd been looking for. In my off time from guarding the portal, I'd traversed the streets of Crossroads, getting the lay of the land. Near what used to be a courthouse was an odd little market, tucked away in a wide alley with fairy lights strung between the two buildings. I'd purchased clothing here once to better fit in, my leather and armor ill-suited for this realm.

But on my inspection, I'd spied a number of shops that could potentially have the information I needed. There was a book shop and an apothecary, both promising options, as well as a seer advertising "readings" at discount prices. Since I'd rather gouge out my own eyes than trust a charlatan speaking in nonsensical riddles, I figured that was a last resort.

The alleyway darkened as it curved, the lights dimming as the door came into view. The thick wooden monstrosity creaked as if it were announcing me, its hinges likely not oiled in the last century. The entrance was filled with haphazard stacks of books, each one with frayed edges and crumbling pages, before the alcove widened into a labyrinth of shelves that were full to bursting.

I would be willing to bet the information I needed was here. I would also be willing to bet that it would take the rest of eternity to find what I needed. The faint scurrying of feet had me bracing myself, so when the shopkeeper seemed to appear out of thin air at my elbow, I didn't so much as flinch.

She had to be a Fae, maybe a brownie or a sprite, though a brownie would never let their domain be in such disrepair. Her head barely reached my elbow, and she squinted up at me through thick glasses that made her eyes seem comically large. The rest of her was just as disorderly as her books. Her white hair shot out at all angles from her scalp as if she'd been struck by one of my lightning bolts, and her sweater was mis-buttoned over a loudly flower-printed blouse.

"What can I do for you?" the old woman asked, a faint tinge of disappointment crossing her features for a moment before stretching into a wrinkly smile.

I had a feeling I'd ruined her fun. She likely scared the pants off of whatever poor soul got the stones to cross the threshold of this place. Bird skulls and petrified spiders hung from the low ceiling like party decorations, their scents mixing with the moldering pages. This likely wasn't the fanciest shop in the Crossroads, but it had potential.

And even though I didn't trust her one bit, I still gave her my request.

"I'm looking for information on gods. Primarily ones that have or had an affinity for the sky."

She tilted her head, her eyes narrowing. "There are more gods and goddesses with sky powers than you can shake a stick at. Can you narrow it down a bit?"

Shit. I didn't have their names or the name of the god that... Shaking myself, I simply shrugged. There were plenty of details I could give her, but something told me offering too much information would be to my detriment.

"No, I can't. I will need to look through all your

books on sky deities." It wasn't a request, and I didn't phrase it like one. She had what I needed—I just knew it.

The old woman bristled, her lips thinning as she drew herself up to her full height. "That would be thousands of books. I'm not pulling all of them for you." She tapped her lip, softening a little. "Maybe if you give me your hand, I could help some. Your palm will tell me what book you need."

A frisson of unease trilled down my spine as the air shifted. The faint odor of molding paper morphed into the more pungent scent of decay. Ever so faintly, a rattle rang through the shop, almost like the patter of rain drops or the tail of a snake. I had a feeling I knew exactly what she was, and my palm wouldn't tell her shit.

It would put me right in the middle of a trap, though.

"I don't think so," I growled, my eyes and fingers beginning to spark in irritation. "How about you pull nothing, and instead, you point me in the right direction of the books I need, and I'll ignore the obvious trap you're trying to set?"

Her form shifted a bit, her glamour so intricate I'd almost missed it. I did not have the mental fortitude to deal with a lamia today—or any other day.

She wasn't a Fae. No, she was a demon, and her cloaking spell was so well-crafted, even someone as old as I was damn near believed it.

At least she wasn't trying to eat a child.

Yet.

"There is no trap, chil—"

"I can almost guarantee I'm older than you are," I growled, losing the limited patience I had. "And you can cut the shit any time now. You're a lamia. It would be out of character for this to *not* be a trap."

She stumbled back a step, likely shocked I could not only see through her glamour but also knew what she was.

"It makes no difference to me how you get your food, but if you so much as sniff in my direction, I will make sure you die slow and screaming. Now, do you have the books I need or not?"

All of a sudden, her glamour dropped, and instead of a withered old crone, there stood a tall blond woman with red eyes. Her body was adorned with scales, and her legs had disappeared into a thick snakelike tail.

With her glamour gone, this could go one of two ways. The first, she would attack, I'd fry her to bits, and I'd have to pray my powers didn't burn this whole building down. The second, she would be nice and cordial and give me what I fucking asked for. If I were a betting woman, option one was looking more and more likely.

Sizing me up, she crossed her arms over her scaled chest. "There are roughly three hundred sky deities and over one thousand books in this building about such gods." A lone eyebrow raised in challenge. "If you don't want me to help you narrow it down, then I'll show you to the section. But if you choose a book and can't pay, I'm eating you and there's not a damn thing you can do about it."

I contemplated frying her on principle.

She swiftly twisted, her tail slithering behind her as she rounded the corner, guiding me to a rather large section of ancient books. "Here. If I have a book on the god you're looking for, it will be here."

The sheer size of the section meant I would be here for a long, long time.

Three hours later, I emerged from the shop, bleary-eyed and empty-handed, more pissed off than I'd been since stepping foot on this stupid realm. I didn't make it even halfway through the section, and feared I'd actually have to give that stupid lamia my hand at some point just so I could figure shit out faster.

Thunder rumbled overhead, and I rolled my eyes at myself. Did I honestly believe after five thousand years, I'd just waltz into the first book shop I found and figure out a plan on the spot?

Pursing my lips, I marveled at my own idiocy. This would take work and dedication and...

A subtle pull in my chest had my steps faltering for just a moment before I forced myself to keep walking. I sort of figured that this was completely unavoidable. I had a mate, and now that I was in his realm, of course he would seek me out.

Of course he would follow me around like a fucking stalker, hiding in the shadows.

And naturally, because I was an unhinged psychopath, I kind of admired that about him.

Because there was no way I was going to seek *him* out. There was no way I would search the city for him. There was no way that I would allow this to progress on my own. And as much as I hated being pursued, I had to give him credit.

The fucker was tenacious.

Traffic had picked up while I'd been occupied, the patrons filling the alleyway like a sea of bodies.

Edging through the crowd, I weaved my way toward the edge of the market, the roofline obscured by the glowing lights. *He* was likely up there, hiding in plain sight. Or at least, that was what I'd be doing, scoping out my prey like the predator I was.

Fur brushed my leg, and I fought off the urge to flinch. Looking down, I noticed the barest glimpse of white fur before an odd sort of glamour flickered over the animal, turning it into a dull-colored down-trodden wolf.

Interesting.

I wondered what other kinds of odd shifters populated a city such as this.

Past the bustling market, the crowd thinned considerably, and I felt like I could breathe again. But that pull, that tug on my senses was still there, like a buzzing in my chest that begged me to turn around, to look up, to...

And despite that incessant needling by Fate, I pressed on, heading for the water. I wondered how long it would take him to find me once I'd crossed the portal. Could he feel me as soon as I stepped foot onto the land like I did with him? It had taken everything in me to not point my feet north, the urge making me a complete hypocrite.

I'd told Caius I hadn't come to this world for

him, and at the very first step, my body betrayed me. And each time I felt that pull, I wanted to scream. I didn't have time for this.

By the time I'd made it to the park, I was seething, the fuckery of Fate making the thunder roil in the clouds just highlighting the very reason I didn't want a mate in the first place.

"I know you're out there," I shouted, finally turning around. "Stop fucking following me."

But in the shadows, I spied the monstrous being prowling closer, it's skin stonelike and yet not all at the same time. It had the face and body of a lion, but a pair of horns curled down to its massive jaw instead of a mane. Giant leathery wings fanned over his back, as a serpent's tail flicked back and forth behind him.

The slow way he was pacing toward me, it was as if he didn't expect me to be able to see him.

"I can see you, you fuck. Stop following me before I incinerate you where you stand."

Lightning crashed into the ground around me—its rarely welcome heat a form of protection I had never wanted yet couldn't get rid of. And still, it was as if I had not said a word because he was still prowling my way.

"I don't want a mate—especially one who can't take a hint."

Then in a split second, I made a rash decision, setting one of those bolts free. It slammed into his chest, knocking him backward until he was a chimera-shaped jumble of limbs on the ground. Instantly, I wished I could take it back, but the damage had already been done.

Then, oh, so slowly his stonelike skin melted away as his bones snapped and cracked, reforming into the shape of a man. That man turned, rolled to his feet as those steel-blue eyes pinned me to the spot.

He was no worse for wear. It was as if I hadn't hit him at all.

"That hurt, Storm Cloud. If I didn't know better, I would think you didn't like me."

His silky voice let loose a riot of butterflies in my stomach, its quiet menace almost a growl. I'd killed more men than I cared to count with that power, and not only was there nothing to show for it, he was *taunting* me.

It was official.

I was in deep shit.

CHAPTER 6

CORVIN

That.

Fucking.

Hurt.

This wasn't the first time I'd been struck by lightning. As a gargoyle, it was a regular occurrence, part of the job description, so to speak. Standing on top of buildings in rain or shine, watching out for my pack had made me rather immune to a plethora of Mother Nature's rage issues. I had willingly sat through blistering hail, a few hurricanes, and more storms than I could shake a stick at, but Styx's lightning was something else.

I saw the moment she decided to hit me with it, too, and the instant remorse as I flew back. Eating pavement, the shift to my human form was an involuntary one as my mate essentially tased me into oblivion.

It was the remorse that gave me hope—not that I would tell her that.

"I don't," she growled, crossing her arms over her chest in a defensive position that seemed to telegraph just how vulnerable she felt. It was either that, or she was harnessing her hands, so she didn't zap me into an early grave.

I blinked and hard, lost in the middle of our conversation. "Don't what?"

"Like you very much. What? Did I scramble your brains when I hit you? No, I don't like you very much. I categorically don't like people who don't listen when I tell them to stop following me."

Tilting my head to the side, I watched her every move. She was steadfast and pissed off and I fucking loved it. "Had to do that much, Storm Cloud? Tell men to stop following you?"

Why did that instantly fill me with a spike of rage?

Why had she had to defend herself like that?

Styx backed up another step, refusing to give me her back.

Smart girl.

"No one on Tartarus is stupid enough to follow

me, and the ones that are, don't stay breathing for long. Are you one of the idiots, shifter?"

So, we were name calling then. "Unless you have another mate in your pocket, I don't see where anyone in their right mind would trail after you and live to tell about it. Then again, men do very dumb things for beautiful women."

She rolled her eyes, her chuckle bitter as she backed up a step. "Beautiful women like me are the reason men die in droves. They drown themselves in rivers, trying to take what's not theirs. Do you want to take a swim, shifter? I bet you'll die just like all the rest."

So she had more tricks up her sleeve. That made me immeasurably proud and a little turned on. I liked that my mate had ways to protect herself. I liked that she was formidable and fierce just like her namesake.

Not that it was helping my case right then, though.

I rubbed at my scruff, kind of wishing I'd been smart enough to grab a go-bag. I wasn't opposed to nudity—most shifters weren't—but this wasn't exactly the best first impression, me naked as a jaybird while trying to make conversation.

"Gargoyles don't do well in the water, Storm Cloud. Stone tends to sink."

Her gaze drifted over my body, lingering on my shoulders before traveling lower and lingering. A second later she shook herself, those gorgeous sparking eyes narrowing.

"Stop calling me that."

Her scent changed ever so slightly, and I couldn't help the hint of a smile that hit my lips. My mate liked what she saw.

She liked it a lot.

At least I had that going for me.

"Well, I'd call you by your name, but you ran away before we could be properly introduced." I put a hand to my chest, allowing the half-truth to spill from my lips. "See, my name is Corvin Blackwell, Alpha of the Blackwell Pack. And you are?"

She shuffled backward once more, and I figured I had about three seconds before she out-and-out ran from me. For as formidable as she was, she sure was a skittish thing.

"Styx."

"Like the river," I added, trying to keep the conversation rolling.

She shook her head. "I don't know what you

mean. There is a river on Tartarus named for me, but…"

Suddenly, her shoulders straightened, her gaze hardening. "I don't want a mate. Getting to know me won't change that. If you know what's good for you, you'd reject me right now."

That sounded like the stupidest thing I could ever do, and I'd trusted Taron Rose for fuck's sake. No, rejecting Styx was an impossibility, topped with a "never going to happen." She was the epitome of the woman from my stories, a walking, talking fairytale.

"And why would I do such a thing? You're beautiful, formidable, packing a biting wit. I'm pretty sure it would take me eons to fully get to know you, and I am up for the challenge. Why would I ever reject you?"

Her gaze narrowed. "Fine. I'll do it. Corvin Black—"

"Don't," I growled, moving as fast as her lightning before covering her mouth with my hand. "*Please.*"

I think it was the "Please" that saved my ass. Thunder crashed above as rain lashed my skin, but no lightning hit me. No, the only thing that hit me were those beautiful eyes and the blade under my chin. When she'd had time to pull a knife and where she'd pulled it from were both a mystery to me. She was so small in my arms, so delicate when I knew she was anything but, and the sheer fact that she was never without a defense damn near made me mindless.

With every fiber of self-control I possessed, I let her go and backed up, raising my arms in surrender. "I'm sorry, it's just... You may not want a mate, but there isn't a rule that says you have to accept me right away. You could just as easily get to know me and reject me later if we don't mesh."

Yes, I was bargaining, but *fuck*. I did not want to lose this woman.

"Or I could gut you like a fish right now and save myself the trouble," she growled, slowly lowering her weapon, and spiriting it away in the hidden sheathe at her back, the biggest point in my favor of the night.

I couldn't help the smile that tugged on my lips. "Maybe later, Storm Cloud."

"What did I say about calling me that?"

Choosing to ignore that request, I pressed on with what was really on my mind. "What I really want to know is why you were in Tasty Tomes. Don't you know the patrons of that shop rarely leave alive?

What were you looking for that had you walking in there?"

The owner, Nadia, had quickly gotten on my radar as soon as I moved here. I made it a point to learn all the nooks and crannies of this city, making sure I wouldn't step on any toes while creating a pack. I could smell the death as soon as I'd walked in the door. I didn't know what kind of supernatural she was, but I knew never to go back into that shop again. Later, I'd learned of her reputation and why no one even so much as looked at her store.

"I don't see how that's any of your business."

She didn't see how putting herself in imminent danger was my business?

Fucking adorable.

I had to remind myself that she wasn't a member of my pack. She didn't know me. She didn't know the lengths I would go to make sure that she was safe.

"That's cute, but you and I both know that you being in danger is at the tippy top of what is my business."

"Don't overstep, shifter. I've been taking care of myself for a very long time. I don't need your help in that regard. And as far as the owner of the book-shop, we've come to an agreement. She doesn't sniff in my direction and shows me what she has, and I won't murder her and burn her shop to the ground. So far, it's working out just fine."

It was probably wrong that the sound of her being so blasé about murder was a complete turn on, right?

"You still didn't tell me what you were looking for."

"And I still maintain that it's none of your fucking business. I'm here to do a job and that's it. Once the job is done, I will go home to Tartarus and never see your face again. I don't want a mate, remember?"

Oh, I remembered. Now I needed to bargain, and that was tough to do naked. It also didn't help that her scent was surrounding me, frying what little brain cells I had left.

"If the job is so important, why not let me help? I could make your time on this plane significantly shorter." I *could*, but I *wouldn't*.

Styx seemed to read my mind, and her retreat to the river started in earnest. "Somehow, I doubt you'd be willing to help me complete my task. Just a hunch I've got, you know?"

But I *would* help her do what she needed to. I would do just about anything already, and I barely knew her. I just wouldn't sit idly by while she hopped back through the portal. I wouldn't let her reject me without knowing me at all.

"I get it. You don't know me, and trust is earned," I conceded, trying my best to not scare her off completely.

Styx's smile was brilliant for one shining second before it twisted, her eyes darkening with a hardness that made me think that winning this war would be hard and bloody.

"Trust is an illusion, Corvin. It doesn't exist—not really."

Then she spun, ripping the sticks out of her hair and pulling off her clothes as she sprinted for the water. Barely breaking stride, she shucked her jeans, and I got one tantalizing glimpse of her perfect ass before she shifted on the fly, transforming into a beautiful black horse. Her silky mane brushed the ground for one single moment before she dove into the river, leaving me behind as she dipped below the surface.

I worried for a moment until I realized she wasn't a horse but a kelpie. Then the drowning comment made a hell of a lot more sense. A part of me wondered what would happen if I followed her into the river. Would she really drown me? Would she wrap me in her deathly embrace and drag me to the depths? Or would she understand that I wasn't going anywhere?

I'd been chasing my whole life and had always felt like the prize was never worth it. Chasing my mother's love, chasing leadership in a pack, chasing acceptance from my brother.

This time, it was different.

My mother, the Syndicates, New York, Ronan— none of them had wanted me.

Styx was fighting with herself because she didn't *want* to want me.

And as crazy as it was, I could work with that.

Shifting back to my gargoyle, I watched the water, letting her pull to drag me down the river with her.

She'd been looking after herself her whole life?

Not anymore.

She's had to fight every day?

Never again.

She could do it herself?

Sure.

But I'd be there to back her up.

Because if there was one person in this world she could trust, it was me.

CHAPTER 7

STYX

The river was the coward's way out.

As soon as I turned from him, I knew I was cheating, but Corvin wasn't fighting fair, either. How was I supposed to keep him at a distance when he was saying all the right things? How was I supposed to remember that I didn't want a mate when he was acting like that?

When I'd knocked him out of the sky, I'd immediately regretted it, but nothing prepared me for seeing *all* of him. His shoulders, his abs, his thick corded neck, and that "V" of muscle leading down to the best cock I'd seen in five thousand years. He'd been aroused, hard and thick and... It had taken nearly everything in me not to give in right then and there.

I wasn't a blushing novice when it came to sex. Over the years, I'd had plenty of lovers, but Corvin was something else. I had never really lusted after someone like that, flipping a switch inside myself so fast I was still trying not to think about falling to my knees and letting him play with me.

Sure, I'd feel the urge every once in a while, and then find someone to scratch it, but never like that and no one permanent. Being Caius' inner circle, there was very little trust to be had for civilians. There were plenty that wished to take the crown, plenty that wanted power for themselves.

Five thousand years, and I'd had no one to come home to. No one to be there for other than my closest friends. No one that just wanted me for no other reason.

Not for the power I had.

Not for what I could give them.

Not for what I could destroy.

And then this asshole walks up with his easy smile and kind eyes, and...

Trust is an illusion.

I'd learned that the day my family died, and it had been a certified fact for five millennia. I trusted four people, and even that was tenuous. There would never be a time that I trusted a man

I'd just met—especially after unsuccessfully killing him.

Why wasn't there a handbook out there for situations like this? Like *How to Reject Your Mate in Five Easy Steps*. Or *How to Ignore Your Mate's Hot Body*. Maybe *Your Mate Won't Reject You. Now What?* or something to that effect. After the slew of books I'd researched just in the last day, there had to be something, right?

Grumbling, I let the water caress my skin as I continued to reside in the one place *he* couldn't follow.

Corvin. His name is Corvin.

There went my inner voice, *the bitch*. For weeks, I hadn't known his name, even though he'd haunted my thoughts, my dreams, and my conscience. And now that I did, I didn't want to use it. Using his name gave him a foothold, carving out a little place inside my brain where he squatted rent free.

At least on Tartarus, I didn't feel his presence. At least on Tartarus, I didn't risk the chance of seeing him again, risk falling into the trap of a good-looking man willing to give me his time.

I didn't risk tying myself to someone who should never know what poison I really was.

After a few hours under the water, allowing my

kelpie form to play in the giant river, I figured I'd run long enough. I emerged from the nameless river, wondering when I stopped thinking of Tartarus as a prison and started calling it home. I might not have exactly loved my life there, but at least I had my river, my home, my friends.

Here there were nothing but new places, new people, and even with a two-week stint here months ago, I was still getting my footing. I moved through the small but well-kept neighborhood, the houses dotting the shore of the river were quaint with neat sections behind them banked with trees. One such house had a line of clothes pinned to a string of twine.

Lifting my neck over the low fence, I stole a shirt, plucking it off the line with my teeth, glad to have something to cover myself since I'd so hastily left my clothes.

I didn't know if Corvin was hanging back far enough that I couldn't feel him, or if I was finally successful at ignoring his presence, but I still scanned the horizon for him, anyway.

Stop it.

Squeezing my eyes closed, I sucked in a lungful of air, allowing the transformation to hit me. The air was still and cool on my overheated skin, but I couldn't find Corvin's shadowy form in the night. A pang of disappointment hit me for a second before I shoved it down.

Stop. It.

It was good for him not to follow me, right? It was what I wanted—to be alone to find the gods who banished me. Then why did it feel like I'd just lost something? Why did it—

Fucking stop it.

Torn, I yanked the shirt over my head, ignoring the buttons entirely, glad that when it settled into place, it practically hit my knees. I missed pants. And my knives. I fished through my hair for my sticks.

Son of a bitch.

Those sticks were the one thing that stayed with me when I shifted. I must have lost them in taking the coward's way out.

See? That's what you get. Now he's gone and who do you have to thank? No one but yourself.

And I was so busy mooning over whether or not I wanted Corvin to chase after me that I missed a vital detail in my inspection of the shore.

That stillness was not the winds finally calming on the water.

It wasn't my tumultuous emotions settling down.

It was a danger I hadn't anticipated—at least not this quickly.

So when magic slammed into me, knocking me off my feet, to say it caught me by surprise would be an understatement.

Unwanted and unwelcome, the magic burrowed into my very cells, absorbing into my tissues, changing the makeup of who I was. Without my permission, I stole that power, not knowing what it was or how to use it, only that it was mine now.

And worse?

It was a reminder of my past, of the wrongs done to me, of a very different *him*. Sucking in air, I tried to keep the memories out, tried to shove it down deep with all the other shit I refused to deal with.

But the rage stayed.

Blood poured from the gash in my shoulder as a mountain of pain seared every nerve ending I had, but I couldn't pay attention to any of that. No, I was stuck staring at the small army of white-robed figures surrounding me. Each one had a symbol on their breast of a bow and arrow, the reminder of their master clear as crystal.

To this day I couldn't forget *his* son, with his foot

on my neck and his bow across his back, a quiver of celestial arrows at his hip. Even though I didn't know their names, his face was burned into my brain. Their master was the son of the god I'd killed, one of the pair who'd banished me.

Thunder rumbled in the sky as lightning streaked through the rapidly forming clouds. I didn't have my sticks to guide it, but I didn't need them—not after all this time. After thousands of years, I'd managed to harness some of *his* power, managed to mold it, carve it into something I could use.

It didn't matter how much I'd wished to get rid of it or how I'd resented the reason I had it. This was the one time I would use it to my advantage without remorse.

The one at the center dropped a staff of light to the ground, the scent of burning flesh high on the air as he cradled his hand to his chest. It didn't take a genius to figure out what power I had now.

Someone *used to be* fireproof. Bet he wished he'd kept his magic to himself. His face twisted, his sneer pulling at his reddening flesh. "His children are coming for you, thief. They are owed their revenge."

I sort of figured five thousand years in prison was revenge enough. What thirst could my banishment not have quenched? What need did they have passed a near-eternity of me locked away? Because they and I both knew the very same thing.

If they could have killed me five thousand years ago, they would have.

Instead, they'd shoved me into a prison world never to be seen again.

Until now.

Underneath the robe of the man in charge, his skin bubbled and blackened, his scorched eyes turning white as if he had looked upon a true face of a god and lived to tell the tale.

Well, not for long.

"Let them come," I whispered, my body shaking with fury as I tried to hold in my stolen power. "I'd love to show them what five thousand years in their prison has done to me."

They wanted to threaten me? I was Styx of Tartarus. I was a murderer, an assassin, a thief, a god killer. But most of all?

I was pissed the fuck off.

My rage boiled over, striking the ground around me like the cage I'd escaped from. Bolts of lightning knocked him off his feet, driving the crowd back some as I ignored the burn in my muscles and joints.

Ignored the way using that power hurt for the first time.

Ignored the new energy racing through my veins like acid.

But as a stray bolt hit another acolyte, I realized just what the power I'd absorbed really meant. Because as soon as that energy hit him, he didn't so much as flinch. Thousands of volts of energy slammed into him at the speed of light and yet it was as if I hadn't touched him at all. It was worse than when Corvin had risen from the ground unscathed. It was worse because as much as I hated that he'd followed me, he hadn't meant me any harm.

These assholes?

Not so much.

That power that I had stolen all those years ago was useless to me now.

Hand-to-hand combat it was.

It took a split second for me to launch myself at my first foe, wrapping my legs around his waist and my hands around his head. Efficiently, I snapped his neck, ripping his skull clean off his body and tossing it at the first person that moved.

No one really realizes how hard skulls are until they're thrown. Sure, they're surrounded by a sort of a fleshy sack, but the weight of them, all those hardened bones to protect the brain? They were something of a weapon, and considering I had none, I'd take what I could get.

The next acolyte ducked, grabbing for the staff of their fallen leader, bringing it up sharply to my injured shoulder. But it didn't burn like before, the only pain I felt was from the still-bleeding gash and the poison-like fingers of that power snaking through my veins.

Growling, I snatched that staff out of his hands and snapped it over my knee. Two sticks were always better than one. The half in my left cracked against his jaw as the right slammed into the knee of the next asshole. And even though I was flagging, in agony with my body begging to quit, I didn't.

My foot shot out, kicking hard as I let a stick fly, the jagged end embedding into the chest of the next guy as I used the other as a bludgeon, damn near smiling as the blood flew. A lash of wicked heat against my back had me falling to my knees, the skin splitting as a blade made its second pass.

Fuck.

There were too many of them, and the burning in my veins was only getting worse. Sucking in a breath, I launched myself at another acolyte, my full-body tackle doing little except knock us both to the ground. A hard hand latched onto my wounded shoulder, fingers digging into the wound as another mindless cult member flipped me to my back.

A bloody sword in his hand, a crazy-eyed disciple started giggling.

"I will be rewarded for this," he said, tightening his grip on the sword. "Glory will be mine."

He enjoyed that victory for a single shining moment before he was knocked off his feet by the biggest fucking gargoyle I'd ever seen.

Gargoyles weren't a thing on Tartarus—or at least if they were, I'd never seen one—so to watch Corvin smash this whack job under his feet was a thing of beauty. Leathery wings slammed through the remaining crowd as his serpent tail whipped back and forth, taking whoever was still standing to the ground. A roar I felt all the way down to my bones was accompanied by a string of fire, and then he started taking heads, biting them clean off their bodies and spitting them out as if they tasted like dirt.

Slowly, I struggled to my feet, grabbing my fallen sticks of light, and helping cut through the rest. By the rest, I meant the last poor soul who'd managed to gather the brain cells to run. I let the stick fly once more, embedding into the runner's back. As soon as he hit the dirt, his body burst into ashes, the staff piece burning him from the inside out.

As it was, there weren't many left, but they couldn't get away from Corvin, his rage and ruthlessness cutting them down as if they were blades of grass.

I tried to stay standing once the last one fell—I really did—but that scorching agony was slowly leaching all the strength from my limbs. My knees buckled, and I slammed to the ground once again as the rest of me gave out.

In an instant I was in Corvin's arms.

"It's all right, Storm Cloud. We're going to get you some help."

The light was fading fast, but arguing with him was becoming one of my favorite hobbies. "I don't need your help," I slurred. "I'll be fine. Just leave me here."

That probably wasn't the best plan, but I'd take it over owing him a damn thing. My vision started to darken on the edges, but I still caught Corvin's incredulous expression as a fair amount of rage lit his human-shaped eyes on fire.

They were oddly pretty in a deadly sort of way.

"The fuck you don't," he growled back, his grip on me gentle but secure.

I probably would have had a biting remark to whip back at him, but my brain and body chose that moment to give up. I'd just take a little nap, and then I'd be right as rain.

Probably.

Maybe.

Ah, fuck. Probably not.

CHAPTER 8

CORVIN

I didn't think the first time I ever held Styx in my arms she'd be on the verge of death.

"Come on, Storm Cloud. I need you to open your eyes for me."

Scalding-hot blood flowed over my arm as I gently clutched her closer to my chest, the fear settling into my bones as reality hit me like a brick.

Who the fuck were those people?

Why had they tried to kill her?

What the fuck was going on?

And then the other questions started racing through my brain as her breaths became labored, her skin pale while she shivered as if she had a fever. I'd never been sick a day in my life. Not even when

I'd been beaten within an inch of it had I ever been this bad.

Would she survive this?

What had they done to her?

How was I supposed to help?

The only thing I could think of was to bring her to the water.

I'd watched Styx for miles as best I could from the air, catching brief glimpses of her shadow as she raced under the surface of the water, her dark body barely visible in the night. She'd surfaced upstream, taking down a deer that had taken a drink from the river at the wrong time. She'd torn into it with her sharp teeth, eating her fill before going back under the water and racing ahead.

In my limited knowledge of kelpies, I knew that they were carnivores, but I had been under the impression that they stuck to people as opposed to animals. I was glad that bit was wrong.

The water flowed over her skin, creating a cloud of red in the dark river, mixing with the inky wave of her hair as it washed the scarlet blood from her shoulder and back. A faint trickle dripped from her nostrils, but her eyes didn't so much as flicker once. Her breathing shallowed, and I wondered if I pushed her under the surface if it would help or if it would hurt her. Kelpies were an odd kind of Fae—both shifter and water Fae alike, straddling the line between the two species.

"Come on, Styx. I know you're harder than that," I taunted, praying that she would sit up and argue with me some more. I'd do anything to see those eyes flash with lightning, say anything to get that sharp tongue back.

"Where is the woman who shot me out of the sky, huh?"

The temperature of her body rose by the second as the blood continued to flow.

"Wake up, Styx," I commanded, infusing my words with the Alpha power I was born with. And still, it did nothing. No movement, no stirring, nothing. "Come on, baby. Open your eyes for me, please."

The water wasn't helping—not even a little. She needed to shift, to heal, but she couldn't do that unconscious and I couldn't make her. Even though I was an Alpha, I wasn't her Alpha. Plus, with her being a kelpie, I didn't know if she even would have a pack at all.

I needed more help than I could possibly give her.

I needed *my* pack. My family.

Without thought, I pressed at the sigil tattooed

into the flesh of my shoulder, calling every member of the Blackwell Pack to me. The sigil had been Penny's idea. In the early days of our pack, we'd been spread all over the Crossroads, and we'd nearly lost Knox altogether to some dipshit with something to prove. Now part of our initiation, Penny tattooed the Blackwell sigil into our skin.

Just in case.

In case we were too far apart, or hurt, or unable to get to help. It was a way to call us all together, a way for me to call my pack to me as their Alpha.

I'd never used it. Not once. Never had to.

Until now.

The magic seared my flesh, and I gritted my teeth against the pain as I clutched Styx closer to me, praying that it worked, praying that help was coming, wishing I had anything to offer this woman besides river water and hope.

It seemed like hours before anyone came.

Knox arrived first, letting out a low whistle when he saw the scatter of dead bodies on the shore. But something odd happened at his approach. I'd never been possessive a day in my life, but as soon as Knox stepped one toe toward Styx, my animal decided he'd come far enough.

A snarl ripped its way up my chest as flames

threatened to erupt from my throat. Unlike my half-brother Ronan, I couldn't wield the flames as if I were made of them. Being a hybrid, I was immune to heat and fire, the chimera form allowing me to breathe fire as well. But I'd never felt it want to erupt from my skin, never experienced the flames begging for freedom while I was in this flesh. Fire burned behind my eyes as blind fury nearly made me mindless.

And I had a feeling it was all due to the woman in my arms.

"Easy, boss," Knox murmured, his hands raised in surrender as his wings tucked into his back. "No one is going to take her from you."

It didn't matter what words fell out of his mouth, if he so much as moved one more step closer to her, I would take his fucking head off.

"Knox, I love you like a brother, so I'm only going to tell you this once. Stop. Don't come any closer to her. Understand? She needs Penny. If you can't find her, we need a healer—any healer. *Now.*"

Knox tilted his head to the side, his gold eyes studying Styx with confusion. "Penny will be here in a sec, boss. She's even bringing her bag."

A tiny niggle of relief hit me. Penny was coming. Styx would be okay.

She *would*.

Jude and Aster chose that moment to show up, his bear form lumbering from the forest in a quick clip with Aster on his back, her human form a rare sight. Aster wasn't a big fan of her human form, and it always took her a few days to knock the cat out of her system before she was back in her right mind.

Aster slid off Jude's back mid-run, her long legs eating up the distance before Knox stood in her way.

"Whoa, there. The boss is a little touchy about who gets near his lady friend. Might want to take it slow."

Aster flipped him off before ducking under his arm, skirting around my second like she was still in her cat form. "It's because you're a dude, dipshit. Since I don't have a penis, I'm fine."

Still, those wild green eyes stared me down as she picked her way closer to the shore. Aster stopped right at the water's edge, a softness I rarely saw crossing her expression before she masked it.

"She's dying, you know that, right?" Aster knelt at the shore, her head tilting to the side as if someone was whispering in her ear. Most likely one of the dead actually was speaking to her, something she managed to avoid at all costs in her animal form.

"She was poisoned. With power. The person they follow, he wants her dead."

Yeah, I caught that.

She shook her head, her eyes blackening with rage. "Oh, fuck you, buddy. I hope you stay in limbo forever, you slimy fuck."

I fought off the urge to yell. "What," I seethed through gritted teeth, "did they say?"

Aster shook her head. "Nothing of use. Just that he hoped her death was painful and that she deserved every minute of agony before she died. Called her a thieving whore."

I shouldn't have killed those men so fast. I should have made it hurt more. Clutching Styx closer, I murmured in her ear what I would do to anyone if they came for her again, promising to tear them apart slower, to make it hurt. Promising that I wouldn't let anyone do this to her again—not ever.

Not two minutes later, Penny's old Wrangler peeled through the quiet neighborhood. No doors, no roof, it was a rusted-out shit box of a vehicle run on magic and dreams, but it got her places in a hurry. Jumping the curb, she squealed to a stop as she and another member of my pack, Diana, jumped from the cab, Penny's witchy bag of tricks in tow.

Diana wasn't a shifter at all. Instead, she was a

Fae with no home and no family, kicked out after she'd disgraced her family somehow. I didn't ask questions—didn't need to—because I'd understood that shit all too well. She skidded to a stop, staring at Styx like she was looking at a goddess or something.

"Oh, she's *old*. And powerful," Diana whispered, her ice-blue eyes shining in awe.

"She's also dying," Aster broke in, her voice rough. "Can you two get the lead out sometime in this century before the boss loses his shit?"

Penny didn't bother with niceties as she snapped open her bag, pulling ingredients almost faster than I could track.

"Tell me what happened, what kind she is, something," she demanded like she was the Alpha and not me.

But how could I explain what I'd witnessed? I'd lost Styx in the convergence of the Missouri and Mississippi rivers. I'd thought she went east but she'd gone west, and I'd had to double back. In that time, she'd gotten ambushed, but that was about all I knew, and the shit didn't make sense at all.

"She's a kelpie with some kind of elemental power mixed in. These guys jumped her. Aster said she was poisoned, but…" I shook my head. "I don't know much else."

And didn't that just prove that Fate hated me? I'd spent ten weeks dreaming about her, trying to get to her, pleading with that fucking portal guard only to be denied at every turn.

Only to lose her now.

I *wouldn't* lose her now.

Couldn't.

"Tell me you can save her, Penny," I growled, not above begging if I had to. I didn't know the first thing about Styx other than she was the most beautiful woman I'd ever seen, had a scent that made my knees week, was a formidable fighter, had a tongue like a razor, and was apparently old as fuck.

I wanted a chance to know more.

But Penny didn't make promises she couldn't keep so she pressed her lips together as she worked her magic. "I can make her a universal antidote, but that might just be a Band-Aid on a war wound. Until she wakes up, I—"

"Just fucking fix her and don't be diplomatic about it," Aster growled, the strain in her eyes causing even me to wince. "She doesn't have time."

I wanted to give a shit that Aster was struggling

under the weight of all this death. I wanted to reassure Penny.

But the thing I wanted most of all was Styx to wake up.

"Open her mouth," Penny ordered, and Diana wedged her jaw open as I tried not to growl at either of them.

Penny dumped a vial of swirling purple liquid down Styx's throat, and Diana pinched her nose so Styx would instinctively gulp it down.

Instantly, Styx's black eyes flashed open, her body convulsing as the potion foamed at her mouth. Then she turned, crawling to the shore before she vomited all over the grass, the purple liquid mixed with a golden shimmer that would be pretty if it didn't remind me of the staff that had made her scream in pain.

"Styx, baby, are you okay?" I gathered her hair in my hand, the help insufficient but all I had. I couldn't touch her anywhere, her injuries too many to count.

"Get back," she croaked before heaving again. "Tell them to move. Run."

"Wh-what?"

She rose to her knees, her formerly black eyes now swimming with gold. Her back bowed as she cried out, her body convulsing as she tried to keep it together. "Get them back. I—I'll kill them. Save them."

But none of that made any sense.

Styx turned to my pack. "*Run,*" she commanded, enough Alpha in her words that anyone not moving already ran like their asses were on fire.

Penny, Aster, and Diana jumped in the Jeep, peeling out in a manner that told me if I wanted to live, I'd better do the same. Letting Styx go, I allowed the shift to take me, my wings catching air as she dove into the water, putting as much space as she could in between her and my pack.

The current took her downstream as her body began to glow like the surface of the sun. Then she let out an unholy scream as that light exploded out of her, detonating like a bomb. A web of golden power domed from her body before bursting like a bubble of heat.

The trees nearest to the river snapped in half, their jagged tips now burning embers as a wall of water carried Styx to the shore, dumping her on the rocks as she coughed and sputtered. I slowly circled before landing near her, allowing my body to shift back as I tried to keep my rage in check.

The wounds on her back were healing, but

they'd leave a scar that only time could erase, and even with that, she might have them for the rest of her life. She'd saved us by going to the water. Had any of my pack been near her, she would have killed them instantly. But she'd done it like something like this had happened before, like she'd been forced to damn near self-emolliate herself just so she wouldn't kill someone.

And according to Aster, the man who'd done this to her knew they were poisoning her. They *knew*.

I should have killed that fucker slower.

Styx took a wobbly step before collapsing, her legs too weak to support her. In an instant, she was in my arms again, only this time, she wasn't bleeding out.

"Don't worry, Storm Cloud. We'll get you all fixed up," I murmured, echoing the words I'd said right before she told me she didn't need my help. "You'll be right as rain soon enough."

She sagged in my hold, still trying to stand. "I'm going to pass out again, so don't freak out and shove any more magic down my throat." She gagged a little. "No more magic."

But as soon as she collapsed in my arms once again, I knew without a doubt we'd need a fuck of a lot more magic.

To keep her safe.

To keep her cloaked.

To keep her breathing.

I'd need to call in a favor, and the price could possibly be a fuck of a lot more than I could pay.

CHAPTER 9

STYX

The last time I'd woken up not in my own bed, I had peeled myself from Legion's floor after a night of far too many magically enhanced drinks. Funnily enough, my head felt about the same as it did then, even though I'd imbibed exactly zero alcohol.

Lucky me.

Corvin's singular masculine scent filtered into my nose as I buried my face in the pillow, reminding me just where I was and whose bed I was in. The slate-gray sheets were soft as butter, and I was pleasantly surprised to be wearing at least something since I'd burned off my stolen clothes. A large flannel shirt that had to be Corvin's covered my important bits, while what felt like bandages covered my back. The bandages were unnecessary, the wounds were already closed up tight, but the thought was there.

Gently, I sat up, grateful that my head decided to play along as I scanned the room. I'd lived in many places over the years. In rivers, in handmade shacks on the shore, in a castle, but after living in opulence for so long, my standards were high. Still, Corvin's room met every single one of them.

The midnight walls were adorned with ornate molding and chair rails, the fireplace surrounded in black and gold carvings. The bed was covered in plush blankets and pillows, the wood just as beautiful and ornate as the rest. But best were the windows. The entire wall was filled with them from floor to ceiling, and the view beyond made my heart squeeze it was so beautiful.

The house was set above a carved inlet from the river, almost like an engineered lake, and all I saw was water.

But better?

The sky was brightening by the second, the coming dawn painting the darkness in pale oranges and pinks, the night falling away to the coming day. If there was one thing I'd missed over the last ten weeks, it was the daytime. I hadn't seen it in so long, all I'd wanted was the warmth of it to fill me again.

The first rays of sunlight hit the inlet, creating tiny diamonds across the water in a scene so stunning, my chest physically ached with the fleeting joy of it.

And it was fleeting.

Those acolytes had found me within a day. Less than, if my calculations were correct.

How was I supposed to make the gods who'd banished me pay if they had an army to back them up?

How was I supposed to get rid of this awful power when I couldn't even save myself?

Sure, I would have eventually exploded without Corvin's help, but who was to say those bastards wouldn't have taken my head off first? Corvin had a whole pack behind him, and I'd nearly killed them all already.

It wasn't safe for me to be here, but until I could figure something out, I wasn't sure I could leave.

If Fate can smile upon the darkest of souls, she can smile upon you, too. Caius had been so optimistic, so blindly trusting that Fate would do right by me. I had half a mind to march across that portal and tell him a big, fat "I told you so."

Grumbling, I moved to one of the doors, praying for a bathroom. After I took care of business, I inspected the place. Like the castle, it had a large shower, a soaking tub, and a large vanity. On the sink was a toothbrush and paste, and three towels of different sizes with a note on top reading "For Styx."

I sniffed my hair. I smelled like the river, and considering how much trash had been on the bottom of it, that wasn't exactly a good thing. If I stayed in this town, I would need to do something about that.

And when did we start making plans?

Plans meant surviving killing the gods who'd killed my family.

Plans meant living beyond my revenge.

Plans meant that I was already changing my mind and it hadn't even been a day.

When did I become so weak?

Snatching the bath towel, I headed back to the shower and reluctantly divested myself of Corvin's shirt and turned on the tap. The soap smelled like Corvin, the woodsy, spicy scent making my whole body clench.

No.

Horny, pissed off, and cursing my body's reaction to even the barest hint of the man, I washed my hair, conditioned it, scrubbed my body, and refused to think about him naked.

Gods, did he look good naked. Like really, really good naked. A wave of need flooded me at the memory of him stalking toward me, his determination, his fire. There should be art devoted to that man's abs and legs and his arms and—

No. No thinking of the man naked.

By the time I peeled myself from the water, the scent of cooking meat wafted under the door, and my stomach howled in protest. Begrudgingly, I slid from the heat of the room, already missing the water as I spied a pile of clothes on a rolled arm settee in the corner. Next to it was a small end table with a lamp and a pile of books, and I fought off the urge to paw through them as I inspected the clothing.

On a closer look, I found that all the clothing, save for the folded shirt, was mine, freshly washed and the knives even sharpened. Hidden in the fabric of my jeans were four metal rods, two of which I'd lost while shifting, and the other two I'd abandoned weeks ago before escaping back through the portal.

He'd saved them.

I fought off the urge to smile, biting my lip so I didn't allow sentimentality to burrow its way into my chest.

Why should it matter that he'd kept them?

Why should it matter that his home was on the water?

Why should it touch me so that he had taken care to save my clothes and my knives?

Why did I keep thinking of him naked?

Oh, who was I kidding? If he did one more nice thing for me I would vomit all over this intensely plush rug and then attack him.

Stupid mate bond bullshit.

Roughly, I pulled on my pants, not at all giddy at the fact that my own shirt was ripped to shreds, and I had to settle for wearing Corvin's. It was purely for practicality. My shirt was in disrepair, and it did not matter one bit that this one happened to smell like him and was soft and made me feel like I was wearing a blanket.

Nope, it didn't matter at all.

Grumbling, I fed my arms through the sleeves after wiggling into my bra, managing not to part with the butter-soft fabric for more than a second.

And no, I was not going to give that any brain power, either.

I swept my wet hair up into a bun, securing it with my abandoned sticks, sheathing the other two next to my knives before hurrying from the room as silently as I could. The hinges of the door were well-oiled and didn't make even a whisper of sound as I absconded down the empty hall toward the staircase, following the scent of food.

After expending as much of the foul power as I could, it felt like the cells of my body were each screaming for sustenance. I needed to eat, and that small woodland animal from last night wasn't cutting it.

As I moved through the hallways, I found the kitchen by scent alone, admiring the way the plush carpeting adorning the dark wooden floors muffled every step. Sticking to the shadows, I spied Corvin at a stove turning meat with a fork. His wide back was hidden underneath a tight black shirt and jeans lovingly encased his ass. I both hated and admired both pieces of fabric for doing their job and preventing me from seeing all of him.

With his head tipped back, his eyes closed for what appeared to be patience, his dark wavy hair swept back from his face, I couldn't help but openly stare at him. Was this what mates did to you—made you absolutely enamored with every single facet of them? Because unfortunately, I was utterly blinded by how gorgeous Corvin Blackwell was.

I had never been taken by anyone in my life the

way I was with him. Five thousand years, and yet, I had never desired anyone, never thought of anyone, never obsessed over anyone the way I did him.

That made him dangerous.

Whatever hold he had on me, whatever bullshit Fate had in store, whatever this bond was, it was dangerous. In a way I couldn't define or quantify, allowing myself to fall into this trap would be the end of everything I was.

Everything I had always been.

It would be the end of *me*.

I contemplated just leaving, running as far and as fast as I could back to the portal, back home to Tartarus and calling it all off. Was revenge really worth it?

My family's faces flashed in my mind, clearer than they'd been in thousands of years.

Yes. They were worth it. Plus, now that the portal was open, I couldn't guarantee that the acolytes—and the gods they served—wouldn't try to cross over and find me, anyway.

And to top it all off, Corvin wasn't alone. Members of his pack sat around the corner, several of them laughing and joking, making him smile. I was equally happy he had bonds like that and so jealous it made my heart hurt. He could so freely give himself to people, laugh and joke and trust them without worrying about an ulterior motive.

I trusted four people, maybe five if you counted Reagan.

Not an entire pack.

I wasn't sure if I could ever trust that many people at once.

"I won the bet, you shit bags, and you're going to pay up one way or the other," a blonde waif of a girl said as she lifted a strip of meat to her lips and crunched down. "I called it a month ago. Boss has a mate."

"That's not fair," a big beefy man with a giant beard grumbled as he gently nudged her shoulder with his own. "You used some witchy juju to figure that shit out. I call bullshit."

"I did no such thing, thank you very much," she countered, flipping him off as she stuck out her tongue. "It's not my fault you can't read the signs. He has been fucking off to an unknown location every day at dawn. I figured he had to be going back to the portal because that's what he was doing for *weeks* before he started getting that hangdog expression all the time. It's just science. One plus one equals mate. *Duh.*"

He went back to the portal every day?

For weeks?

Why hadn't Oberon told me? Why…

Squeezing my eyes shut, I tried not to let the guilt pull at my insides. No wonder I had been dreaming of him. No wonder I'd been unable to get him out of my head.

I'd left him.

Not once had he left me.

"What I want to know is—what does the 'guinea pig for witchy magic' role entail? Because the bet did not cover ultimate experimental privileges on pack members," another girl demanded, sweeping a long fall of dyed black hair off her shoulder.

"Oh, you'll see," the blonde said, tapping her fingers together as an evil smile spread across her lips.

And I was so busy watching them interact that I didn't notice Corvin's eyes on me at first. Even in the shadows, I hadn't fooled him one bit, that cosmic tie between us selling me out immediately. And when I met that steel-blue gaze, everything in my body seemed to stop at once—my breath, my heart, my brain.

I was at his mercy, and I fucking hated how much I liked it.

But he didn't out me, he simply gave me a gentle smile as he brought a platter filled with food to the table. His pack tucked in, reminding me why I'd come downstairs in the first place.

My stomach took that opportunity to give me away, the unmistakable growl of hunger revealing my eavesdropping. The best I could do was walk in the room and show myself before the questions started.

But the welcome wasn't as frosty as it probably had a right to be. I'd nearly killed everyone in this room, and all I got were smiles and a chair pulled out at the table.

"For the love of the gods, give this woman some food before she devours us all," the black-haired girl said, but the venom was missing from her words, even if they were closer to the truth than she realized.

"I have a 'no eating women or children' rule. You're safe," I deadpanned, taking the offered plate and seat.

The girl's eyes widened a bit before narrowing to slits. "I can't tell if you're joking or not."

Not being a big joker even in the best of circumstances, I simply raised an eyebrow, allowing her to figure it out for herself. Corvin took the seat to my left at the head of the table and started filling my plate in earnest. Strips of meat and fluffy yellow clouds of something were mounded in the open space while cuts of juicy fruit filled the rest.

I would need about ten of these to feel full, but that was future me's problem.

But as I started to eat, I felt everyone's eyes on me, likely waiting for an explanation of some kind. One I couldn't give them. Still, I was eating Corvin's food in front of his pack. This was the one time I couldn't tell him to go fuck himself.

The silence stretched uncomfortably as Corvin's pack waited on tenterhooks to see if I would break. I wouldn't. I had outwaited and outlasted many enemies over the years, and I'd never broken once. Plus, watching them squirm was quite fun.

Eventually, it was the tall man with the hooklike nose and gold eyes that broke. He was oddly attractive in a way completely different from Corvin.

"Okay, I can't wait anymore," he growled, pulling his light-brown hair into a knot at the base of his neck. "What the fuck was that? One second, you're dying and then you're using Alpha mojo to make us run, and then—"

"She fucking exploded, that's what. You do that

often?" the big burly one grumped, still digging into food just as fast as I was.

"Knox, Jude, it's bad form to just start interrogating guests before they've eaten," Corvin scolded, his smile gentle. "We have to wait until her mouth is full before we ask the real hard hitters."

Naturally, he'd said that as I stuffed my face with the fluffy yellow stuff. It was savory and buttery and so good I moaned. I ignored them all in favor of tasting the bread. It, too, was fluffy and flaky and... I swear if Corvin could cook like this, I would probably have to reconsider my stance on that whole "mate" thing.

"What is this?" I asked once I swallowed, ignoring all the other questions.

Corvin frowned, staring at the bread. "You've never had a biscuit before?"

I shook my head. "Or the yellow stuff. Or the meat. We have different food in Tartarus. It's not bad food—actually all of it is phenomenal—but not this stuff."

"I swear to the gods, it's like she's from Mars or something," the black-haired girl muttered as I took another heaping bite. "Those are eggs."

"Eggs of what?" I asked around my food, the buttery goodness turning to ash in my mouth. I had a "no eating young" rule, and there were plenty of things that I did not want to eat the eggs of. "I'm eating young?"

Corvin covered his mouth as he chuckled. "Unfertilized eggs of chickens—small birds bred to produce the eggs for food. The eggs are used in many dishes, and the birds will produce them whether we eat them or not. You're not killing anything."

Fair enough. Still, that swallow of food was a doozy.

"Are we really talking about the ethics of egg consumption over here?" the blonde griped, staring at me like I'd grown another head. "This lady damn near dies in your arms, and we're discussing biscuits and *eggs*?"

There was a third woman sitting quietly as she nibbled on a circle of meat, staring at me like she knew what I was. Her red hair flowed over one shoulder as her blue eyes seemed to see all the way through me. She knew a lot more than what she was saying but I had to correct the blonde.

"I wasn't dying. Hurt, yes. Dying, no. I might have been close to death, but trust me, I've been alive for a very long time, and I can assure you death does not want me."

The black-haired one frowned heavily, staring at me like she couldn't quite figure me out. "But you were dying. I mean, I felt it. There was enough death on you to take out an entire city block."

I simply shrugged. How could I explain to her that Tartarus was full of death? That I had killed so many that it was likely embedded in my very cells? That I had taken more lives than I could count? That I'd hurt more people—both intentionally and not—than I could even fathom?

"Do you sense death on me now?" I asked, watching as her brow furrowed and sweat dotted her hairline.

"Yes. A lot of it. It's like you're one step away from the grave."

"That's just me, sweetheart. And I'd be willing to bet if you went to Tartarus, you'd see plenty of that around. Death magic, shadow magic, and darkness is pretty much all Tartarus is, and I've been there for a very long time."

Most likely she was a death Fae of some kind, probably mixed with a shifter of some sort. Most of Corvin's pack—except for the redhead—were of mixed breeds, and that I understood. There were many mixed breeds in Tartarus, the portal changing us all significantly in one way or another. Those with shifter blood turned into shadow shifters, the portal making us more bloodthirsty, more violent, more ruthless. Those with other magics were changed as well, their powers tuned more to darkness or death as time continued on.

And people like me who were both shifter and *not* at the same time? We changed, too.

"That doesn't make any sense, you look fine but..."

"Aster, she said she was fine," Corvin murmured, filling the empty space on my plate with more food. "And it doesn't matter who those people were. Once Isaac gets here, no one will be looking for her again."

My gaze flashed from my food to Corvin's face. In it there was a dogged determination that wouldn't be easily swayed. My eye twitched, a white-hot bout of rage making the whole house shake with the booming thunder outside.

Of all the high-handed, bullshit, macho-man behavior.

"What have you done?" I asked, rising from my chair as I pressed my hands onto the thick wooden table so I wouldn't zap him where he stood.

"I called in a favor."

CHAPTER 10

CORVIN

Thunder shook the very foundations of the pack house as Styx's eyes flashed with wrath.

Normally I'd be intimidated, but I'd carried her limp body across town in Penny's Wrangler, praying that she didn't decide to die on me. I'd held her in my arms as I dressed her, watched over her while she slept, and then when I'd realized there was no other way, had I made the call.

Did I want to know every single facet of information about the people who had nearly taken my mate from me?

Abso-fucking-lutely.

But I wouldn't hound the cagey woman for details until she was calm. Right then, rage was the prevalent emotion and getting answers was secondary to her not burning my house down.

"I told you no more magic. It wasn't something I said in the heat of the moment, Corvin. Who. Did. You. Call?"

My brother Ronan shared his mate with two other men, their bond not common but not unheard of, either. Isaac was also bonded to my brother's mate, the master vampire a former enforcer for the now-defunct Clan Tepes. I'd had plenty of dealings with Isaac over the years, and as long as he didn't spill my secrets all over Destiny and Dragomir, calling in this favor wouldn't hurt.

Much.

"A friend from New York—back home," I amended when she gave me a confused frown. "He and my brother are mated to the same woman. I'm probably going to owe him more than I can pay, but you need to be cloaked so those people can't find you again. They were trying to kill you. You get that, right?"

Thunder clapped outside, rattling the windows and making the lights flicker. The once-bright morning was now a squall of a storm, the rain battering the house as if we were in the middle of a hurricane.

Her eyes flashed with the same lightning that hit the ground right outside the back door. "The sword to my back was a bit of a clue. Nearly blowing up your entire pack, nearly getting my head cut off... Yeah, I'm aware that they were trying to kill me."

I might have had my fear of losing her, but Styx had lived it. My experience was periphery but hers was the war. Eyes flashing, fists clenched, arches of electricity flowing between the metal rods in her hair—it all made me realize that her rage hadn't even begun to reach its peak.

"What I want to know is," she whispered, her tone deadly, "why you think taking on my problems as your own and not asking before making decisions about my. Fucking. Life. Is even in the realm of okay?"

I was an asshole. I knew that without question.

But at least this asshole would keep her breathing.

Then the fact that we have a live audience to this little row filtered into my brain.

You're the Alpha, dipshit. Act like it.

"I realize this is like a soap opera for you guys, but I really need you to step out," I said, meeting Knox's eyes over Styx's head. He knew damn well what I wanted, and I didn't have to say a word.

Knox let out a low whistle, shaking the group out of their stupor, each of them rising from their chairs, taking their plates, and absconding with a platter before leaving the room. Styx and I needed to have a conversation, and we needed to have it now.

"Why no magic?" I asked, skirting around my chair as I stalked closer to her. She wanted to be pissed, fine. But if I couldn't protect her in the only way I knew how, she needed to tell me why. "What's the big deal?"

Styx's lips pressed together into a thin line as she shook her head. It was as if she were holding herself back, holding it all in. That dam needed to break.

Taking my life into my hands, I crowded her, latching onto her sparking fingers, pulling her to me so her chest was flush with mine. She smelled like my soap, and I fought off the urge to bury my nose in her neck and bite.

"Tell me, Storm Cloud. Make me understand why you won't accept basic protection."

And when the dam finally broke, I wasn't prepared for what she said.

"I steal it," she whispered, those gorgeous eyes hitting my shoulder instead of staying on mine. "Not on purpose, but..." She looked at the ceiling, likely not even seeing it. "Do you hear that thunder outside? The rain? I wasn't born with that power. I was born a kelpie—just a plain, everyday kelpie with nothing added, nothing special, and I was fine with that."

I squeezed her waist, urging her to go on.

"This power? It was thrust upon me. I didn't ask for it. I didn't want it, but I stole it on accident. And then it got every single member of my family killed. It got me thrown into Tartarus. The place is a fucking prison. Did you know that? Where they put the people that they can't control."

I had no idea how long she'd been there or what guilt she might have been carrying, but damn if it didn't make me want to pull her closer.

"So when you blew up at the river..."

She shook her head, gritting her teeth for a second before showing me those beautiful black eyes finally free of the lightning of her rage. "They ambushed me. One of them used their magic on me, and I stole it. That's not even the right word. I *absorbed* it. I took it from him."

She pulled out of my arms, planting her ass on the edge of the table as she ran her hands over her face.

"That's what happens when I'm hit with magic

or touched by magic. I absorb it. I take it away from the person who touches me with it. Sometimes it stays with me forever like the thunder outside, like the lightning. Sometimes I can get rid of it. Sometimes I have no choice *but* to get rid of it."

Hence the reason she exploded. She'd had no choice in the matter at all. The power she'd absorbed was like poison. Whoever had attacked her had poisoned her on purpose, maybe?

"So when you say don't use magic on you…"

She rolled her eyes as she twisted the sleeve of my shirt in her hands. "I mean, don't fucking use magic on me. I've never experimented with it, so I don't know how it works. I just know not to use it."

I pulled the sleeve from her grip, urging her to look at me. "Tell me how I'm supposed to protect you. Give me another way to keep you safe, and I'll call Isaac off. I'll do what you ask, just give me a better option."

"I don't know, okay?" she growled, shoving off the table and starting to pace. "I didn't expect them to find me so fast. I don't even know how they managed it. Maybe it's the power I use, maybe it's me. Maybe they knew as soon as I crossed the portal. All I know is I am a walking bullseye and if I don't get the fuck out of here as soon as possible, I could be bringing them straight to your door."

Okay, I'd had about enough of this. Catching her on a turn, I pulled her to my chest, backing her up against the pantry door. "How about we give Isaac a choice? He can choose to help you of his own free will, or he can choose not to. Maybe he knows of another way to cloak you that doesn't involve touching you with magic. But you do need to be cloaked because you're not dying on my watch. I offered you help long before I knew the risk, and now that I do—"

"You are being ridiculous. I don't need your help."

I fought off the urge to growl. Instead, I tipped her chin up and stared into those fathomless eyes of hers, trying not to get lost in them.

"Yes, you do."

"You need to get the whole 'mate' shit out of your head. Helping me now isn't going to change my mind. The only thing it's going to do is put you and your pack in danger."

Dipping my nose to her neck, I took in her heady scent. Over the perfume of stress and apprehension was the blatant call of need. I affected her just as much as she did me. She just wouldn't let herself have me.

"You've already changed your mind, Storm Cloud," I whispered, fighting off the urge to nip at the tender flesh of her neck. "You just won't admit it to yourself yet. But don't worry. I'm a patient man. I can wait."

Trembling, she fisted her hands at her sides. "Don't you get it?" she whispered. "I'm a bad bet."

No, she wasn't. She was the mother of all prizes, a being so elusive and wild that just existing in her orbit was intoxicating as fuck. "Why don't you let me worry about that?"

"And get you and your pack killed in the process? Yeah, I can see how that's not going to weigh on my conscience at all."

My thumb brushed over her full bottom lip as I fought off the urge to kiss her right where she stood. "It's not your pack. It's mine. I'm their Alpha, and they trust me to know what's best for them. If they trust me, why can't you?"

She shoved at my shoulders with a little more *oomph* in it than I expected from her. Then again, I did watch her tear a man's head off with her bare hands, so maybe that was my bad.

"I told you already, trust is an illusion. It doesn't

exist—it never has. What you're talking about is faith, and I don't have that, either."

No trust *and* no faith? Time had not been kind to my little Storm Cloud.

"Well, that's too bad, but don't worry. I'll have enough faith for the both of us."

Styx opened her mouth, probably ready to tear me a new one, when the man of the hour waltzed into my kitchen like he owned the place.

"I realize you two planned on a much longer argument," Isaac drawled, "but I have places to be."

Of course Isaac would have already arrived. Word was that his court had a witch in their pocket who could do portal potions that allowed him to jump across long distances in a matter of seconds. I'd tried getting Penny to give that a go with little success, and given how much energy it had taken her to cloak this home and property, she'd done more than enough.

Styx straightened, eyeing Isaac like she was trying to decide whether she wanted to kill him first and ask questions later or let him speak. She went with option two.

"I take it you heard our little discussion, then?" Her eyes flashed with her power, making Isaac smile.

"Of course. Eavesdropping is a pastime of mine. I know a Fae with your same predicament. She's something of an anomaly in the Fae culture. We call them Echoes, though when Ender takes a power, it eventually fizzles out once she uses it for long enough."

Ender was Ronan's kin, his half-sister on his father's side, and she had been instrumental in taking their father down and reshaping what New York was today.

"But fun fact?" Isaac said, his smile widening as he seemed to get a kick out of Styx's inspection. "Ender can't take my power because it isn't used on her directly. She only takes active powers and attacks. How much are you willing to bet that you're the same?"

Come on, Storm Cloud. Give him a chance. My mental urging wasn't making her move any faster, so I threw in a carrot.

"If you want to get the drop on people, it's best to work in the shadows, right? They can't attack you if they don't know where you are."

Styx sucked in a breath through her nose, her eye twitching ever so slightly, and I knew she was about to give in.

"Fine, but if you suddenly can't cloak people, that is not my fault. You were warned."

Isaac chuckled. "For what your boyfriend is paying, I'll take the risk."

"He's not my boyfriend," she growled, fingers sparking once again.

"Mate, boyfriend, fuck buddy, whatever."

"Again, he is none of those things," she insisted, and while it was sort of true, it also stung a little.

I searched the ceiling for patience. "She is my mate, but she's a little hesitant to pull the trigger on that. So, if you could get your nose out of my love life, that would be just peachy."

"Fair enough."

Isaac slowly withdrew a blade from his pocket, showing it to Styx like she'd either bolt or gut him where he stood. Personally, I'd bet on door number two, but that was just me.

"I need a drop of your blood. I prefer not to take it the old-fashioned way," he said, pointing to his fangs. "You can cut yourself or I can cut you. You choose."

Styx eyed his blade before pressing a single finger to the tip, her scarlet blood welling onto the metal before she drew it back. Isaac brought the knife to his mouth, licking off the drop before his eyes widened. He staggered back a step, knocking into the table before hitting his knees in the middle of the kitchen.

Blood dripped from his nose as he clutched his temples, a roaring scream ripping from his lungs as he worked his magic.

Styx staggered back from Isaac, her hands covering her mouth as she stared at him in horror.

After a few moments, Isaac's screams died down, but he didn't stand. No, he sucked in huge breaths as he tried to get his bearings.

"Fuck the deal we made, Blackwell. I don't want payment from you."

I yanked him up by his shoulder. "Now wait a minute here—"

He shoved me off, his gaze boring a hole into Styx. "I want payment from her. *If* I do this—and it is a big if—*she* will owe me a favor of my choosing."

"No," I growled, stepping in between them.

"I accept," Styx whispered, brushing me aside to shake Isaac's hand.

Isaac took it as he wiped at his bloody nose. "You could have warned me. I would have prepared myself better."

"She did," I growled, not liking his hand on her one bit. "Now get your paws off of her, asshole."

Isaac let her go, but gave me a quizzical expression. "You have no idea who she is, do you? What she's done. What's she's cap—"

Styx moved faster than I'd ever seen, gripping Isaac's throat in her hand and lifting him off his feet. "If you want to keep that tongue, I suggest you keep your mouth shut."

"If you kill me," he rasped, "the cloaking dies with me."

Styx seemed to be thinking it over, her eyes crackling in time with the thunder outside.

"How will you honor their deaths if you let their murderers go free?" he croaked, his face turning purple.

Honor whose deaths? Who had she lost? What the fuck was he talking about?

Styx lowered Isaac to his feet. "If I hear a word of my origins on another's lips, I'll know exactly who told them. I've been a hunter for a very long time. I'll find you one way or another. No favor or cloaking in the world will save you from me, understand?"

Isaac had read her blood, and the secrets he now knew, Styx would kill to keep.

"Understood. Do you accept this bargain? Cloaking from your enemies for as long as I live in exchange for one favor of my choosing."

"No killing women or children. No hurting those I am loyal to. And no dicking with the portal to Tartarus," she clarified, her tone stating that she would kill him if he refused.

"Obviously. What kind of man do you take me for?" Isaac had the gall to ask, rolling his eyes.

A dead one if he didn't quit fucking around.

Styx sighed before grasping his hand again. "We have a bargain, vampire."

Quickly, she released him, stepping away as if she didn't want to be anywhere near him. Did the truth of her past make her uncomfortable, or was it just that Isaac had power over her?

Either way, it made sense to remove him before she decided him knowing who she was made things too complicated for her. Wrapping an arm around his shoulders, I moved him bodily from the room, ushering him to the front door while he still had the use of his legs.

Isaac pulled a potion bottle from his pocket, but he paused before he could use it. He turned it in his hands, not saying anything for a good long while.

"She reminds me so much of Cira it hurts," he murmured, his voice pitched so low I knew only I could hear him. "Strong but broken, fierce but kind, beauty created from the ugliest of origins. I've cloaked her as best as I could, but even I have limits. She needs to solve her problem fast."

He moved to leave, but stopped short, hesitating for a second. "Treat her with care, Blackwell."

With that, he exited my home, crossing the warding before smashing the portal potion and winking out of sight.

I had already planned on treating Styx with care.

I just hoped it was enough.

Staying in that kitchen with Isaac's blood on the floor—blood I'd made him shed just from him reading my sordid history—made me want to scream. Anyone knowing that much about me made me consider killing him on principle, but the protection of his cloaking was a benefit I'd never had.

Granted, I'd never needed it, but...

The glass door led to the rear of the property and the inlet, the water calling my name over the scent of food and blood and fear. Somehow, I'd managed to lose my appetite, a feat I didn't think possible.

Before Corvin could come back, I took my exit, allowing the rain to kiss my skin, hoping that it would wash away some of my anxiety. Sure, Isaac said he could cloak me, but what was one vampire's power against two gods? He could make his bargain and his claim all he wanted, but I was smart enough to know the truth of it all.

His ward would fail.

They would come.

And I wouldn't be able to save Corvin or his pack.

If I were smart, I would jump in that water and swim as fast and as far as my legs could carry me.

If I were smart, I would run back to Tartarus. I would ask Caius for help, and I would reject Corvin if only to save him from what was coming.

If only to save him from me.

I picked my way down to the dock, the call of the water almost too much. Slipping off my boots, I allowed myself a single moment to think it over. Running wouldn't stop Corvin from following me. It wouldn't stop him from getting hurt at my expense. He would seek me out one way or another, because it didn't matter what cloaking power Isaac had, mate bonds were stronger than any magic on the market.

Corvin would find me.

He would try to protect me.

And he would die doing it.

Pulling up my jeans, I planted my ass on the dock, dipping my toes to touch the cool water. I had been solitary for so long that being around this many people made my skin itch. There were so many personalities, and I knew most of them were hiding, scared away by my lightning and my thunder, running away from my rain.

I pulled my feet from the water, turning so my belly was resting on the dock, all so my fingers could play in the only thing that was even remotely similar to home. A trio of fish, silvery in their scales, came to see what the fuss was about, their fins tickling my fingertips as the rain continued to pelt me.

Corvin would want the truth. He would want to know exactly what Isaac had seen, and I had no intention of telling him—not really. Because how would I possibly broach the subject of what had happened to me—of what had happened to my family?

How their deaths were my fault.

How my sentence was my fault.

How they hadn't even wanted to come here, but I'd thought this new world would be good for us.

How I'd caught the eye of a god as we crossed to Earth realm, and he'd become obsessed.

How I'd refused him.

How...

Swallowing, I squeezed my eyes tight, trying to ignore the thunder rumbling in the sky.

Years I'd been praying for vengeance, and now I was more worried about this pack—these people—than I was about the blood I owed to the family I'd lost.

I should be ruthless. I'd been that way since I'd landed in Tartarus, and yet...

"You'll freeze to death out here," a woman said, her presence catching me off guard.

Instantly, I found my feet, a blade in my hand before I even thought about it. It was the redhead from the breakfast table, her pale-blue eyes wide as she held her hands up in surrender.

I was off my game. There was no way this woman could sneak up on me if I had been paying attention. *See?* This was what mooning over feelings got you. Snuck up on by a fragile little girl.

"Unlikely," I muttered, stowing my blade. "I like the cool weather, and the water is much warmer than out there." There was mountain runoff in the river, the deepest parts of it nearly freezing. I absolutely loved it.

Caius' castle was built into the side of a volcano.

I welcomed the cool breeze and chilly water more than I could possibly say.

"It hasn't rained this much in years. You are either going to wash out my tulip bulbs or we're going to have a mud pit soon enough." Her gaze roamed over the soggy earth, and I spied the drenched flower garden near the house. "I'm Diana by the way. We weren't introduced before."

I didn't know what tulips were, but I got the gist. Closing my eyes, I pulled in a breath, trying to calm my tumultuous thoughts. By the time I opened them, the rain had stopped, the thunder quieted, and the clouds rolled back to reveal a cool winter sky.

"Sorry about that. Better?"

Diana rubbed at her damp sweater, the sun's rays doing little to warm her. "That'll do. You planning on making a break for it?" She tilted her head to the side. "You're a kelpie, right?"

Did I want to make a break for it?

Yes and no.

Could I even call myself a kelpie anymore?

Yes and no.

And while it was still true I didn't want a mate, the thought of leaving Corvin behind after he'd sacrificed so much already, after he'd helped, after he'd come to my rescue... It seemed like a slap in the face to up and leave now.

I didn't typically do that to people who didn't deserve it.

"I just like the water," I answered, staring out at the river, hoping it had the answers to my problems.

She had a secret sort of smile on her lips that told me she knew something I didn't. "Oh, I know." She paused, seeming to contemplate something for a minute. "Did you know this house wasn't on the water when it was built originally?"

My gaze swept over the natural curves of the inlet, noticing the lush vegetation even in the middle of winter. It had to be an earth Fae's doing for sure.

"Corvin came here from New York about a year or so ago and had this house built. I think he knew he was starting something here—wanting a pack for himself after the Syndicates went bust. But the river was all the way over there." She pointed in the distance. "About two and a half months ago, the boss asked Jude and I for a favor—requested that we carve out this inlet and build a dock. He wanted to make sure that water touched the property. Said it was imperative."

She eyed me like a was a bug she was studying. "I wonder who that was for?"

I swallowed hard, biting my tongue so the bittersweet ache of it didn't drag me under. All this time he'd been helping me, carving out a space for me in his life. And all I'd done for him was turn and run away.

All I'd done was tell him no.

All I'd done was deny him.

This had to be one of the nicest things anyone had done for me in my entire life. No one had ever done something like that for me without cause or reason, without asking for something in return.

"I didn't even know his name then," I croaked, trying to deny what we both knew. "How could this be for me?"

Her gaze softened, a secret smile pulling at her lips. "You know better than that. Who else would it be for?"

I didn't have an answer for that.

"I'm not going anywhere," I assured her, knowing that it probably didn't matter what I said. She was likely babysitting me on her Alpha's orders. "You don't have to stay out here with me. I know you're cold."

"That's not the only reason I'm out here." She

sat on the cool dock, rubbing at her arms for warmth. "I wanted to take your measure."

This wasn't the first time I'd been told I wasn't good enough. Might as well get it over with. "And what's the verdict? Have you come to the same conclusion I have? That your Alpha is probably better suited for someone else?"

And why did that sentence feel like I just swallowed thorns? Why did the thought of him finding another make me want to vomit and cry and scream all at the same time? Why did it make me want to find this imaginary bitch and cut her from end to end and wear her lungs as earrings?

And why did the truth of it just cut me to the bone?

It didn't make any sense.

I didn't make any sense.

I didn't want a mate—didn't deserve one—so why did it suddenly hurt to breathe?

"No," she murmured, shivering now. "I think the only person who thinks that is you. I learned a long time ago that Fate always comes out on top in the end. Her chess moves far outweigh what we can see with our own two eyes."

My laugh was bitter as I held out my hand, pulling her up. She needed to go inside, and I doubted she would with me out here. "Fate hasn't been kind to me a day in my life. I doubt she'd start now."

Snagging my shoes, I led her back to the house, knowing I'd need to plan my escape soon enough. Staying here any longer would only make it harder to leave.

And I would need to leave.

Right?

So why couldn't I?

Thirty minutes later, I was thumbing through Corvin's books when he swept into his room, his eye nearly twitching as a dark cloud of his emotions surrounded him like a cloak. He didn't stop at a respectable distance from me, either. No, he crowded me, herding me so my back was against the wall, his jaw set and eyes wild.

I didn't know what had happened between him ushering Isaac out and now, but whatever it was, it had changed something in him.

"Tell me," he ordered, his demand straightening my spine.

"Tell you what?"

His head tilted, silence reigning for a single moment. "A complete stranger to you knows your entire life story and your mate does not. Doesn't that bother you? Because I have to admit, it bothers the fuck out of me."

I fought off the urge to tell him I didn't want a mate. It hadn't done any good so far—why would it do any good now?

"If I would have known my blood would tell him everything about me, I would have never given it to him."

Corvin simply nodded, like my answer didn't surprise him in the least. "Isaac told me that he can only cloak you so much, that the people that are looking for you are likely more powerful than he is. That you don't have time to fuck around about finding them and killing them first."

I didn't know why, but I didn't think Corvin would tell me that truth. And with every good, nice, pure thing about him, my walls crumbled just a little bit. Already I'd been worrying about his pack, his life, instead of my own revenge.

Was this what mates did to you? Made you think about people other than yourself? Made you not as selfish?

Was this what Caius had become? The darkest among us turned soft as mush for the right woman?

But I already knew the answer to that. It was a resounding yes.

"I figured as much," I murmured, training my eyes on the column of his throat rather than meeting his steel-blue gaze. I had to admit it was a good throat, strong and thick with just a hint of stubble on his jaw. I wanted to mark it, taste it. Just a little.

Focus.

"Tell me what's happening," he urged, his hot hands on my hips like twin brands. "Tell me who's after you. Tell me something, Styx."

And just like that, I crumbled, giving in when I had no business allowing this man anywhere near my problems.

"I don't know who is after me," I admitted, saying it out loud for the first time ever. "I don't know their names. That's what I was looking for in the bookshop. I was researching sky deities. That's about all I have."

That wasn't exactly true. I knew what they looked like, but unless those books had five-thousand-year-old pictures, the makeup of their faces wouldn't exactly be of any help.

Corvin backed up a step, his fingers lifting my chin so I had to look in his eyes. "You've been in prison for who knows how long, and you have no idea who sent you there?"

When he said it like that, I sounded like an idiot.

But if I knew their names, I would have asked Caius ages ago. I would have had a plan. But Nadia had been right. There were hundreds of sky deities, and too many to count that had lightning abilities. Narrowing it down would take forever, and I was one person with no time to waste.

"Yeah, that about sums it up."

Corvin nodded, a calculating look in his eye. "Sky... *deities*. As in gods?"

At my hesitant nod, he drew away from me, catching my hand in his and pulling me toward the door.

"So we go back to the bookshop, expand our research. Two heads are better than one and all that."

And damn it all, I let him take me to that store, once again leading him right into the belly of the beast.

CHAPTER 12

CORVIN

Tasty Tomes was about the last place I wanted to be. The shop was musty, the owner was a people-eating sociopath, and I worried that the information that Styx needed wasn't even here. But I'd told my mate that I would help her look through these musty, crusty books, and I was a man of my word.

The section on deities alone was ten bookcases deep, each filled to the brim with information that could be true or could be a load of bullshit. And the shopkeeper, Nadia, wasn't exactly the most helpful of creatures.

Glamour solidly in place, the small woman toddled around the stacks of books, pestering Styx for more information. Styx warned me of what was hiding under that glamour, and to say I was not a fan would be an understatement.

"I don't know who you think you're fooling with that glamour," Styx muttered, thumbing through a book that was written in a language I didn't under-stand. I supposed I could have asked a witch for a language matrix, but we'd been in a rush.

"What if I have more customers?" Nadia grumped, pulling another three thick leather-bound books from the shelf to add to my mate's stack. "I can't just go slithering about. I would like to eat dinner sometime in the next year."

"I thought you only ate customers who couldn't pay up," Styx accused, her finger following the ancient squiggles as if she understood every word.

"No, I told you if *you* couldn't pay up, I would eat you. There's plenty of reasons to eat people nowa-days. Sometimes they dog-ear pages, break bind-ings, don't shelve the books back where they're supposed to go. Plenty of reasons. You let one thing go, and then they're burning your whole library down."

She sounded like a librarian with a grudge, but who was I to say?

"I would prefer not to know any of this," I muttered, thumbing through one of the few texts on sky deities that I could actually read. There were texts in ancient Sumerian, Latin, Arabic, Aramaic, but none in more recent ones that I knew.

Nadia rolled her eyes. "And I would prefer your mate to give me something I could actually use instead of being stingy with the details of what she's looking for, but here we are." She turned to the stack of books Styx had already skimmed through and discarded. "A weapon, an ability, *something*."

While I knew that the white-robed psychopaths had the sign of an archer on their chests, I wisely kept my mouth shut. Styx didn't trust Nadia, and she was smart not to. Lamias weren't known for their honesty.

"You could give me your hand, and I could—"

"I believe we've already had this conversation. I said no. No, you cannot have my hand. No, you cannot have my blood. No, you cannot do whatever creepy lamia bullshit you have in store, okay? The answer is no."

Nadia seemed offended, but it was tough to discern what was part of her glamour and what was actually her. Whatever she'd paid for the thing was not enough. It was damn near impenetrable. "I was simply trying to help. I have no intention of eating you. I have a feeling you would taste like river water and that is not exactly my favorite flavor."

Styx slammed the book shut, spearing the small woman with a glare so fierce it was a wonder she didn't die where she stood. "And snake isn't one of mine, but if you fuck around, I'll still have you for lunch."

This was getting us nowhere, and as soon as Nadia fucked off, I could ask Styx more questions. "Ladies, could we get back to the task at hand?"

"I just don't understand why she's being so cagey," the lamia griped, pointing at Styx like I didn't know prying information out of my mate was the equivalent to attempting to open a welded-shut box with a butter knife. "She wants a book. I want to sell her a book. If she told me what she was fucking looking for, I could actually be of service."

Maybe the lamia had actually been a librarian at one point.

"The absolute last thing I need is your nosy ass in my business," Styx muttered, turning another page. "How was I supposed to know there were hundreds of sky deities in this stupid world?"

"How many deities do you have in yours?" I asked, my curiosity getting the better of me.

"A few. Not a thousand books worth. And only one that actually matters."

Nadia stalked off in a huff, grumbling about cagey kelpies and how Styx had better not mess up her books. Styx snorted as she turned another page, settling in to sit cross-legged on the floor surrounded in piles.

"What's Tartarus like?" I asked, wanting to talk to her about something—*anything*—that wasn't this. Yes, we needed to find the people after her, but I could tell the search was drowning her spirit.

"A lot like here in some ways. There's no sun, but there are twin moons that give off a lot of light. We have volcanoes and acid-filled lakes, but also a wide sea that goes on and on, and my river. There's also a dead spot that is kind of frightening—even for me—but there's still civilization. There are families and species of plants that we'll never find here. There's life and we've built a real community. I mean, of course the worst of the worst are housed there, but I don't know..." She shrugged, scanning the next page. "I've lived there so long, it became my home."

"Do you have a home—a house—I mean?"

She shook her head, blindly giving me more information than she ever had. I didn't know how

I'd convinced her to open up to me, but I was damn glad she had.

"No, I live in the castle with Caius and Reagan and most of the court."

Was the instant white-hot jealousy rational? Absolutely not, but that didn't stop me from asking my next question.

"And Caius is?"

Styx pried her gaze from the book, her squint telling me I hadn't exactly been subtle with that question.

"Caius is the primordial god who created Tartarus. He's my king and his mate Reagan is the queen. He found her when the portal opened. It was a whole 'key to the cage' situation. Who knew the key to his cage would be his mate?"

That sounded like a story I'd like to hear one day —if she'd tell it. "And you have friends there, yes? People you care about?"

Styx frowned, turning another page. "A few. I figure you've met at least one at the portal— Oberon? I have a few others. Not a lot, nothing like your pack, but I've never needed much."

And wasn't that the truth? I doubted Styx would complain even if I held a gun to her head. She just wasn't made to sweat the small shit.

"Lovers?"

Was I a jealous asshole for asking? Yes.

Did I give a shit? No.

She pulled a face that made me laugh outright. "Gross. No. Never, ever. Not in a million years. Caius and Oberon are like family."

"I meant—do you have someone back home? A lover? Not—"

Dawning realization crossed her expression before it shuttered. "*Oh*. No. I'm not a big relationship kind of girl. I'm not saying I've never taken a lover—it's just being on Caius' court means not really being able to trust other people."

And as relieved as that made me, it also hurt, too. Because how long had she been alone? How long had she been in Tartarus with no one to comfort her? No one to come home to?

"You don't trust anyone, anyway," I murmured, pulling up a spot of floor next to her and snagging a book.

"True."

Her smile was small, but that tiny lift to her lips was practically a toothy grin according to Styx.

"What about you?" she asked. "I remember you saying something about New York. Are you not from the Crossroads?"

I shrugged, not wanting to delve into my past, but figuring she'd find out eventually. "No. I was born and bred in New York, a member of the Ward Syndicate for most of my life, even though I'm a half-breed. My father was a gargoyle, but my mother is a fire Fae. The Wards didn't like my kind much, but since gargoyles are rare and deadly, they accepted me and my dad well enough that we didn't feel the prejudice too much."

"Was it just you and your dad or…? What about your mom?"

If I shrugged any more, I would wear my shoulders out. "Laena wasn't exactly suited for motherhood. She didn't really want me, she only got pregnant with me to make her lover jealous enough to leave his mate. It didn't really work out too well for her."

Her eyebrows reached her hairline, but she didn't say anything. No "I'm sorry," no "That sucks," and a part of me really appreciated that. There was nothing about my origins that I could change, and sympathy wouldn't fix it anytime soon.

"I got banished from New York about a year ago and moved here to start a new pack," I admitted, figuring the truth was better than a lie. I wasn't that good of a liar, anyway.

"Banished?" she asked, her skepticism clear enough that she might as well have been waiving the 'bullshit' flag in front of my face. "For what?"

"Nothing as cool as stealing power from a god. More like backing the wrong side of the fight. I fixed it in the end, though, which is why I got banished instead of got dead."

A decent amount of rage hit her eyes before she was able to mask it, and a part of me gloried in that little bit of hope.

"It's not as bad as it could have been. I have my own pack here, and I like it better. It's less cutthroat, even though it's still a No Man's Land. Back home is a different animal entirely."

Styx returned to her book, but I could tell it took effort. "If you say so."

The loud screech of the door opening had both of us jumping to our feet. No one in their right mind came into Tasty Tomes of their own free will, and despite Isaac's protection, I still got this odd trill up my back that something wasn't right. Instinctually, I put myself between Styx and the door, even though I couldn't see it over the bookcases that nearly reached the ceiling.

I knew Styx could take care of herself, but something in me wanted to prevent her from getting so much as a paper cut. I'd seen enough of her blood to last a lifetime, and I wanted no part of having it happen again.

Over my shoulder, I silently directed my gaze to her, and my woman already had a blade in each hand, with lightning flashing in her eyes. She flipped one of the blades, so she held both in one hand and then signaled that she was going to look around the corner.

But I didn't want her to have to go first. I didn't want her to have to protect herself. When I shook my head, she gave me a single raised eyebrow that basically told me to shut the fuck up because I wasn't her Alpha.

Fair enough.

Styx flipped the blade back into her other hand and silently crept around the corner leading toward Nadia's office rather than the front door. I sucked in a breath, trying to get a scent over aging books and the mark of death that permeated the very walls of the shop.

And over all that, was a remarkably familiar scent.

Styx had called them acolytes, but I thought they were closer to cultists—off to try and kill my mate for a crime she'd committed ages ago. My question was—how had they even found her?

Nadia.

And Styx had already assumed the lamia had sold her out, because her first order of business was to head for the office rather than the front fucking door.

The shake of a snake's tail had both Styx and I freezing in our spots, and we listened as Nadia greeted her new patrons.

"Can I help you?" Nadia greeted, her fake old-lady voice like ice as that rattle got louder.

"Mind your business, old woman," a man growled. "We're just looking for a girl. Black hair, kind of bitchy. Seen her around?"

"Get. Out," Nadia hissed. "And sssstay out. Or I'll make ssssure you never leave."

Styx and I rounded the corner, sticking to the shadows as we watched one of the white-robed goons shove Nadia into one of her shelves. Her back hit, the shove knocking several books to the floor before that glamour disappeared, and in its stead was six and a half feet of lamia demon, her red eyes looking at her lunch.

Nadia's tail whipped out, encircling the acolyte that shoved her, his body wrapped up tight before he even knew what hit him. The other two men scattered, realizing the error of their ways.

Instantly, Styx took off, heading left while I silently debated on going with her or catching the other acolyte before he could make a run for it. The decision was no contest. I raced right, picking through the bookcases, listening for footsteps over the screams of the asshole becoming Nadia's meal.

Without another option I raced for the entrance, hoping one of those assholes was stupid enough to try and leave. I managed to catch my prey as he lunged for the thick wooden door, his fingers barely scraping the handle before my claws latched onto his shoulders and tore him back.

He landed in the middle of one of the bookcases, his body snapping the shelves before falling in a heap to the floor. The wood case collapsed, raining books on him as he struggled to stand. A staff of light appeared in his hand, and I knew better than to let it anywhere near Styx. Grabbing his wrist and his throat, I drew him up, slamming him into another bookcase, the wood splintering around him.

"Tell me the god you serve, and I might let you live."

That was little less than a half-truth, the "might" part of that sentence heavily implied. There was no way I would let him live. He wouldn't so much as step a foot outside that door. As soon as he gave me the information I needed, he would be dust along with his other friends back at the river.

Instead of answering me, the fucker spat blood in my face before what used to be his tongue fell to the floor.

Had this fucker bitten off his own tongue to avoid being interrogated?

I had to give him credit for the dedication—even if it wouldn't save his life.

"Since you've got nothing to say," I growled, snapping his head clean off his body. I wasn't taking any chances with whatever magic these fuckers might have had, and beheading killed most creatures whether they wanted it to or not.

With one down, I stalked through the stacks, my single focus down to finding my mate and making sure she was safe. Following her scent was difficult, but the call of our mate bond was too strong to ignore.

Three turns later, I found her with the acolyte's jaw in one hand and the top of his head in the other, his body was still twitching on the bloody ground. But Styx didn't have a single scratch on her and that's really all I cared about.

"You manage to get anything out of him?" I asked in lieu of running my hands all over her body to make sure not a single ounce of magic hit her.

"Of course not. If I had, I'd be screaming the god's name at the top of my fucking lungs." She dropped the head and the jaw, disgust stamped all over her face.

"Hey, Nadia? You want seconds?"

Nadia slithered around the corner, her scales bright and eyes a deeper red than before. "Look what you've done to my booksssss," she scolded, her taloned fingers fisted at her hips.

"Get over it," Styx grumped. "It's a lot better than the place burning to the ground, isn't it? Which would have happened had I used my powers. Blood or burning, pick your poison, demon."

Nadia huffed, crossing her arms over her chest. "I swear no one respects libraries anymore."

"This isn't a library, it's a bookshop, and had those guys used their power in here, I would have exploded the damn thing. Be grateful."

But I was more worried about how they had found Styx in the first place. Were they following her? Did they automatically know where she was? Or did the power running in her veins call to them in a way that Isaac couldn't contend with?

Or had the lamia sold her out?

"Did you tell anyone that Styx was here?" I asked, my tone perfectly pleasant, even though my face probably said if she gave me the wrong answer, I would rip her apart. She wasn't the only venomous creature in the room.

"Of course not. Do you realize she's my first patron in a year? Not since you walked in and immediately walked right back out, have I had another person so much as set foot in my shop."

It was tough to feel bad for Nadia. Maybe if she stopped eating her patrons, she would have a better reputation.

"I've been picking off Crimson Rose trash to stay fed." Her face twisted as if the idiots weren't exactly tasty. "I don't know if you know this, but vampires aren't exactly a filling meal."

"Just because she's a customer doesn't make you loyal to her. You *eat* your customers."

Nadia sniffed, her nose raising high in the air. "She didn't make a fuss about how I get my meals."

So, the lamia liked Styx because she didn't judge her? That was new.

Styx regarded Nadia as if she couldn't quite figure her out. "I'm a kelpie. Why would I give a shit if you eat people? *I* eat people—amongst other things—but still."

"Doesn't matter," the lamia huffed, waving away Styx's comment. "I'm not a traitor. And I especially don't like assholes who hurt my books."

I surveyed the mess. Neither Styx nor I had exactly been kind to Nadia's shop when we'd taken care of the threat.

"I'll send a few of the pack to help you clean up," I offered, but Nadia waved me off.

"Don't bother. Most shifters don't like coming in here, anyway. They sense me as a predator and then it'll turn into a real mess. I'll fix it myself."

But the shop had been made and Styx couldn't come back here. "How much for fifty of your books regarding sky deities? Specifically, ones that have to do with archers?" I asked, pointing to the bow and arrow insignia on the acolyte's bloody chest.

Nadia squinted at me, her calculating eyes shining like rubies.

"A drop of blood from you both," she haggled, knowing full well that under no circumstances would she be getting even a taste of Styx's blood.

Styx stepped in between us, the sound of thunder reaching my ears even through the thick stone walls. "You may have three of my hairs and no more in exchange for every book you have about a sky deity with relation to archers. And you will get my blood *never*."

Nadia eyed Styx, likely trying to see if she would be able to talk her down.

But I knew my mate was one of the most stubborn beings ever created, and soon enough, Nadia would know it, too.

"You got all of these for *three* hairs?" Aster marveled, staring at the stacks of books taking up the majority of the dining table.

"Let's just say I'm good at negotiation," Styx replied, arms crossed over her chest as Knox, Jude, and a couple of other pack members brought in more boxes.

"More like Nadia didn't want the rest of her books destroyed in the spirit of research," I grumbled, pinching my brow.

But the books were the least of my problems.

I had been forced to recall every member of the pack—even the ones out on patrol—because of what had happened at Tasty Tomes. If we had been followed to the bookshop, there was a chance we had eyes on us now. My goal was to keep my mate happy, the lightning strikes from giving her position away, and to circle the wagons to make sure we all were safe.

Ten hours later, it was as if Tasty Tomes had exploded all over the kitchen. While Styx, Penny, and Aster studied the books, Knox and I made sure everyone was accounted for, had a room to sleep in, and had a belly full of food.

Usually, the pack house was just for me and the lieutenants, but we had plenty of room and the property was big enough to expand. Knox and I had been throwing around the idea of building cabins for mated couples and families on the land so we could keep the pack together. In New York, most people had apartments, so it was easier to be co-located, but high-rises weren't exactly the rage in this part of town.

By the time I'd clawed my way out of my office and back down to the kitchen, I found Styx alone, an abandoned cup of coffee at her elbow, fast asleep on a book that had to be at least five inches thick.

At some point in the night, she'd taken out her sticks, allowing her hair to fall around her shoulders and down her back, and standing in that doorway, watching her rest, I had to fight with myself not to kiss her.

It wasn't time—not yet.

But that didn't mean I won the battle with myself.

Without thinking of the consequences, I grabbed her hair sticks, shoved them in my pocket, and lifted her into my arms. At that point, I figured I'd get a knife to my throat, but instead, Styx just wrapped her arms around my neck, snuggling into me like she was a contented house cat.

I froze for a second, barely breathing as I waited for her to spring out of my arms. When she didn't, I swept from the kitchen, carrying her upstairs. It was only when we got to my room that she fully woke, her arms retreating from my neck, like if she moved slow enough, I'd forget how she'd snuggled into me.

"I know you're awake," I whispered, setting her on the settee so she could get her bearings. "Space is limited for the time being, so you're bunking with me tonight. You can have the bathroom first."

Sleepily, she tugged off her boots and padded to the bath, the fact that she was still wearing my shirt hitting me in the gut, not for the first time today. Ten minutes later she was back, hair mussed, teeth brushed, yawning as she rubbed her eyes.

Fuck, she was gorgeous. All bronze skin and dark eyes and—

Bathroom, dumbass.

But by the time I was done, Styx had settled onto the settee, curled into a ball with the quilt from the bed tucked around her. Only the bathroom light cast a paltry glow on the room, but even I could see how uncomfortable she was. Despite her small stature, she barely fit on the tiny couch.

"What are you doing?" It may have come out as a growl, but fuck it, that's just how it was going to be.

Frowning, she looked over her shoulder at me. "Trying to sleep. What are *you* doing?"

"I'm wondering why you aren't in bed."

Those lines between her eyebrows got bigger. "I am in a bed. You said I was bunking with you. This is me bunked."

I pinched my brow for maybe the hundredth time today, praying that someone, somewhere would grant me the patience it would take to convince this stubborn woman of the facts.

"Styx, in what world would I allow you to ever sleep on the motherfucking couch while I slept in a bed?"

She rolled her eyes, turning back to her makeshift pillow of her pants. "I'm fine."

I swore to the Fates if this woman said she was fine one more fucking time...

Once again, "Fuck it" was the only right answer. If she didn't want to listen to reason, I would just have to take matters into my own hands.

Without a word, I turned off the bathroom light, scooped her up in my arms—blanket and all—and deposited her on the bed. Ignoring her squawk of protest, I yanked the blanket from her grip, settling it over the rest of the covers before tucking her in.

Then I shucked my shirt and jeans, pulled on a pair of sleep shorts, and slid in the bed next to her.

"What are you doing?" she hissed, clearly scandalized if the glare she shot at me were any indication.

But we'd covered this already. *We* were going to bed, and damn if I was going to tell her again.

Gently, I turned her, tucking her into my side as I settled into my pillow.

For the first time all day, I breathed a sigh of relief. She was safe, no one could touch her, and she was right where she was always supposed to be— with me.

"Corvin?"

I peeled open an eyelid. "Can you argue with me tomorrow, Storm Cloud? I'm tired, baby."

Styx's breath hitched, her whole body drawing tight for a single long moment before she relaxed into me.

"Okay," she relented, "but just for tonight."

Sure thing, Storm Cloud.

Keep telling yourself that.

CHAPTER 13
STYX

Just for tonight.

What a crock of bullshit.

My arm reached out to the now-empty side of Corvin's bed, his warmth gone as the light from the morning sun filtered through the wide windows. Disappointment slashed through me like a blade, my heart aching at the fact that I'd woken up alone.

What kind of fuckery had the mate bond bullshit done to me?

I'd never slept next to anyone in my life. Always a solitary creature, I had never trusted anyone—accepted anyone—ever. Anytime I had taken a lover —if you could even call them that—I'd always left before we could even reach this step. And I'd never brought someone to my home, never slept next to them.

I scratched an itch and moved the fuck on. And at no time had I ever in my life cuddled anyone —ever.

I didn't know what kind of witchcraft Corvin had or how the mate bond was changing me, but I didn't like it one bit.

I had so easily given in to him the night before with his soft demands and the secure weight of his arm across my belly, folding like a shirt and relaxing into him, as if I were meant to be in his bed, meant to be in his arms.

And the worst part of it all?

I had slept better than I had in eons right next to him. No dreams of before, no dark shadows of my past, just easy rest snuggled next to the safety of his presence.

Sleep had never come easy to me, not even before I'd been banished. But last night I had been as contented as a house cat sleeping the best sleep I had ever had in my fucking life.

Just for tonight, my ass.

I hadn't even fucked the man yet, and I was simpering over him like a fawning schoolgirl.

How was I supposed to reject him—reject this—if I slept like a baby in his arms?

If I missed him when he was gone?

If I dreamt about that steel-blue gaze every time we were apart?

How was I supposed to protect myself against him?

How was I—

Grumbling, I swept from the bed, pacing in front of the window like a crazy person. Hell, even the sight of the water didn't calm me. All it did was remind me of what he'd done. Of what he'd requested of his pack just for me. How he'd carved out a spot for me here before he even knew me.

How he'd gone back to the portal every day while I'd been gone.

How he'd saved my life—not that I'd ever admit it out loud—at the edge of that very river.

My plight was made worse by an entire night of his scent surrounding me—of him surrounding me. Of his breaths in my ear. Of his strong body holding me so close. It made me wonder what those breaths would sound like when he was inside me. What his body would feel like slicked with sweat as he powered into me, making me scream.

His gargoyle was a chimera in form. Did that

mean Corvin had fangs? Would he bite me? Would I like it?

My core clenched.

Hard.

I'd been right that night when I'd blown him right out of the sky, and he'd gotten up like I'd just flicked him in the shoulder.

I *was* in deep shit.

The deepest.

After handling my morning business and brushing my teeth, the mirror over the sink showed a bedraggled mess of a woman with pink cheeks, bright eyes, and something close to hope in her gaze. I barely recognized myself.

Where was the woman who could barely even look at a mirror? Where was the assassin, the murderer, the ruthless killer of men?

I must have left her back on Tartarus with my damn sense.

And on top of all that, I wished I would have thought to actually pack a bag before my hasty trip to this realm. While I could buy the items I needed here, it had been short-sighted to simply leave my home with nothing but the clothes on my back and half a plan.

I'd honestly thought I would return within a

day, not bothering to think of my future beyond that.

Short-sighted didn't even begin to cover it.

I finger-combed my long hair before putting it up on top of my head, securing the mass of it— as always—with my sticks.

Before I could contemplate my need for new clothes or get a chance to put on pants, Corvin slipped into the room with a tray of food in his hands. I couldn't recall a day in the last five thousand years where I had blushed in front of anyone, nor could I ever remember dealing with a morning after.

Corvin and I hadn't even had sex yet, hadn't even kissed, and yet I was still standing in the doorway to the bathroom like he'd taken my virginity the night before instead of simply cuddling me while I'd slept.

If I could curse Fate to her face, I would.

"The kitchen is overrun with most of the pack. I figured you wouldn't want to be around that many people you didn't know, so breakfast." He lifted the tray just slightly, gesturing to the mound of disks covered in an amber-like sauce topped with a fluffy white cloud.

"I take it you've never had pancakes before." He

set the tray on the small side table next to the settee. "You're going to love them."

But I didn't so much as move, frozen by the thoughtfulness and the knowledge that he had made that breakfast just for me.

"It's not poisoned, I swear," he said with a chuckle before leaning down and cutting a triangle out of the top pancake and popping it into his mouth. "See, no poison."

And I couldn't exactly pinpoint when I had moved from the doorway to the bathroom, all the way across the room next to him, nor could I understand why that tiny smear of amber liquid on his bottom lip was the most mesmerizing thing I'd ever seen in my life.

I also couldn't quite discern why my gaze was locked on said lips, or why I wanted to run my tongue over them before nibbling them just a tiny bit before maybe doing something else.

"Do you want a taste?" he murmured, his husky voice pitched so low it was the most sensual of growls. A growl that did something to me, made my core clench, made my fingers itch to touch him, made a flash fire of heat race over my skin.

But I didn't move.

I was frozen once more, afraid to act, afraid to lose that iron hold I had on my control.

Afraid that if I let him in even an inch, he would take a mile.

I don't know when it happened, but one second, I was staring at Corvin's lips, and the next, my back was pressed against the wall beside the settee, and he was millimeters away, his lips so close to mine I could feel his breath against my skin and the heat of him filtering into my bones.

No part of him touched me, but he was vibrating with the need of it, a fire blazing in his eyes like the night of the river.

"Tell me I can kiss you."

Part-request, part-order, and I couldn't find it in me to tell him no. I also couldn't tell him yes.

His hands found my waist under my shirt, the blunted tips of his growing talons pressing into my skin like ten tiny brands.

"For the love of fuck, Styx. You aren't wearing any underwear." He sucked in a sharp breath through his nose, his eyes flaring when he scented my need. "You're telling me I slept next to you all night while you just wore my shirt and nothing else?"

His forehead touched mine, his lips so close they

brushed mine with every word he said, with every breath he took, and still, I didn't answer him.

"Let me kiss you, Storm Cloud. Just once. Let me taste you."

I wanted it so bad, needed to know if those lips tasted as good as they looked. What could one taste hurt?

Oh, so slowly, I lifted onto my tiptoes, pressing my lips to his. Without me telling it to, my tongue swept out, tasting the sweetness on his bottom lip before I lost every single ounce of control I had.

Corvin pulled my sticks, letting the waves tumble down my shoulders before those hands were in my hair, turning my head, positioning me so he could take over, ravaging my lips in a kiss so mind-bending I forgot control completely.

My hands fisted into the fabric of his shirt, pulling him closer as his tongue swept into my mouth, exploring every millimeter, every stroke making me hotter, needier, ravenous. His thigh fit between mine, pressing against my center. My desire was likely soaking his jeans, but I could not give that first fuck because it put pressure right where I wanted it.

His hand wrapped around the back of my neck, tilting my head as his arm did the same around my back, hoisting me up on his thigh as he rocked me, shooting bolts of pleasure everywhere but especially my aching clit.

"Fuck, baby, you're so fucking wet. I bet I could make you come just like this, couldn't I?"

I fisted his hair, guiding his lips back to mine as he gripped my hips in earnest, those talons sharper but never breaking the skin. I couldn't help the moan that tore up my throat as his hold tightened, his slow, methodical torture so fucking good it was tying me in knots.

His lips trailed down my neck, nibbling, tasting, driving me insane.

My hands fisted in his shirt again, but this time I tore it off, ripping the fabric right off his shoulders. I wanted his skin. I wanted it on mine. In all the ways. In every way.

Corvin was gentler with his shirt, pulling it up and over my head, leaving me naked and under his smoldering gaze. He'd seen me naked before, sure, but this was different.

"I want to lick you everywhere. I want to make you come on my thigh, my fingers, my tongue. I want you screaming for me. But I especially want these," he said, cupping my aching breasts in his large hands, his thumbs brushing over my nipples, nearly making me come out of my skin, "in my mouth first."

His head dipped, taking one stiff bud into his mouth, his tongue teasing the tender flesh until I couldn't control my hips anymore. I rubbed myself on Corvin's thigh like a cat in heat, chasing my pleasure as he wound me around his little finger.

"That's it, baby, use me. Let me watch you fall apart."

But I couldn't. I needed something more, and the needy whimper that came out of me told him so.

"Tell me what you want, Storm Cloud, and I'll give it to you. Anything you want. It's yours."

My head thudded against the wall, desperation making me unfocused. "I want more."

His chuckle was wry. "I gathered that. Say the words and it's yours."

I didn't know why I was so shy all of a sudden. I hadn't been shy a day in my life. Still, I swallowed thickly and forced myself to tell him what I wanted.

"Your fingers. I want your fingers."

Those flames in his eyes flared, his hold on his control slipping just like mine was. "Can I taste you?"

I thought about his mouth on me for about a

second before I nodded, the ache in my sex making me whimper.

Then the wall wasn't at my back anymore, replaced by the softness of his bed. Roughly, he pulled me to the edge of the mattress, before kneeling between my legs, his warm breath skating over my sex. His tongue flicked over my clit once, twice, before he devoured me in earnest, his fingers filling me to the brim as he feasted on me.

I held on to the sheets for dear life as he worked me over, melting me, molding me, changing me into the mindless creature that only wanted pleasure. My release reached up and grabbed me, drowning me in a bliss so acute, I thought I might die from it.

I know I screamed—I had to have—and I did not give nary a single fuck, either.

Corvin was winning the war, and he damn well knew it.

Pulling him up, I tasted myself on his tongue as I kissed his beautiful lips, my release addling my brain into doing something probably stupid. My hands reached for his belt, but before I could yank it free, he had both my wrists in his grip above my head.

"Not just yet, Storm Cloud. That was for you. I don't need anything in return."

The fuck he didn't. I rolled my hips, his ridged length practically bursting from his jeans.

"You sure about that?" I taunted, rubbing myself on him again, enjoying the way his eyes rolled up into his head.

"I'm trying to be a gentleman," he growled through gritted teeth, his eyes squeezed tight. "I need you to let me do that."

Well, shit. When he put it like that...

"Very well. I'll just remember that I owe you one." I tightened my knees on his hips, flipping us both so I was on top of him. "And I always pay my debts."

Corvin looked like he was in agony, his muscles pulled tight as he fought off the urge to snatch me back under him. He didn't have to say it, I knew that look. I'd worn that look not five minutes ago.

But a cold splash of water dosed us both when a pounding came on the bedroom door.

"Boss?" Jude's deep bear growl came through the wood. "We've got a problem. We need you downstairs. Now."

Then he said something that twisted my insides.

"Penny's been hurt."

Penny.

The girl who'd done her level best to keep me breathing.

The girl who'd known Corvin had a mate before anyone else.

The girl who'd helped me search hundreds of books for the gods who'd banished me.

She was *hurt*.

Corvin and I moved as one, snatching on clothes and shoes and bolting for the door. I followed him and Jude down the stairs in a quick clip to the kitchen, the books relegated to the floor as a bloody Penny took up the whole of the table.

Aster held a soaked cloth to her neck as Knox and Diana tried to stem the flow at her wrists. Her hair was stained scarlet, the *drip-drip-drip* of her very lifeblood hitting the floor was all I could hear.

Not the shouts of Aster begging for Penny's healer's bag.

Not Diana's cooing reassurances in her ear.

Not Corvin ordering his people out.

Not Knox calling a healer while he tried to hold Penny still.

I didn't hear anything over those drops, and I didn't see anything but the ripped shirt and bra, the torn jeans.

Tying my hair on top of my head, a singular type of calmness settled over me along with the rage. My fingers moved of their own accord, touching my knives, my extras sticks, reassuring myself that I was as armed as I ever was.

Treading through the throng of pack members, I made it to Penny—not to reassure, not to keep her breathing, but to catch her attacker's scent. She reeked of vampire saliva, the bites at her neck and wrists done in such a way that they wouldn't close on their own—not without a shift.

I couldn't do anything to help her—only her Alpha could—but I did have a special set of skills that I would gladly put into action.

Corvin brushed Diana aside, getting close to

Penny, and ordered her to shift, her keening cry of agony followed by the swift snaps of bones breaking.

Penny would live.

Her attacker would not.

I would make sure of it.

Slipping out the back door in the midst of the commotion, I set out to do what I did best.

Hunt.

If the vamps were smart, they'd already be running. As it was, the leather-jacket-wearing dipshits were too busy yucking it up to realize they were in danger.

Each jacket had a red rose embroidered on the breast, the insignia of a gang of morons too full of themselves to notice how close to death they really were. These same men had tried to throw their weight around at the portal, too.

It hadn't worked out for them then, and it wouldn't work out for them now.

It had taken twenty minutes to follow the trail of Penny's scent and blood and tears to this sprawling warehouse to the south of the city center. It would have taken longer to find my ass with both hands than it was to get the drop on these assholes.

But as I listened to them brag about hurting the "wolf girl," I realized all too quickly that it hadn't been just one vamp. They'd all watched their friend hurt Penny, they'd enjoyed it, got off on it.

My kill list grew by the second.

"Did you hear her squeal?" a dark-haired vamp crowed, adjusting his crotch as he took a swig of amber liquid straight from the bottle. "Shifters make the best noises. You should have let us get a piece." His arm shot out, tagging a blond vamp's shoulder, knocking him sideways.

Fangs flashed as the blond growled, shoving back. "The wolf girl is *mine*. You don't get to touch what's mine."

The dark-haired one backed down, a calculating gleam in his eye. "Sure thing, man. But we all need to take Blackwell down a peg. The way he's moving through this city can't stand. Taking out the river gang, killing Mosby, taking over the rail lines. Maybe we all need to take some of his sweet pack pussy in exchange for his transgressions."

These cowards wouldn't go at Corvin directly like men. Instead, they would attack the women of the pack like cowards. If there was one thing I hated more than anything, it was a coward.

"You're just looking for pack pussy to keep your dick wet," a bald vamp jeered, kicking the barrel fire they were surrounding, knocking the sparks of the blue flame into the air. "Can't say I blame you. Did you see that kitty cat they've got? I'd love to get a sample of that one. Bet she cries real pretty."

If I had ever thought of allowing them to live—which I hadn't—that idea was long gone now.

"Too bad she got away before you could claim her," the quiet one in the corner taunted, his eyes red and fangs descended, like he was spoiling for a fight. "Did your balls finally drop yet, or do you need to fish them out of your throat after she made you cry like a little bitch?"

The blond kicked over the fire in his haste to square off with the quiet one, the blue flames spreading over the stonelike floor. Men roared their displeasure, but the two didn't pay them any mind as they whaled on each other like teenage boys with more balls than sense. They were no better than Legion's young recruits, squabbling like children.

Using the distraction to my advantage, I emerged from the shadows, yanking the bald vamp right off his feet, silently jamming my dagger into the base of his skull before he could make a sound. To his friends, he was there one moment and gone the next.

"Hey," one barked, "where did Bill go?"

The rest grumbled in turn, not knowing where their friend went, and once their confusion was at its peak, I tossed his heartless, headless body back into the light at their feet.

The shadows of the room clung to me as I skirted their panicked stances, the warehouse offering plenty of darkness even in the middle of the day. Each window—of which there weren't many—was coated with black paint, allowing not even the bright winter sun access.

I couldn't complain.

Just like Tartarus, the darkness called to me, and just like Tartarus, I embraced my darkest side.

I went after the dark-haired one next, his desire to hear Penny squeal his undoing. In the shadows, I made him squeal—right before I plunged my fingers into his chest and ripped his heart out. I could have done it with my knives, could have made it clean and quiet.

I didn't.

One by one I picked them off, making sure to leave the blond for last—for Penny. She needed her revenge, her penance for what he'd done to her. He might not have taken everything from her, but I saw the fear in her wide eyes, her shattered illusion of safety.

She wouldn't ever get that back. I knew that all too well.

A part of me wondered why I cared about the girl, why the need to protect her and Corvin's pack had tuned my brain to this singular focus. She was no one to me—barely even an acquaintance—but seeing her blood, scenting her fear, knowing exactly what it was to have your family try to piece you back together...

I'd been in her shoes a very long time ago, and something in me had just snapped.

No one got to touch her and live to tell the tale.

No one got to harm a hair on her head.

And each one of those bastards had died for their role in making her bleed. For their plans to make all Corvin's pack bleed. For their laughs at her pain, for their callous jeers and crotch grabs, for their dark thoughts and ill intent.

His friends had paid their penance already, but the blond?

He would suffer.

He hadn't even had the good sense to run, too

busy searching the inky blackness of this warehouse for the culprit, ready to fight me instead of realizing that I was the oldest, deadliest thing in this room.

Catching him was too easy.

I would dance out of the shadows, cut a tendon here or there and race back. By the time I'd gotten bored, he was on his knees quivering with fear, the scent of his piss-soaked pants making my nose wrinkle in disgust.

Still, I needed to ask him some questions.

Being a five-thousand-year-old water Fae had its perks. The best one? People often forgot that they were made up of about eighty percent water. Vamps —with their penchant for drinking their meals— bumped that up to about ninety. I doubted this poor excuse for a vampire had ever felt the sensation of his blood attempting to escape his skin or the distinct awareness of his organs ripping themselves apart.

It wasn't pleasant.

"Who else hangs out here?" I asked, clenching my fist with the express purpose of making his blood boil.

Writhing on the ground, he shook his head, his screams echoing off the metal walls. *Fine.* He needed a touch of relief then. I released my hold on his blood, and he coughed wetly, his lungs slowly healing for a second.

"I asked you a question. Answer it, and I will make sure you stay breathing. Don't, and I will make sure you go insane before I'm done with you. Understand?"

His bloody eyes found mine, and he nodded.

"Good. Who else frequents this shithole of a warehouse?"

He coughed again, clearing his throat. "No one —not anymore. It's just us."

He could be lying, then again, it didn't seem to be a brain trust of an operation.

"Are you working with anyone else? Someone who will notice you missing?"

His gaze flared. "Ye-yes. A coven of witches on the east side. Across the river. We-we—"

"Let me guess," I offered, knowing his answer before he gave it. "Thieves? Have a proclivity for river boats? Think piracy is a good time?"

Blondie nodded. "Ye-yeah. How'd you know that?" His eyes widened as he tried to shuffle back. "You-you're the bitch who killed James and his crew. Made them drown themselves."

Ah, yes. One of my many talents.

I reminisced on my first dip in the river once we

crossed. A group of pirates had tried to take a river boat, aiming to rob, maim, murder. Twelve pirates had died that day, but I'd missed the witch leading them. As long as she wasn't on the river, I didn't give a shit, but I didn't like that she'd lived.

"And they'll miss you?"

Maybe as cannon fodder, but I doubted there had been any skill in this lot.

"Su-sure."

That smelled like a lie. Tightening my fist, Blondie's eyes rolled back in his head as his screams rent the air.

"Try again. Who will be looking for you?"

He gasped when I set his blood free, scarlet tears staining his hair much like Penny's had been.

"No one, okay? Uziah let us swing after Blackwell took the train lines. Said he didn't want to contend with a pack. And the coven won't talk to us after one of their witches died on our watch."

My smile must have been straight out of Tartarus because he tried shuffling back. "That's good. Final question, and then it'll all be over."

His nod was frantic, the end to his misery almost in sight.

Oh, you poor, stupid child.

"Why Penny? Of all the people you could have picked, why her?"

His face shuttered, closing off as if I'd flicked off a switch. He'd just put it together that I wasn't here for the train lines or the pirates. I was here for the sole purpose of taking my pound of flesh.

"She's *mine*. That little bitch thinks she can reject me? Fuck no."

It was as I'd thought. Fate had been cruel to the healer, choosing the worst, most cowardly for her instead of someone she deserved. History was repeating itself, only this time, I could save her like I'd wished someone would have saved me.

And I didn't even have to steal any power to do it.

"I see." The desire to rip him from this earth and stomp his soul under my boot was strong. So strong, I was damn near blind with it.

But Penny needed her vengeance—I couldn't steal that from her.

And why did I care?

Why did I give a shit about Corvin's pack? Why did I want this girl to be safe, to be whole, and not tied to this pitiful excuse of a man? Why was I set out to protect Corvin's pack members? To make sure not one of them got the same treatment as Penny had?

I was falling too fast and too hard, my heart tying strands of rope to this realm, to this pack, to this place. I needed to reject Corvin before it was too late. Before I couldn't leave.

Before I fell and couldn't get back up.

So why couldn't I?

I sensed more than saw when Corvin found me, the bond calling to me deeper than it had been before. Shame clouded my thoughts for one bitter moment, wondering what he'd seen, if he cared, before I shook my head and stomped it down, too.

I didn't care if he thought me a monster. I was one. Unapologetically, I protected my people—I had for thousands of years, and I wouldn't stop now.

She's not your people. He's not your people. They are not your people.

Blondie tried to scramble away, his eyes landing on Corvin before mine did. Too bad with a simple squeeze to my fist, he couldn't so much as twitch.

"I found the one who hurt Penny," I murmured, unable to look him in the eye. "His friends watched. They planned on going after Aster and Diana and all the rest of the females to teach you a lesson. I killed them, but I'm saving him for her."

To kill. I thought it, but I didn't say it.

"He thinks she's his mate, tried to claim her by force. I won't let that stand, Corvin. If she doesn't do it, *I* will." I swallowed, trying to find the right words.

Blondie had to die. Today. I wouldn't let Penny go through the same thing I had. Not while I had breath in my lungs.

"You have to be swift with things like this or it will get away from you," I warned. "Take it from someone who has been alive for a very long time. Predators will always be predators. Liars will always be liars. Sadists will always be sadists. If we don't stomp this out now, he'll take Penny against her will. And if it's not her, it'll be someone else."

Corvin nodded before taking a slim device from his pocket. After pressing a few buttons, Knox's voice spilled from the thing.

"Yeah, Boss?"

"Bring the pack to the warehouses on the south side. Penny too. Styx has a present for her."

"A present? I just got her settled—"

"Now, Knox."

We sat not speaking while I held Blondie still, the silence only punctuated by the vamp choking on his own blood until the rest of the pack showed up. The bloody warehouse doors peeled open, letting the light in for the first time, revealing the worst of my wrath.

"Sweet mother of the gods," Knox murmured, "what the fuck happened here?"

"Like I said," Corvin rumbled, "Styx got Penny a present."

Jude rounded the corner with Penny cradled in his arms, his eyes widening at the aftermath of my hunt. Penny's sad eyes landed on the blond vamp in my grip, her expression blanking.

The bear set her on her feet, but it was Diana and Aster that held her up. She was shaky and weak, and it took everything in me not to crush my fist and remove every single ounce of blood in him.

Her gaze went from him to me. "You found him? For me?"

She said this like I just given her a mound of jewels or a new puppy. She was touched that I had aided her revenge and damn did it make my heart swell.

This isn't your pack. She isn't a member of your herd. She is not your family—none of them are.

"You needed your revenge. He didn't deserve to live. Two birds, one stone."

And even though I shrugged as if none of this

mattered, as if none of them mattered, as if I wasn't already crumbling to dust at their feet, it did.

All of it fucking mattered, and I had no idea how I was supposed to let them go.

"You saved my life. I helped you get your revenge. Makes us square, right?"

Her eyes flicked back to Blondie, the blue taking on a golden hue as her bones snapped and cracked, as she transformed into her wolf. Her growl rent the air as she limped toward Blondie.

And I fought off a smile as this dainty little girl, with a healer's touch, clamped down on his throat and ripped it out.

Knox and Jude stayed behind to clean up Styx's mess, her utter ruthlessness proving to me that she actually gave a shit about my pack—probably more than she'd admit to herself.

My pack piled into their vehicles, heading back to the house, and I lost Styx in the crowd for about a minute before I sensed her walking away from us all.

She was running again.

After all of that, after what she'd done for Penny, after making sure that her revenge was served, after what we'd shared, she was still leaving. And it pissed me the fuck off.

I stopped Diana and Aster. "Make sure everyone

gets home and settled. Don't leave Penny alone. Yes?"

Aster rolled her eyes. "Of course, Boss. You didn't even have to ask."

Diana only nodded, her gaze tracing over the bloody body parts and in the direction of my mate, her worry clear. "She needs you more than we do at the moment. We're fine."

Her statement had my teeth on edge, but I left my pack, following Styx in a very familiar direction. As always, she was headed for the portal, and the truth of it was, I wasn't sure I could blame her.

"You're just leaving then?" I growled at her back as she picked her way over a crumbling street. "Tough to not take that personally, Storm Cloud."

She hadn't met my eyes once since the ordeal with Penny. I couldn't tell if she was ashamed, if she was pissed, or if she was just done with me.

"It's not meant to be personal," she whispered. Still not meeting my gaze, still not stopping, her strides pressing forward as they cut down the lane.

"It is personal, Styx. Everything you do, every breath you take, is personal to me."

"I can't do this," she growled, finally stopping, finally showing me those sparking eyes, finally facing me. "You saw what I did in there, how ruthless I can be, what I can do. You think I don't know that it changes how you look at me?"

That had me stumped. "Why would it? Why would it change anything at all? You defended a member of my pack as if she were your own. Why would I not be proud of you for that? You think I wouldn't do the same?"

It was as if I hadn't told her how much I was in awe of her. Honestly, it was as if I hadn't said anything at all.

"See? This right here. I can't do this, this worry. This constant push and pull and wonder if I should reject you to save you from me or from the danger that I face, or if I should just give in and live in this place with you and care for your pack. They're not my pack, and yet, I couldn't stop myself."

I rushed her, sparking fingers and all. "They can be your pack. This can be your home. Or we can go to Tartarus together. Or we can decide later. You keep thinking you have to decide now, and you don't."

"But I do," she growled, her teeth bared as if she were simply dying inside. "I've spent the last five thousand years in prison, and every single day here feels like I'm ripping myself apart because I'm not finding the gods who banished me. I keep getting distracted. I keep wanting to see your face. I keep wanting to defend your pack. I keep wanting all of this shit that I. Can't. Have."

Was I hallucinating or did she just say five *thousand* years? Not five or fifty or five hundred.

Five.

Thousand.

It dawned on me for the very first time just how old Styx was, just *who* she was.

"You're not named for the River Styx," I murmured, adjusting the faint knowledge I had of my mate, reorganizing it in my brain as I tried to fathom just how long she had been waiting. "The River Styx is named for you."

She blinked, confused at the direction I was taking. "And how the fuck would I know that?"

She had a point there.

"There's a myth, though, now I doubt it's a myth at all. About you. About a river of death that killed a god." The truth crashed through me, changing everything I thought I knew. "That's why you were banished. Not that you stole power, it's because you killed a god, right?"

Her lips firmed into a thin line as she stared at the roiling clouds. "There were extenuating circumstances, but yes, I did kill a god. Whose power do you think I stole?"

Stunned, I just stood there, still processing the new reality I'd found myself in, but leave it to Styx to get to the heart of it all. "You said there's a myth? Tell it to me."

I still had the book in my library somewhere, the fairytale of Styx about the wild woman who refused to be tamed. "My father bought me a book when I was a child—an old one with crumbling pages and a cracked spine. It had many myths in it, but my favorite was about an old god killed for his hubris after he swam in a river of death—the river of Styx."

At her silence, I continued, wondering how much of the tale I'd learned as a boy was true.

"The story goes that Odaar, king of the gods, followed a woman through an ancient portal—a woman so beautiful, he was mesmerized by her. But she was wild and free, and she ran from him. But as far as she ran, Odaar would not let her go. Styx warned Odaar not to follow her into the river, that her waters would take his life, but he chased her anyway. The waters came for him, stealing his power, but still he swam, trying to reach her. Knowing that he would not survive, she wrapped her limbs around him and drew him down to the bottom where he never surfaced again. The myth goes on to say that he still lives in the river with her, killing any of those that dare to disturb their happiness."

Styx clenched her jaw, her eyes blazing with her lightning, her whole body shaking with rage. "It's a beautiful story," she whispered. "But that's all it is—a story. It didn't exactly go down like that. Not at all."

As a boy, I had always loved the myth about the wild woman who refused a god. How she refused to be conquered, refused to be beholden to anything or anyone. I had always wondered what it would be like to be loved by someone like that. But just the look on her face told me that the myth was just that—a falsehood, a fairytale, a lie.

"Tell me how it really went."

She stared off in the distance for a good long while as thunder and lightning cracked over our heads. With every boom, her shoulders reached her ears, as if she hated that sound more than anything.

"It's true, he did follow me through the god portal. My family and I came from Avalon—the Fae realm—through the portal, hoping for a better life." She scoffed at herself, rolling her eyes. "No. *I* convinced my family that the unrest in Avalon would reach us, and we needed to move. I had been convinced that danger was coming."

She shook her head, her eyes welling with tears. "I thought I knew what was best. I didn't feel like we could live as freely as we should. I had no idea what freedom really meant."

Sniffing, she found a large piece of rubble to sit on. "We had a life here for a little while, but I guess I had caught his eye and he followed us—*me*. Initially, I refused him. He was pushy and arrogant. Rude. I'd always wanted a fated mate, and I knew he wasn't mine."

I had a feeling the bad part was coming, and I crouched at her knees, waiting for it to come.

"At first, he accepted my answer, until one day... he didn't. Until one day, it didn't matter how many times I said no, he was going to claim me whether I liked it or not. Whether I wanted it or not."

I fought off the urge to snatch her to me, to hold her close as she told me her story. Forcing myself to stay still, I refused to let the rage take me over, forcing myself to listen to the rest.

"After he took what he wanted, he didn't like my reaction. Didn't like that I hit and bit and scratched and tried to run. In his rage, he hit me with his power. I'd never taken a power before—didn't even know I could. I didn't know what would happen. I didn't choose it, but I laid there hurt and crying and damn near dead and he started yelling that I had stolen it from him. He tried to choke the life out of me, and his power just came out of me. I struck him and he died. Burned up right in front of my eyes."

She'd been sentenced to five thousand years in prison for getting raped by a god and killing him for it?

"What happened next?" I growled, trying not to lose my fucking mind.

"My parents were trying to help. They were dragging me to the water, trying to keep me breathing, but his children came. My sisters, my nieces, my nephews—they were all gone in a matter of seconds, killed without cause or question just for helping me. My parents died next, and then they tossed me into Tartarus. Alone. In the dark. No friends, no family. I landed in the water, and it took a long time to heal both my mind and my body. Any man who came within sniffing distance of the water died."

That seemed fair. If I'd lost my whole family because some asshole wouldn't leave me alone, I'd be murderous, too.

"For a long time, I killed. Until Oberon and

Caius came. Until Legion and Pol. We reformed Tartarus. After Caius took me under his wing, I had a purpose, a goal. They had all been imprisoned, too, and eventually they became my friends—my family."

She shrugged as if her story wasn't the most heartbreaking thing I'd ever heard. As if it meant nothing. As if after all this time—to her—it was just a story. I knew it wasn't. Because even though Odaar was dead, his children still remained.

Children that were looking for her.

Children that wanted her dead.

Children that had damn near killed her. Twice.

No wonder she was running from me. The last time a man had chased her, she'd lost everything.

It made me sick to my stomach that I had idolized that story. That I had dreamt of it. That I had wished for my very own Styx to drag me down with her. They were all just pretty words for vile things, rewriting history in the victor's handwriting. I'd never wanted to burn a book before, but I did want to burn that one.

"Why don't you reject me outright?" I whispered, not wanting it, not wishing for it, but knowing it could be her only option all the same. "You said you didn't want a mate, and I didn't listen.

I'm listening now. If you don't want me, I'll accept it. It'll kill me to do it, but I will."

Because it would feel worse than just the thought of it did right then. It would cleave me in two.

"When I was banished, I swore to myself I'd never take a mate. That it was my clinging to the mere thought of a mate that might never come that had gotten my family killed. It was the reason I denied him and because his death prompted it all, that I didn't deserve one. I promised this to myself for centuries, millennia, over and over again. Punishing myself for what had happened to them."

Her words made my heart lurch in my chest. "It wasn't your fault any more than it was Penny's. Can't you see that?"

She finally met my gaze. "But every time I think of rejecting you, it burns me up. Because if I reject you, it doesn't just hurt me, it hurts you, too. I don't want to hurt you, Corvin, but I fear I will no matter what I do."

Her words caught me off guard, the promise they held so sweet, I needed to protect it, nurture it, keep it. Cupping her face in my hands, I tried not to take, tried not to demand. Unless she asked me to, I'd never demand anything of her again.

"I'm going to help you," I swore, my vow tying me to her with a thousand strings. "I'll help you avenge your family. And when I do, maybe then you can think of a life more than just the guilt that isn't yours to own. Maybe then you can—" I swallowed, cutting myself off as I stared into those fathomless eyes. She didn't need the pressure of what finishing that sentence would be.

Maybe then you can love me, I thought, unable to stop myself from hoping.

"Whatever it takes," I insisted, hoping she believed me.

Styx's lips brushed mine in a gentle kiss so sweet it felt like a vise was squeezing my chest.

"Okay, Corvin. I..." She swallowed, eyes shining before she continued, the most beautiful words coming out of her mouth. "I trust you."

I was struck by a flash fire of fear, the enormity of it all nearly dragging me under.

The woman who didn't trust anyone.

The woman who believed trust was an illusion.

She trusted me.

Only me.

Gods, I hoped I never let her down. I didn't think either of us would survive it.

trust you.

When the fuck had that happened? When had I gone from trusting no one to giving Corvin the very heart of me? I barely trusted Caius, and I'd known the man for... well, *forever.*

Yet somehow, in telling my story—really telling it—it made me realize that Corvin was nothing like...*Odaar.* He was nothing like the god who'd set this awful wheel into motion. He was nothing like Odaar's children.

Corvin was good and safe and... The heat of his palms filtered into my cheeks, his steel-blue gaze like a spear directly into my heart.

I trust you.

Had I ever told anyone that? In all those years, in all that time, had I ever had faith in anyone?

My eyes trailed down to his lips. I couldn't kiss him—not like I wanted to. We had things to do—him and me—and if I got sidetracked, I'd never get the courage to do them.

Still... I caught his bottom lip between my teeth, nipping just a little, needing that taste before I could get to my feet and walk straight to the gallows.

When had I gone from pushing him away to needing him closer? And I did. The thought of being away from him twisted a knife in my gut, which was why he would be going with me. He had to.

This would absolutely, positively suck, would likely cause bloodshed, and definitely a bruise or two... or five. And someone would definitely need stitches. Threading my fingers through Corvin's, I got up, dragging him behind me as I continued on my course.

"Where are you going? Or rather—where are we going?" he asked, and unfortunately, I had to tell him the truth.

"Home," I growled, eyes forward, shoulders back, headed for the portal that—if I had any luck at all—would not have Oberon guarding it.

"What do you mean home? Home is that way," he said, hooking his thumb behind us.

Sighing, I halted my progress and stared up at the sky, hoping for an answer that didn't involve Tartarus at all. Unfortunately, this sky was ill-equipped to grant my wishes.

"I have to talk to Caius. I need fresh clothes. And weapons. And way more info than I currently have. Now that I know his name, I might be able to get information on his children. Caius might know something."

I paused, wanting him to understand that this was our only option left.

"I've searched damn near all of the books Nadia gave us, and not only did I not find myself in any of them—not that I thought I would—I haven't seen his name once. That doesn't give me a good feeling that I'll find them at all."

I couldn't kill what I couldn't find. And I couldn't ask Caius if I couldn't even say his name out loud.

Corvin pressed a kiss to the back of my hand, seemingly in awe at the sight of our fingers threaded together. "And you want me to go with you?"

That was such a loaded question. Did I want to go to Tartarus? Technically, yes. Did I want Corvin to be subjected to my family? A resounding no. But did I want to be parted from him to go alone?

Also no.

I squeezed said fingers in response, not wanting to actually have to ask. "I assumed that was implied."

Corvin pulled me toward him, dropping my hand as he wrapped his arm around my waist. "You think you can give me a minute to get my affairs in order?"

"What do you think my friends are going to do, put you to death or something?" It wasn't a far cry from the possible, but I'd do my best to make sure he stayed breathing.

Corvin's eyebrows hit his hairline. "Or something. All I know is if Penny or Diana or Aster brought their mate home, I know Jude and Knox and I would put them through the ringer. Considering your ringer is in Tartarus, I'm just covering my bases."

I really hoped no one even considered touching Corvin. Lightning flashed in the sky as a deep booming thunder rattled the very pavement under our feet.

"No one's going to touch you," I growled, trying

to get my jaw to unclench. "Not if they know what's good for them."

Corvin blinked at me, a sexy smile curving his lips. "Anyone ever tell you you're fucking gorgeous when you're pissed off?"

I raised a single eyebrow. "Not twice."

"That's my girl." He pulled the slim device from his pocket, and once again Knox's voice came from the receiver.

"Yeah, Boss?"

Corvin's smile didn't fade even a millimeter as his steel-blue gaze pinned me to the spot. "I need you to hold down the fort for a couple of days."

Knox's sigh gusted from the speaker. "I figured as much. Where are you going?"

"Tartarus." But there was no fear in his eyes or waver in his voice. He wasn't scared to go with me— no, he was determined.

Knox paused for a long moment. "That gives new meaning to going to Hell and back for a woman. Is she going to lookout for you, or do I need to send an emissary to keep your ass in one piece?"

Both Corvin and I knew that an emissary wouldn't get past Oberon, so while Knox's offer was kind, it was also moot.

"Styx is very keen on my survival. I think I'll be fine."

I was glad he had enough confidence for the both of us.

"Keep an eye out for Penny, though, okay? If she needs us to come home, press the mark. I don't know how it'll work with the portal, but give it a go if you need it. Otherwise, leave word with the portal guard."

Mark? Did he mean the pack crest on his shoulder? I'd admired it briefly the few times I'd seen it. Then again, the times Corvin had been shirtless, I'd likely been admiring other... parts of his anatomy.

"Sure thing. I'll make sure everybody stays home."

That brought me a measure of relief. With me not on this world, their threats should be diminished—especially since the Crimson Roses were now a thing of the past.

With that, he hung up, and we set out to the one place I didn't particularly want to go.

Together.

"You have got to be fucking kidding me." The words were harsh, but Oberon's smile was smug. "You sure know how to prove me wrong, don't you?" That statement was poised at Corvin, but my friend's eyes never left my and Corvin's joined hands.

Of our little group, I had met Oberon first when he'd been dumped into Tartarus, broken, bloody, and pissed the fuck off at a whopping betrayal. I'd considered stabbing him to death from the very first moment I met him, and occasionally, I wondered if I made the right choice sparing his life.

Kind of like right then.

"What can I say? I'm a likable guy," Corvin replied, but it was almost as if he really wanted to dump one of my oldest friends on his ass.

Then again, this asshole had sat on the fact that Corvin had returned to this very spot every single day for ten weeks straight with no breaks. Every single day at dawn, he had been trying to get to me, trying to talk to me.

Given my past, I could see why Oberon would want to keep him away. The last time a man had been obsessed with me, it had brought my ruin.

But Odaar wasn't my mate. Never had been.

Corvin was.

A shudder worked its way through me as the

realizations kept on coming. Admitting that—even to myself—was as if I'd just climbed the tallest mountain. But I needed my head together to deal with this, and mooning over the fact that Corvin was my mate, and I *might* accept him, was not on the list of shit I needed to focus on.

"You'd have to be," Oberon muttered. "Wait till I tell Legion and Pol. I haven't seen something this entertaining since Nog got his new chew toy."

I had a feeling I knew who'd spilled the beans to Caius about Corvin in the first place. *That little shit.* I had half a mind to gut him and show him his intestines before he passed out. But that fun was for later.

"Move aside, dumbass. Before I go tell Legion who bought up all of his favorite fruit from the market vendors and hoarded it out of spite."

Oberon paled slightly. "You wouldn't dare."

I tilted my head to the side, eyes narrowing. "Oh, wouldn't I?"

Oberon crossed his arms over his chest, ready to negotiate. "Fine. And I won't even alert Legion or Caius or Pol that you're coming. Is that enough to buy your silence?"

I thought about it for about half a second. "Maybe. I'll have to think about it."

"I suppose that is as good as I'm going to get, isn't it?" Grumbling, he stood to the side. "Never thought I'd see the day you fell for the mate bullshit."

I didn't have the heart to correct him on the particulars of Corvin's and my situation. "One of these days it's going to be your turn, and when it is, I am going to point and laugh at you until I'm blue in the face."

Oberon's smile slid off his lips. "You and I both know it's never going to be my turn. Good try, though."

We'll just see about that.

Corvin and I crossed the swirling portal, the familiar atrium of the castle a welcome balm to my addled nerves. The fragrant blossoms of the pomegranate and persimmon trees filled my nose, as the darkness enveloped me like a friend.

I loved the sun, but Tartarus brought a level of safety I didn't have on Earth. Turning, I watched Corvin's face take in this little slice of my home, checking for any sign that he hated it. Eyes wide, mouth open, the wonder in his expression made my heart squeeze.

"It's so beautiful." His gaze fell from the trees to me. "This is your home?"

Before I could answer, Pol waltzed in, an evil gleam in his eye. This was exactly what I'd wanted to avoid.

"Don't start," I growled before the asshole could even open his mouth, stepping in between Corvin and my so-called friend. Naturally, Corvin stepped to the side, refusing to allow me to save him. "I need to talk to Caius, grab some of my clothes, and then I'm gone. Please do not make me regret coming here."

Corvin squeezed my hand before pulling me to his side. "Oh, come on, Storm Cloud. If your family wants to make sure I'm good enough for you, I'm game."

Pol's eyes widened as he sputtered out a shocked laugh. "You call her 'Storm Cloud'? And she let you?" He crossed his tattooed arms over his chest, his expression three paces past put out. "When I gave you a nickname, you threatened to fry me from the inside out and feed my entrails to whatever that thing is that lives in the ocean. This is bullshit."

Corvin shrugged. "She tried. It didn't work."

Pol's expression blanked for a second before it morphed into something like impressed.

I'd had about enough of this. "Is Caius in? This

isn't exactly a stroll through the flowers here. I need information."

Pol sobered, his penetrating gaze making me uncomfortable. "He's in with Legion, getting ready for the war games to start."

War games? Again?

I rolled my eyes. "Am I still banned from playing?"

"You'll have to ask the king, *Storm Cloud*," Pol jeered, turning to the hallway.

My smile was pure evil as I shot a lightning bolt directly at his left butt cheek. Pol yelped, jumping a foot into the air as Corvin and I skirted around him, heading for Caius' office.

"Only *he* gets to call me that."

CHAPTER 17

CORVIN

I had no idea what I was expecting from Tartarus, but my brain couldn't even contemplate the reality of it. Instead of fire and brimstone and death—which given Styx's description, I already knew was bogus—it was an opulent castle with onyx walls and plush furnishings.

It was a home—a home fit for the beauty and grandeur that was Styx.

Sitting in the middle of the room in a large black chair that could only be described as a throne was Caius, the king of this realm, a primordial god in the center of his own creation. Once upon a time, he'd been called the "Soulless One" or the King of Monsters, but I doubted any of that could be true.

I had once idolized a god for his love of Styx, enamored by a fairytale instead of seeing it for the betrayal it really was. There was no doubt in my mind that Caius had received the same twist of history Styx had.

And while they'd welcomed Styx back home, the apprehension of me was thick in the air. I couldn't blame them. I likely would act the same if one of my pack brought a stranger into our midst—a stranger from another world. Caius' dark eyes were just as fathomless as Styx's, and they stared into me as if he were taking every bit of my measure—as if he already knew every bad deed I'd ever done.

It didn't matter to him that Styx could take care of herself any more than it would matter to me if Aster were in her same position. I'd still be skeptical.

And rightly so.

"Corvin Blackwell. Alpha of the Blackwell Pack." Caius said this without even a hint of inflection, either waiting for me to break, to run, or to hide behind Styx.

I did none of the above.

"Formerly of New York, you were banished by your brother, correct?"

Well, that one stung.

"Yes, there was a... *change* in leadership last year. I listened to the wrong advice and chose the wrong side. But my help did manage to assist in his mate gaining power and creating a House. And while I'm ashamed of the part I played, I don't see how I could have done it any differently. Sometimes we trust people we shouldn't."

Understanding dawned in his expression, and he gave me a little tip to his chin. Trusting those I shouldn't was a running theme in my life, but I refused to feel sorry for it. After all, it had brought me to Styx. If I hadn't been banished last year, if I hadn't brought myself to Crossroads, I would likely have never met her.

Styx's head whipped to me, her flashing eyes narrowed. "Your *brother* is the one who banished you?"

If I didn't know any better, I'd think she was pissed off on my behalf.

While the banishment still stung sometimes, my part in the upheaval was still my fault. "My support of his father nearly got his mate killed. Even tangentially, it was still partly my fault. Banishment was less than I deserved. I can't say I'd be as merciful in the same position."

I thought of the men I'd killed for even so much as sniffing in Styx's direction, for thinking of harming her, for even being party to the men who did her harm.

No, I wouldn't be as merciful.

Not even a little bit.

Styx crossed her arms over her chest as she eyed her king. "What? Did you get information from Oberon and then send a minion to have him investigated? Overstep much?"

"Of course not," Caius replied, his smile part-evil, part-taunting. "I talked to Broca."

Styx muttered something about a "fucking goat lady" under her breath and rolled her eyes.

"Are we doing a full interrogation here, or can we get started? My men are getting antsy."

Another large man stood to the king's left, his long hair caught back in a queue, his body encased in armor. The war games were due to start as soon as their general arrived, and our appearance had disrupted the schedule.

While Styx and I had come here for a reason, the act of saying "why" hadn't exactly crossed her lips. I doubted we'd get to it until she could say a certain name, and I had a feeling she was still working herself up to it.

The big man snorted, giving me the once-over. He'd done that a lot over the last few minutes, his assessing gaze likely choosing how he would torture me once he got the chance. "This is the one you were mooning over in the bar? He seems a little puny for you, but who am I to judge?"

Styx pinched the skin between her brows. "I was *not* mooning over him. And just because he's not meant to decimate entire nations, doesn't mean he's puny. I hit him with lightning, and he just shrugged it off and got up. That's more than I could say for *you*."

Caius covered his mouth, but I could tell he was holding back a smile. "Didn't you piss yourself and drool uncontrollably for at least a week the last time she hit you?"

Legion looked affronted. "That was one time."

I figured laughing right then was a ticket to a prison I would not escape from, so I clenched my jaw and kept my face blank.

"Fine. If you're so tough, why not join us? Klyn only agreed to fight because your mate is still banned." Legion gave me another once-over, but this time, it was as if he was assessing my capabilities. "We don't allow full shifts, but you can join if you want."

I was riding the high of Styx finally *not* correcting someone about me being her mate, that I barely registered what he was offering. Cutting my gaze to Styx, I silently asked her thoughts. This was either a carrot to get me easily killed or a test—a test I wanted to pass. Her eyes tightened, and just like in the bookshop, we were having another silent conversation.

Should I?

Her lips tipped to the side. *If you want. Up to you.*

Tilting my head, I shrugged. *Think it's safe?*

She winced. *Hard maybe.* Then her face got the expression she wore right before someone got killed. *If it's not, someone will pay.*

Good to know she had my back if needed.

"I'm in. But only if she watches. The last thing we need is for you to get killed because I got a paper cut or something."

Legion's lips tipped to the side in the same almost-smile Styx rarely wore. He moved to slap me on the shoulder, and I was smart enough to shift the arm to stone before he made contact. Legion wasn't expecting that, and his eyebrows rose in surprise before his smile grew in earnest.

"Oh, we've got this in the bag. They're not going to know what hit them."

The coliseum-style arena was filled to the brim with combatants, the field teeming with every brand of supernatural in Legion's army. The general seemed at home in this space, as if his entire life had been for this very purpose. Up in the stands was a plush private box area where three women resided.

On the right was a pretty brunette that could be Reagan, Caius' mate. At the center was a hooded woman, her arms crossed as if she were attempting not to touch a single thing, and then there was Styx. My mate pointed two fingers at her eyes and then directed them to Legion as if to say, "I'm watching you."

She pointed to the girl and then back to me.

"Gods, she's got it bad," Legion muttered, adjusting his armor. "You'd better not get hurt out here. She just threatened to take out Tori if you get so much as a scratch."

So, I wasn't the only one she had silent conversations with. I guessed after five thousand years together that kind of bond was expected.

"Out of the two of us, I haven't been the one

almost croaking in the other's arms, so I don't know what she's got to worry about," I muttered under my breath, a little touched that she cared and irritated that she didn't think I could handle it.

This wouldn't be my first battle, and it was for damn sure not my first war.

Legion's eyes cut to me. "What the fuck does that mean? Explain. Now."

Ah, fuck. The bastard had heard me.

I put my hands up in surrender, paintball gun and all. "Oh, no. I am not spilling the beans. You'll have to ask her. I just got that woman to trust me. I'm not fucking it up just because you're a nosy asshole."

Legion's gaze hardened, and I remembered that Styx had told me he was usually the lead interrogator to traitors. Given what Styx considered "advanced interrogation techniques," I did not want to know what he'd do to me if it came down to it.

"Respectfully," I added, mostly to avoid a spear in the back or him removing my fingernails.

"Styx doesn't trust anyone," he growled, his steely stare never wavering. "Never has. I doubt she even trusts herself."

Isn't that the truth?

But also, it tore a hole in my chest to think

about. Five thousand years, and she'd never told anyone what she'd told me—if not her story, then admitting she had even the smallest amount of faith in me.

I needed to protect it, savor it, tend it, because that flame could so easily die out.

"Be that as it may, I'm still not telling you anything. If you want to know what's going on with Styx, you're going to have to ask her." And likely, I'd catch shit for his overpowered hearing, but it was what it was.

"We'll just see about that," he muttered.

My gaze tracked the woman in question as she leaned on the partition that separated the box from the rest of the stands. Those sparking eyes were like a caress, her attention so acute, it was as if she could reach me from there.

Then again, I'd seen her lightning. She likely could.

"I'm kind of surprised no one has threatened my life if I hurt her," I said, likely signing my own death warrant.

Legion gave me a sidelong glance. "We don't have to. If you do, she'll likely gut you and feed you piece by piece to the fishes. But you knew that already or you wouldn't be here."

"Just making sure her family is as ready to go to battle for her as she is for them—as she already has for mine."

Legion tipped his head up. "Always."

Then the horn sounded, starting the battle, and it was game on.

Sticking close to Legion, I ducked behind a stone obstacle, his signaled commands so much like Styx in a fight, I felt like I had an advantage. I wasn't a huge fan of guns, preferring to use my teeth or claws in a fight. However, in the last two hundred years, I'd been forced to use them enough that I could hold my own.

Peeling left, I let a partial change free, turning my arms and neck to stone as I cut through the arena. A bullet whizzed by my ear, telegraphing where my target was, and I realized this arena, with all its obstacles and tight corners, made it feel like I was right back in New York. The feeling of home was bittersweet, but that didn't mean I wouldn't use it to my advantage. Within the span of a single moment, I had aimed, fired, and knocked the guy out of the game along with his two buddies.

Granted, one got me in the arm, but the paint slid off the stone as if it were water.

"No fair," the guy roared, pissed at the three

bright-green splotches of paint on his armor, but all I heard was a dark chuckle from Legion as I shrugged and moved on.

"It only counts if it sticks. Looks like you're shit out of luck."

Grinning, I cut around the throng, avoiding the rain of bullets as I picked off our opponents one by one.

And all the while, I felt Styx's eyes on me, my silent cheerleader urging me on.

Sometime later, I was sweaty, bloody, and bruised, but also laughing my head off at the sore losers covered in paint as they retreated with their tails—some metaphorical and some not—between their legs. I'd held my own out there, helping Legion's team take the first victory of what would be a week's worth of grueling games. Legion's woman, Tori, was still breathing up in the stands, so Styx hadn't been too worried about me.

Once we'd said our goodbyes and peeled off, Styx grabbed me by the hand, and for the first time, I caught her scent. Ducking behind a pillar in a dark corridor, I crowded her, reveling in the heady perfume of her desire.

"Like what you saw out there, Storm Cloud?" I murmured against the delicate skin of her neck, all the partial shifts out on the battlefield making my fangs come out and play. My back ached to let my wings free as I fought off the urge to rake them against her skin.

Desperate to get myself under control, I managed to get a hold on my fangs, but the wings erupted from my back, tearing through my tattered armor as if it were little more than tissue paper.

Styx had no such roadblock, her biting kisses to the underside of my jaw nearly stealing every bit of reason left in my brain.

Her hands fisted in my tattered armor, ripping it from my shoulders as her electrified fingers raked over my skin. Her hands hooked in the waistband of my pants, yanking me closer, turning my brain damn near all the way off.

My hands found the underside of her thighs, and I hauled her up, pressing my aching cock against her scalding center. It didn't matter that we were both mostly clothed, I could still feel the heat of her through the fabric.

"I forgot what you looked like when you fought."

Had she forgotten? Or was it more the last time she saw me in battle, she was damn near dead?

That thought sobered me, reminding me of what we were doing in Tartarus—what I'd promised her to begin with. But then her hand cupped my cock over my pants as she hooked her legs over my hips, and I was lost again.

"When that barrier collapsed, I thought I'd have to come down there, but then you just mowed through them all and—"

Raking my fangs over her pulse point, her breathy moan made my cock pulse. I needed her so bad. I caught her wrist in one hand, bringing it up and over her head as I pulled her tank off her other shoulder, bra and all. Trailing kisses down her neck, I reached the heaven of her lush breast, raking my fangs over her dusky nipple before laving away the sting.

Then her free hand reached for me, and I had to bind that one, too.

With both arms over her head, her delicate but strong wrists in my hand, I could fuck her just like this. I could watch her come apart, I could...

I rested my forehead on her collarbone, her delicious scent not helping me fight for control one bit. It was a losing battle, anyway.

"I need to touch you, Storm Cloud," I growled, her scent so close to driving me mad that I had nearly lost all humanity.

She circled her hips, just about the only thing she could do with her arms bound, pinned against this wall. "Then touch me."

Fuck.

The things I could do to her...

Dropping her to her feet, I spun her, pressing her overheated body against the cool stone wall. My clawed finger found her shirt and pulled it up and over her breasts before I yanked at the button at her waistband, dragging her jeans and underwear over her hips.

Her scent made my knees weak, the heady perfume of her desire so good I had to get a taste.

I couldn't fuck her. Not right now, not yet, but I could show her just how good it would feel when I did.

"Hands on the wall, Storm Cloud. Don't move."

Her luscious ass called to me, begging me to mark it, to bite it, to spank it. Tipping her hips back, I sank to my knees, sinking my teeth into her ass cheek. I didn't break the skin, but oh, how I wanted to. Instead, I tipped her back more, and lapped at the lips of her pussy, tasting the honey coating her sex.

She bucked, and I spanked her ass in answer, earning me a low breathy moan. "I said don't move."

Retracting my claws, I pet her wet center, just touching, teasing, waiting for her to disobey me so I could spank her again. I was rewarded not five seconds later when she squirmed, my hand leaving a bright-red print on her bronze skin.

Damn did that look pretty.

"Corvin," she moaned, her forehead pressed against the stone, "*please.*"

Styx likely hadn't begged a day in her life, but damn if it wasn't the hottest fucking thing when she did it for me.

Granting mercy, I stood as I filled her with my fingers, her groan of satisfaction almost as good as the way she fucked herself on them, her wetness coating one hand as my other covered her mouth.

"That's it, Storm Cloud. Take what you need."

One of these days, it would be my cock filling her, her wetness coating me as I let her moans fill my ears. I just had to be patient.

Styx stiffened in my arms, the walls of her pussy fluttering around my fingers as she lost it, her moans barely contained by hand. Then she sagged, and I held her limp body to me while I righted her clothes. There was movement in the hall, and if we didn't fix our shit, we'd get discovered. I might not care about me, but no one would look at Styx.

No one.

"Feel better?" I asked, a hint of smugness to my tone, but I'd earned it.

Her electric eyes flashed at me over her shoulder. "Much. Though this is the second time I've gotten my orgasm and you've had none."

Oh, I was aware. "One of these days, I'll let you take advantage of me, Storm Cloud."

She licked her lips, and I knew as soon as she got me, I was going to be a goner. I likely already was.

Turning, she kissed the underside of my jaw, her teeth raking the skin hard enough for me to know my Storm Cloud also had fangs. My dick pulsed, whimpering from the confines of my pants.

"I'll hold you to that. Seeing you fight was sexy as hell."

"I gathered." Her scent would stay with me until the end of time. Resting my forehead on her shoulder, I pulled her body flush with mine.

Control.

I needed it and didn't have it. Not at all.

"Though, I prefer your gargoyle form, to be honest," she murmured.

I straightened, pulling my sweaty brow from her shoulder. "You just wanted to see me naked. I see how it is."

Then she did something I'd never seen before. She tossed her head back, and she laughed, the melodious cadence music to my fucking ears.

My heart squeezed in my chest, the swell of pride almost taking me out at the knees. Gently, I pressed a kiss to those still-smiling lips, swallowing down that laugh as if it would fuel my soul.

Fated mate or not, dream woman or not, I loved Styx in that very second. My heart belonged to her from the moment she knocked me out of the sky, but now?

She owned my soul.

I would kill for her—and had. I would die for her. I would move rivers and mountains. I would do anything if it meant she'd be mine and I'd be hers.

Anything at all.

I just had to not fuck it up.

CHAPTER 18

STYX

There were plenty of times that I had told Caius a boatload of shit he did not want to hear, but this was the very first time that the shit had ever involved me.

Okay, so that wasn't exactly true. But it was the first time that it wasn't my fault.

I took the opportunity to talk to my king while Corvin was showering, my coward ass unable to go through this with an audience.

"What do you mean they want you dead?" he growled, and I had to wonder if he had a hearing problem. I couldn't figure out a way to say that any clearer than I already had, but it seemed one of my oldest friends didn't quite understand the predica- ment I had found myself in.

"Considering an army of acolytes have already tried to take me down, I don't see what desire they could possibly have other than stone-cold murder. Then again, they might just want to abscond with me for afternoon tea."

Caius' eyes narrowed, unappreciative of my sarcasm.

"Start from the beginning," he ordered.

Of all the people in this universe, he was just about the only person I would allow to do that and keep breathing.

"Where would you like me to start? Five thousand years ago, when I went across the portal the first time, the second time... I'm going to need you to be a bit more specific."

Caius sat forward on his throne, his shadows seeping from his very body like hands ready to throttle me if I didn't get to talking. "Start wherever you want, just tell me what's going on."

I was used to giving him advice, not the other way around. No one told me that it would suck this bad.

"When I was banished here, I didn't know the name of the god I'd killed. That changed when Corvin told me a story that he'd loved as a boy about the god Odaar and the River Styx." I swallowed, bile hitting the back of my throat. "Did you know that's the first time I've ever said his name out loud? I didn't even know it before yesterday. I still don't know the name of his children, but fuck if they aren't determined to put me six feet under."

I had the urge to wash my mouth out with soap and decided that *his* name wouldn't be spoken. Not again. Not from my lips, anyway. Somehow, it felt like saying his name gave him power—power over me—even though he was long dead.

I fucking hated it.

"I don't know how they found me or why they were even looking. Maybe it was all the times I used his power on the Earth side. Maybe they just knew when I crossed, or it could be a hundred other scenarios."

I thought of their snide faces surrounding me, so smug as if I was an easy mark. As if I was a clever little prize to give to their bullshit gods. As if I was the same girl on the shore of that river pleading for mercy.

"The day I went back to Earth, a group of acolytes came for me. This is straight conjecture, but based off of what they said and the insignia on their robes, they follow his son."

I remembered his quiver of celestial arrows, the

way they shot through the air embedding in my sister's chest. The way her body burned up instantly. That quiver never seemed to run out of arrows as he hit each one of my sisters, each one of my nephews and nieces.

It had happened so fast.

"I was surrounded. No armor, no weapons, and they'd poisoned me with power while they were protected from mine. I..." The memory of that terrible burn made me shudder. "They nearly killed me. If Corvin hadn't come when he did, they likely would have. I haven't even been able to admit this to him yet, but he saved my life."

I didn't tell Caius about how I'd almost killed Corvin's whole pack. How he'd cloaked me, saved me, how he'd brought me to his home instead of leaving me behind—mate bond or no. That said nothing about when they'd found me at the bookshop. How they'd bitten off their own tongues rather than be interrogated.

Nothing made sense—not Corvin's persistence, not the acolyte's faith in their gods, not the makeup of the universe. Fate was a crafty bitch—I'd give her that.

Caius was silent for a long time, his assessing

gaze cutting me to the quick. "So they just want you dead, is that it?"

"You'd think they'd be over it by now, right? But it seems like they were pretty keen on cutting off my head."

"And you can't find any information about them?"

Oh, how I wished for something—anything—that would tell me who they were.

"I didn't even know *his* name until Corvin told it to me. But out of all the books I looked in, of all the sky deities I researched, he's just not there. And what's funny is, other than the story Corvin told me, I'm not sure he's in those books at all. And why would he be? He died five thousand years ago. Why would history remember him?"

And considering how many books I'd read, it was like trying to find a needle in a stack of needles.

"I knew of him," Caius remarked, disgust twisting his mouth. "He called himself the 'King of the Gods.' He was a pompous asshole too full of himself to realize that nobody really gave a shit about some wannabe leader of a sky deity called himself."

That sounded about right. In all his pursuits, he

had just assumed I knew his name. Assumed I knew his story. Assumed I knew his power.

"I don't know the children's names, though. They weren't really on my radar—not to say that he was—but that was a long time ago." He sighed. "I had no idea *you* didn't know who he was, though. As soon as you told me your name, I knew who you were. I thought what you did was justified and your punishment..."

I'd never told Caius everything, but he'd known, anyway.

Figures.

"Just as well. I kind of like the fact that they've basically been stricken from history. Gives me a little warm and fuzzy even if it doesn't help. Corvin said he'd help me find them, but I don't see a way how."

Caius sat back on his throne, his fingers steepled in contemplation. "You really told him everything?"

His question was almost incredulous as if he couldn't really comprehend how far I would fall or how fast.

"He went back to the portal every day while I was gone trying to find me, but he didn't fight Oberon, even though he likely could have," I murmured, the reasons so simple and so *not* all at the same time. "He changed the course of the very river to make sure I had access to it. He saved my life. He offered me protection, even though it would have cost him gravely. He cooked me food."

But Caius wasn't allowing me to give him those paltry answers. "I've given you protection and food and access to a river, and not once have you told me everything. You love him."

Lifting a shoulder, his statement twisted my insides. And what was love, anyway? Was it this ache in my chest from being apart from him? Even though I knew where he was and what he was doing, it still made me want to race to his side.

Was it this longing in my gut to know every single facet of his life before me? To be there every day, learning more about him, being there for his pack? Was it how I wanted to show him every part of Tartarus, introduce him to every person I cared about?

Was it how he held me when I slept? How he put me first, how he was proud of me?

Was it how I felt safe with him?

I didn't really know what love was, but the rest? I knew that.

"I trust him. Isn't that enough?"

"For you, maybe, but that man loves you. He's probably loved you since he was a boy and didn't know it. He's changed the shape of his world just so you have a space in it. What does that tell you?"

Grumbling, I pinched the bridge of my nose, sinking into the cushion of my seat as I tried not to admit the very worst thing ever.

"That you were right, you bastard. Happy?"

A single raised eyebrow was all I got in return. I forgot how I hated that eyebrow. "That depends. Are you actually going to allow yourself to be happy? Are you going to break any of your rules? Are you going to let him in?"

How the fuck did he know about my rules? Oh, right. *Fucking Broca.*

"I told him the very worst thing about myself. How is that not letting him in?"

"You and I both know you only did that as a defense mechanism to shove him away. To see if it would scare him off."

I absolutely loathed that he was just as ancient as I was and knew every single one of my tricks.

"It didn't work, though, now, did it?" I muttered. "And the more he sticks around, the less and less I want him to leave. Is this really what mating feels like? Because I'm not a fan."

"Oh, come on. There are worse things."

"Like what?"

Caius' smile was three parts evil and ten parts absolutely giddy. "The fact that you're probably going to have to talk to your least favorite person to get the answers you need."

"Don't say it."

"But it's so much fun to see you squirm. You're going to have to talk to Broca."

Well, fuck.

By the time Corvin found me, I was in a grumpy mood, Caius was trying not to outright laugh at me, and Reagan had returned. Pol was also in attendance, the asshole just waiting for the show as Broca took her sweet-ass time getting to the castle.

Broca was a glaistig, an awful half-goat, half-woman of a soothsayer full of hot air and bullshit premonitions. So far, she had yet to give a single shred of vital information to anyone else besides Caius, and even that had always been suspect.

Since the moment I'd met her, I'd hated her, her curling language and half-truths irking my nerves far more than they should. Maybe it was because she always pretended to know more than everyone.

Maybe it was her lack of warnings that were filled with riddles and games.

Or maybe it was how if she knew so much, why did she hide that knowledge away for herself, leaving us all to swing?

Or... it was the very way she spoke. It was like *him*. Always indirect, always hiding what she really meant. As if she intended to deceive, to trick. *He* had spoken that same way, hiding who he was while expecting me to just *know*.

She was the prime reason I thought all psychics were complete charlatans and hated them on sight.

Glamour solidly in place, she waltzed into Caius' office, her fake visage dialed toward ethereal beauty with long red hair and a clingy green dress instead of the haggard half-goat woman we all knew she was. Her eyes alighted on Corvin, a shrewd gleam in them as she approached.

If she so much as touched him, I would make her regret it for however short the remainder of her life would be. Corvin caught my left hand, lacing his fingers through mine, completely ignoring the arches of electricity that spanned like webbing between them and the soothsayer's approach.

My free hand rained sparks to the floor as the scent of ozone filled the room, but Corvin didn't so much as flinch. I was just glad they hadn't caught the rug on fire.

"I see you stopped running," she remarked, eyeing him like a juicy steak. "I knew you couldn't do it forever. And why would you want to?"

You need her help. Do not attack the bitchy goat lady.

It was best to stay silent. Otherwise, I would probably rip her in half.

"Caius imparted that you needed something from me. Information. I was under the impression you did not like my guidance."

I shot a withering glare at Caius. As fun as this was for him, he was also the only one Broca would actually listen to. But did he back me up? No. He simply smiled as I tried not to murder the goat lady where she stood.

"If I had another option, I wouldn't ask you for a thing."

Her smile was cruel. "You have plenty of options. You just don't like them. Tell me—what makes you think I'll give you any others?"

"I don't," I admitted, losing what little patience I had. "I think you will screw me around and leave me with nothing just like you have always done. Anytime someone comes to you for information, you like to taunt and tease and speak in riddles, but you don't actually help with anything. Even when someone comes to you for guidance, even when someone asks you outright for your help."

Her green eyes flashed, gearing up for a fight.

"You've hated me since the moment you met me. Why is that?" she asked, but wasn't she the psychic? Didn't she already know my answer?

"Because you speak like *him*," I hissed, meaning the god who'd gotten me trapped here. The god whose very name made me want to throw up. "In riddles and half-truths, and you leave everybody to swing, lost in the dark even though you know the answers—or you at least pretend to. Of course I don't like you."

"Does he speak in riddles?" she asked, nodding to Corvin.

I didn't even want her to look at him. "No, he doesn't. He is straightforward and honest, and I can trust him. Unlike you."

"Then why do you need to go looking for the other gods?" she asked.

So, maybe she did know more than she let on.

"Because my family deserves their revenge. I deserve it, and more, if I don't go looking for them, they'll come looking for me. I'll put the people I care about in danger."

"And you care more about honoring the dead than protecting your new family?" she offered, taking the chair across from me and abandoning all pretense of glamour. Gone were her human-shaped legs in favor of the goat ones, her red hair was now threaded through with a silvery gray, her skin wrinkled, teeth yellowed, but those eyes were still a brilliant green.

Did I care more for the family I lost rather than Corvin's pack? Did I consider them my new family? I didn't know the answer to that. I didn't know how to quantify what was in my heart.

I did know I would protect the living before I avenged the dead, but that was about all I knew.

"I care about not dying or getting the people I love killed. Above that, I'm flexible."

Would it hurt my soul to let them live? Probably. But I'd do it if I had to. My fingers tightened on Corvin's, and he drew me closer to him, bumping his shoulder with mine. His warmth was reassurance, peace, even with her here.

Broca gave me a crooked smile. "Flexible? You haven't been flexible a day in your life." Her attention turned to Corvin. "But you, boy. You have bent yourself in knots." She tilted her head to the side. "And you have shadows to you, too, don't you?"

Then she gasped, her green eyes clouding over, as she angled her head and peered at Corvin as if she was imparting the greatest wisdom.

Storm clouds move across the skies,
Deep and fearful through her guise.
She blinds her eyes and silences her screams,
The power sought burning at her seams.
The war drums pound as an ally lies,
The time to act not on her side.
She twists the arrow, her soul torn in two,
Love or vengeance she must choose.

And how did I know it would turn into this?

Broca stood from her seat, her glamour firmly in place, dusting off her hands like she'd done me a service. I fought off the urge to tackle her to the ground and shock her until she gave me something I could use.

Unfortunately, I didn't get the chance.

"Because my visions are too abstract for you," she said, giving me a perturbed sniff, "the gods you seek are Xyla and Idall—neither of which you'll find in your books. They've been stricken from history, lesser gods without what they seek. I can't give you more than that, so take what you can get."

That I could appreciate. At the very least, she saved me a ton of reading. "Appreciated."

Love or vengeance she must choose.

That line echoed in my head, and I squeezed Corvin's fingers.

Abstract or not, I had a feeling I knew what it meant.

CHAPTER 19

STYX

By the time I'd packed a bag and we'd said our goodbyes, my head was a mess. Reordering everything I'd thought about myself—everything I swore I'd never do and everything I'd promised I'd never be—made me practically a zombie as Corvin led me to the portal.

The rules I'd set out for myself didn't fit in this new reality.

I swore I'd never take a mate.

But here my mate was, caring and kind, fierce and loyal. And I wanted to break that rule—even if it meant he'd be saddled with me for the rest of his life. Because he was the first bit of joy—of real happiness I'd had in such a long time that losing it now would wreck me forever.

I swore I'd make the gods who'd banished me pay.

But if Broca's premonition was to be believed, I would have to choose between them and... *love.*

The love I never thought I'd have, that I never thought I deserved.

The portal swirled in front of us, and for a split second, I wanted to stay on this side. I wanted to hide us away, holing up in my chambers as we figured everything out. Here it was safe—he was safe.

Hesitating, I squeezed his fingers, pulling him back from the edge. Five thousand years in what used to be my prison, and I didn't want to leave.

Not if he was here.

Not if I could keep him.

"What is it, Storm Cloud?" he asked, gently setting my duffle on the ground. "Having second thoughts?"

The smile on his face when I'd packed my things, it had hit me like a ton of bricks. With every article of clothing, it was like a brand-new promise. A statement saying that I would be with him long enough to need each item, I would use everything, I would...

Stay.

But the look on his face now said very different things. It was sorrow and pain and rejection. It was agony.

He thought I was refusing him.

Again.

Rejecting him.

Again.

Corvin had been tossed out on his ass, rejected by his brother, his mother, his old pack. He'd come all the way to Crossroads only to get rejected over and over again by my stubborn ass, even though he'd carved out a space in his life just for me.

"No, it's just—" His pain made me want to curl up and die or ease it somehow, whatever I needed to do so that look never crossed his face again. "This is the happiest I've ever been. What if... what if I ruin it? What if I hurt you, what if I get you killed? Right now, you're still safe. You could cross that portal and never see me again, and you and yours would be—"

"Miserable," he growled, the heat of his hands cupping the back of my neck, his lips brushing mine as he spoke. "I would be miserable. Insufferable. I would claw my way back to you, begging you to—"

I covered his mouth with my own, realizing he was just as lost as I was. I couldn't set him free—not without ruining him forever. Heat swirled over my skin as he yanked me closer, his chest crushed against mine as if even a millimeter of space between us was too much.

"Take me home," I murmured against his mouth, nipping at the swell of his bottom lip. The unsaid "with you" implied.

He pulled away, those steel-blue eyes seeing right through to the heart of me. But that inspection was almost too much, so I yanked him toward the portal. He barely had the chance to snag my duffle from the ground before we were crossing, heading back to his pack, his home.

As we crossed the park with the train station in sight, a strange yet familiar sensation prickled across my skin. After our time in Tartarus, I didn't notice the lack of a moon right away, the pitch-black night falling over my skin like a physical touch. It was only when I felt the twist to my belly as a bolt of white-hot desire speared through me that I realized a little too late.

During *Februlune*, Legion had locked up a whole realm away from Corvin, and still the double new moons had nearly driven me mad. This time there was only one dark moon, but Corvin was right next to me, his scent surrounding me, his warmth like a flash fire on my skin.

This is so much worse.

I was completely unprepared for the onslaught.

Sweat dotted my forehead as I pulled off my jacket. Every step we took, my jeans rubbed against my oversensitive skin, every move making my shirt whisper over my flesh.

"Corvin?" Was that breathy sound really my voice? And why did that single word make him freeze in his tracks?

His steel-blue eyes were overtaken by orange flames as his nostrils flared, his grip on my hand like iron.

"*Fuck*," he groaned, reeling me in, dipping his nose to the soft shell of my ear, a purring growl vibrating his chest. "You smell like fucking heaven, Storm Cloud."

Then he shook himself, jaw clenched, shoulders straight. "I need to lock myself up. I'll call Jude or Knox. They'll keep me in the basement. I'll—"

Once again, I silenced him with my kiss. His tongue brushed mine, and it was as if I could feel it against my clit. My sex pulsed, my knees went weak, and I fought off the urge to strip Corvin naked and fuck him in every way I knew how in the middle of the park.

I'd seen worse on Tartarus.

"The last time I went into heat, I had to be locked up because I would rip apart anyone who got in my way. That was a world away. What do you think I'll do to Knox or Jude if they try to stop me now with you right here?"

The brand of his hand on my ass nearly made me lose it. "I should not be turned on at the thought of you ripping someone apart to get to me, but fuck if I am." He swallowed, his throat bobbing as his jaw clenched tight. "Tell me what you want me to do, and I'll do it. If you want me to run, I will. I can. I'll fly away so you can't reach me. But…"

"No," I growled, my fingers fisting in the fabric of his shirt. "No more running."

He dropped my duffle before plucking me off my feet as if I weighed nothing. My legs instinctively went around his waist, pressing my aching center against his stomach. I couldn't help it, I moaned. I'd already seen Corvin naked and aroused, and just the thought of his cock inside me had my hips grinding against him.

"If you want this, I can—"

"Fuck me so hard I feel you for days afterward? Make me come over and over until I'm a sex fiend that craves you every second of every day? Brand me with your mark?" My sex clenched hard at the thought of him marking me.

Changing course, he carried me into a thicket, the trees tall and densely placed, hiding us from the wide-open expanse of the park. On Tartarus, the forest was dangerous during this time, the moon-called shifters unwieldy and wild.

Here the city was quiet, safe, sleeping, fucking, or fighting elsewhere.

My back found a tree, the rough bark against my thin shirt adding just a little bite to the already-mindless way I was trying to rip Corvin's clothes off. "If I fuck you here, someone could see. Then I'd have to kill them."

If he had to kill someone, then that would be time spent not making me come. "How fast can you get us home?"

His fiery eyes squeezed tight. "Twenty minutes by train. Fifteen by car. Three by air."

Biting my lip, I circled my hips. Three minutes *and* I got to see him naked? I called that winning in my book. "Air it is."

Corvin set me on my feet as he pulled off his jacket, divesting himself of the rest of his clothes before his bones snapped and cracked, reforming into the monstrous shape of his gargoyle. Easily over ten feet tall, the chimera stood before me in all his majestic glory, his stonelike skin nearly black as night. The portal was changing him, making him darker, more savage, as it did all of us.

I snatched my duffel from the ground, fitting it over my shoulder as he put his belly on the earth so I could climb on his back, his giant leathery wings surrounding me.

"Make it fast, Blackwell."

His name barely left my lips before we were shooting into the air, moving faster than any falcon. The wind screamed past us as he carried me over the city, the river winding below like the tail of a serpent. We touched down before I even got a real glimpse of anything, his movements sharp and with a determined purpose.

Soon as my feet hit the ground, the duffel was off my shoulder and I was in his arms, enjoying the experience of his skin under my palms as he clutched me to his chest.

Fangs touched my neck as he tore through the house, the gentle press of them earning him a shiver as a flash fire of need broke out across my skin. In retaliation, I gave him a touch of my own fangs, my animal side so close to the surface that I could barely think straight.

My back hit a wall as his bedroom door slammed behind us, my feet finding the ground. A hard hand pressed me back, keeping me still as he heaved out a tormented breath.

"Last chance, Storm Cloud," he growled around thick lion fangs, his cat-shaped eyes blazing with fire. His wings were gone, but his body practically vibrated as he held himself still. "There's no going back after this. You'll be mine and I'll be yours and—"

"I choose you," I whispered, covering his mouth with my fingers, my heart swelling as desire rose like the tide. "Even when I was running, I couldn't get you out of my head. I want this—you. Always."

Corvin crushed me to his chest, his hot mouth on mine as our tongues dueled for dominance. A rip sounded before cool air hit the skin of my back. A second later, my jeans were gone, and I had a fleeting thought that I was glad I had a duffle full of clothes before his lips closed around my nipple, his fangs scraping the sensitive flesh.

A ravenous moan tore from my mouth, the blistering heat ripping through me, making me mindless. I ached everywhere, and only he could fix me.

"Please," I cried out, only to be rewarded with his rough hand on my pussy, his thick fingers petting my clit before they worked their way inside, filling me, stretching me. Those nimble fingers curled, hitting my G-spot, and my hips snapped as I chased the pleasure, my release so close I could taste it.

"That's it, Storm Cloud, use my fingers, come all over them," he growled in my ear, the scent of his skin—of his need—only ramping up my own. His sharp fangs raked over the sensitive skin of my neck and then I was gone, lost in the white-hot bliss as my release slammed into me.

But just as soon as that release hit, my heat did me no favors, scorching my whole body as if that first orgasm only poured fuel on the fire.

Then my back found the cool sheets of the bed and Corvin's fingers left me.

"No," I moaned, my aching need making me feel like I might combust at any second.

"Patience, baby. I'll take care of you."

But I couldn't wait, I flipped us, pressing my heated skin against his as I reached between us. His hard length practically seared my hand, and I wanted it so bad I could taste it.

"Fuck patience. I need you now."

Notching the head of his cock against my opening, I watched his face as I took him in inch by inch.

Full. I was so full, and I wasn't even halfway down, his cock stretching me almost to the point of pain. My walls fluttered, barely able to squeeze around him, and as he bottomed out, I thought I'd probably bitten off more than I could chew.

"Gods, baby, you're so fucking tight."

I wasn't tight, he was just so godsdamned big.

He sounded like he was in pain, but I was so close to coming with just him inside me and he hadn't even moved yet. Eyes flaring, jaw clenched, he gripped my hips, his sharp claws nearly breaking my skin as he took charge.

In an instant, I was on my back, his body covering me, his hot hand at the back of my neck as he set his mind to turning me inside out. His punishing thrusts wrenched moan after moan from my throat.

Our eyes met, electricity crackling between us as the world faded away. It was just us, no gods, no pack, no Tartarus. Just Corvin and I in this bed trying to destroy each other. Claiming each other.

"Don't stop," I pleaded, my release so close it threatened to drown me. I wanted his fangs in my skin, my blood in his mouth. I wanted his groans in my ear.

"Never."

That sounded like a promise, a vow, and as my climax unfurled, I got everything I wanted. Corvin's fangs cut into the sensitive skin of my neck, drowning me in ecstasy as half of the mate bond slid into place, tying him to me with a thousand invisible threads, his desire, his bliss filling me full to bursting.

I screamed out my release as lightning crackled through the room, my fangs lengthening in my mouth. Completing the bond, I struck, slicing into Corvin's neck, his sweet blood sliding down my throat as the final ties bound us together.

Forever.

CHAPTER 20

CORVIN

Steam rose from Styx's skin as the cool water rained down on us both. She rested against me, her head on my shoulder as I massaged shampoo into her scalp, her moans of pleasure not sexual for the first time in hours.

She was exhausted, but the heat would not release her so soon. By her scent alone, I didn't have much time before it would strike again, yanking us both under.

"How are you so good at that? It feels like you're touching me everywhere," she groaned, tightening her hold on my shoulders, pressing her body so close to mine.

"I used to have long hair once upon a time," I

answered before reaching for the sprayer nozzle. "Lean back, baby. Let me rinse you."

She tilted her head back, exposing the column of her throat and the now-healed mating mark at the junction of her neck and shoulder. My cock twitched, trapped between our bodies, and her legs tightened on my hips.

Soap sluiced over her bronze skin, and I watched each bubble on their path down the most perfect body in the known universe.

"I can't imagine you with long hair," she said, her scent sweetening as she reacted to mine.

Her fingers laced through my shorter strands, pulling my head back, and then she licked my mating mark. I lost the hold on the sprayer in favor of grabbing her ass, yanking her close so her soaking pussy rubbed against my dick.

"I'll grow it out if you want," I murmured against her lips, not exactly following the conversation, and not giving that first shit. She could've asked me anything right then and I'd spill any secrets I had.

She nibbled on my bottom lip. "No thanks, I love it just like this. Especially the scruff. I love the way it scrapes against my thighs."

Her skin heated, the steam fogging the shower glass as her hips rolled.

"Remember me making you come in Tartarus?" I asked, stilling her movements as she whimpered out her protest.

I smacked her ass, loving the way she moaned and fought to seek out her pleasure.

"Yesss," she hissed, her fangs growing in her mouth. "I remember."

"I wanted to fuck you just like that then, so bad I almost lost it right there in that hall. I had to take myself in hand in the shower afterward, and even then, I was still so fucking hard for you I could barely see straight."

Her eyes flashed open as she climbed from my lap, and gods help me, she pressed her body against the stone wall, her luscious ass tilted back like a present. She looked back at me over her shoulder as she gave me the sexiest smile I'd ever seen.

"Like this?"

Unable to hold myself back, I moved, catching her wrists in my hand and pulling them over her head.

"Almost."

Roughly, I yanked her hips back, notching my cock at her soaked opening. Styx's whimper was all the begging I needed, and I pressed inside, the heat of her scalding me from the inside out.

"So fucking tight, so fucking good." I rolled my hips, testing, teasing, needing her mindless. "Are you going to be my good girl and keep your hands there? Or am I going to have to tie you up?"

She only moaned, which was answer enough. She wouldn't keep her hands there, I would have to tie her up, and as much as she loved being called my good girl, she was very, very good at being bad.

I'd tie her up next time.

This time she needed to get fucked.

The sun threatened to breach the clouds, the morning coming too soon for my tired bones. After the third day, Styx's heat finally broke, the fever-like desire banking enough that we could get some sleep. It had been nearly fourteen hours, and I still felt like I needed about a week of rest before I was back in fighting shape.

Pressing biting kisses to her spine, I attempted to wake her, her breakfast cooling at her hip.

"Is that bacon?" she asked, her husky voice sexy

as fuck after days of screaming out her release.

"And coffee. And pancakes."

She lifted her head from the pillow, pulling her mane of hair out of her eyes, a tether of rope still attached to her wrist. It was broken and frayed—the bonds ill-suited for a shadow shifter. I'd have to remember that for her next heat.

Her fathomless gaze landed on the cakey disks as she licked her pouty lips. My cock kicked against my zipper, and I marveled how, after days of nonstop mating, I was still horny.

Maybe it was the mate thing, and maybe it was just Styx. She'd affected me since the day I'd set eyes on her, and she would likely do so until I was in my grave.

Maybe even then.

Or maybe it was due to the fact that she was still naked. And smelled like a well-fucked woman. And...

"I suggest you eat before I forget you need sustenance and eat *you* for breakfast."

Styx's eyes flashed before she snatched the bacon off the plate, her hunger making her take action as she shoved it in her mouth.

"My breakfast first, then your breakfast," she said, a devious smile curling her lips.

Damn did I love that smile.

"I don't get it. I could not possibly need more sex, but..."

But here we were trying not to fuck each other into early graves because we craved each other more than air. "I know. But we should try to leave the room for a little bit. At least to reassure everyone we're still alive."

Styx snorted before she stole a pancake off the plate. "I guarantee they know. Do you think we need to invest in a sound-dampening spell? Especially with everyone here."

Was that a blush rising in my mate's cheeks?

"Aster already took care of it after the first round. She said that if she had to hear every mated couple we had fuck over the new moon heat, she'd vomit herself to death."

Styx let out a dark chuckle. "How many mated couples are in the pack?"

"Four couples not including us, and a few solitary ones as well."

Styx's smile dropped. "Penny?"

I swallowed hard, thinking about what she'd gone through over the last few days. Penny had killed the mate Fate had chosen for her, ripping out his throat after he tried to hurt her in the worst of ways. The new moon coming so fast was just a painful reminder of what she'd survived.

"Knox locked her up at her request. She had offers to help her through it, but it's too soon after everything."

Styx sat up, her expression pained. "Should I… talk to her? I know I'm not the best with feelings, but I could…"

My ancient mate was doing her level best to be a good friend. Gods, did it make me love her more. "If you want. There are some things I'll never understand because it hasn't happened to me, but talking to someone always helps."

She swallowed hard, uncertainty written all over her. "What if I say the wrong thing? I didn't exactly deal with everything the right way when I—" She cut herself off, shaking her head.

"How did you deal?" I asked softly, wanting to know everything about her, even this.

She winced, stuffing another pancake in her mouth, likely so she didn't have to answer. She'd told me some of it, but I had a feeling she'd glossed over most of the story.

Styx blew out a frustrated breath and rolled her eyes at herself. "I may have gone on a century-long murder spree?"

She said it like a question, as if noncommittally confessing it eased the blow somehow.

"And by murder spree, you mean?"

She stared at the ceiling instead of meeting my eyes, a sure sign that whatever it was, was pretty bad.

"I may have lured men to their deaths by making them drown themselves in my river before I devoured them whole for roughly a hundred years," she blurted, before stuffing her mouth with another pancake.

That was one way to go about it. "I take it you're not proud of that time in your life?"

She winced again and gave me a noncommittal shrug. "I'm not, *not* proud of it. As bad as it sounds, I don't feel guilty about what I did. It was the time where I hated everything with a penis, and rightly so. They would see a beautiful, naked woman at the edge of the river, and think 'Oh, that's nice, I'll take that.' As soon as they got within my power's range, I made them drown themselves."

My eye twitched. So it wasn't just Odaar trying to take what wasn't his, it was every man she'd killed. For a hundred years. I swallowed down my rage, blanking my face, and hoping she couldn't feel it through the bond.

"In a way, it was almost like I was culling the herd. If they had even a thought in their head about being a rapist, they drowned. It's tough to feel bad about that—especially after what happened with Penny. How many women did I save? How many kids? How many men who couldn't fight them off? My river is littered with their bones, and I can't say I'm sorry."

"I really can't argue with that," I said, admiring her logic. "I agree, if someone looks at a naked woman and thinks she's fair game, whether she gives you consent or not, that's a rapist. Yeah, I think you probably did the right thing."

"Really?"

"Yes."

"There were plenty who didn't chase me, who asked if I was okay and moved on. I let them live. I didn't kill *everything* with a penis. Oberon's still alive, isn't he?"

She had a point there. "You didn't have a support system. Penny does—a support system that includes you. If you want to talk to her, you should. You might muddle through it, but having you at her back gave her the strength to do what she needed to do. It will probably give her the strength to move on, too."

Styx seemed to think about that for a second as she nibbled on a piece of bacon. "You're pretty good at this Alpha thing. You know that, right?"

That was a compliment of the highest order—especially from someone like Styx.

"I'm glad you think so. I'm glad I got a second chance at it. I didn't do so hot the first time around. I was too worried about playing politics, and not enough about the people under me. I thought I could be the big man, and it turned out that in this kind of job, worrying about the people underneath you is more important than anything else."

"Now you're thinking like Caius. And that is a compliment."

"Compliments always sound like the truth coming from you," I murmured, tasting the sticky syrup on her lip.

"It's because I don't hand them out freely. I only give them when people deserve them. Would you like to hear my thoughts on your prowess in bed? I can give you lots of compliments in that regard."

I pulled her plate away as I rolled her beneath me.

"Tell me all about it," I growled, nipping at her neck.

It was time for my breakfast.

CHAPTER 21

CORVIN

That little bubble of peace we'd latched onto could only last for so long. Even with Styx cloaked via Isaac and the local branch of the Crimson Roses out of commission, there was still a city full of unaffiliated supernaturals with no laws or policing who did a plethora of dumb shit on any given Tuesday.

During the new moon festivities, there had been a disturbance at the very same docks that we'd staked out what seemed like ages ago. The river pirate issue had quieted a fair bit since then, but now the docks were in ruins, the local businesses shuttered and unusable, and I had a feeling that particular foe wasn't quite as squashed as I thought it had been.

Knox hadn't been able to find any information on the boat leading to the home base of the pirates or to whoever they were shacking up with. During Styx's interrogation of the last of the local Crimson Roses chapter, those pirates hadn't been alone. They'd been employing vamps like muscle—not that it had saved their asses. And they had an entire coven devoted to their particular cause, holed up on the east side of the river.

Styx surveyed the crumbling dock, her unreadable expression a testament to her control. Her emotions filtered through my body, and they were dialed toward vengeance. She didn't patron the businesses or the people who owned them on this dock. She wasn't affiliated with them in any way, and yet, she hated every square millimeter of damage, feeling like each one was a personal affront to her very existence.

Styx—as much as she pretended not to—cared a great deal about other people—especially innocent people. She hated seeing blameless civilians hit with loss just because of the luck of the draw, and I couldn't say I blamed her.

I wondered what Caius would do in the same situation. Styx had been his adviser for more years than I could possibly fathom. I highly doubted the primordial god would let such disrespect slide.

"I'm going to have to take over this whole fucking river, aren't I?" she muttered, her eyes flashing as a distant thunder rumbled, the threat faint but there all the same.

The thought of her claiming the river as her own, of making a real home here, of choosing to make her mark on Crossroads filled me with so much relief and joy, I didn't know what to do with myself. Even though my emotions likely filtered through her whole body just like hers did to me, I tried to play it cool.

"It's up to you, Storm Cloud. But if you want a home base here, and you like this river—"

She let out a frustrated scoff. "I'd like this river a fuck of a lot more if there weren't so much gods-damn trash in it," she snapped. "What is it with people just throwing shit in the water? Did you know there are whole cars under there? Ships? Bodies? It's ridiculous."

She had no idea what kind of a toilet the Missis-sippi River had been once upon a time. At least now, with the lack of humans, there was a little decorum. A little respect. Not much, but it was better.

"You think that's bad? It used to be so much

worse. Think of all the fuel they used to power those riverboats before humanity decided to take a shit. And not just riverboats, ships, and cargo vessels, too. This river used to be a major passage to ship goods and people. It spanned nearly the whole country back when this place used to be a country."

"They dumped fuel in the water?" she asked incredulously, aghast at the violation of what she considered sacred. "On purpose?"

Sometimes. And anything else they thought they didn't need.

"The boats used to run on fuel, and as they burned the fuel, it would pollute the river. Considering this river spans most of the continent, that's a lot of pollution."

Styx gagged a little, her whole body shuddering in disgust. "Well that just jumped up my to-do list, right after we handle whoever's fucking with these docks. You know it's a sad state of affairs when even Hell isn't this bad."

I found her fingers with my own, pulling her to my side.

"I thought you said Tartarus wasn't Hell."

"It's not Hell but it is a prison world. And even there, we don't poison our water or toss trash in it because we're too lazy to clean up after ourselves.

We might be damned monsters locked up for our crimes, but destroying natural resources isn't one of them." She stared out at the dark water, her brow furrowed.

"Don't worry, Storm Cloud. We'll help these businesses get back on their feet, and then you can do whatever a five-thousand-year-old kelpie does when she's making a home for herself."

Grumbling, she burrowed her face in my chest, her arms going around my middle as she pouted for a hot minute. Then she lifted her chin, her expression thoughtful. "I thought this was a No Man's Land where everyone's out for themselves, and no one helps anyone. Reagan made it seem like it was so cutthroat."

If this were New York or Portland, maybe, but I'd found Crossroads full of people who just wanted to do their own thing without being tied to a House. It was nothing like the Syndicates. Even with the Crimson Roses element, the lack of organized crime —save for these damned river pirates—was something I had to get used to.

But there were a few that had been run out of both places, run out of every House, and those were who we needed to watch out for.

"Some of the area is. Those parts are completely

merciless, and many of the people are only out for themselves, what they can get, what they can steal. But that's not how I run things. If I claim a territory, I'm going to run it how I see fit. And I don't leave people to swing in the wind when somebody attacks them. I don't sit idly by when people need help."

I wasn't exactly sure when I'd claimed the docks themselves. Maybe when the pirates started coming on land did my influence reach here. All I knew was that it was likely my fault that these businesses had been attacked, and I wouldn't let them feel the brunt of my poor management of the situation.

Styx narrowed her eyes on me, tilting her head to the side as she chewed on her bottom lip. It was like she was trying to figure me out.

"Corvin Blackwell, the collector of lost souls. I can't decide if that is the kindest thing I've ever heard, or the most naïve. This"—She gestured to the docks—"is either bait or a message. You know that, right?"

I did indeed know that. Anything having to do with this particular dock would have always sent me on red alert, which was why I had Knox do a fly over, and Jude sense the earth before we'd ever moved in. It was why I'd asked Aster to check for death traps, and Penny to sense any spells.

It had been clear.

We could have ignored everyone here, however, letting people suffer wasn't in my wheelhouse—not unless they deserved it. Still, Styx had been around for a long time. If she sensed something was up, I wanted to know about it.

"What makes you think it's bait?"

She eyed the destroyed boats at the dock, the ruined buildings that had once operated as restaurants and shops—not necessarily luxurious places but they'd served their purpose.

"The damage is *just* enough," she muttered, eyes narrowed, her suspicions rising with every moment we stood here. "It's not so much that no one could ever rebuild, but it's not enough if we're dealing with people with a grudge."

"The day you came back we killed a witch and three vamps working with them after they murdered a boy on one of the trains."

Styx held up her hand. "I'm not saying what you did was unjustified. I think I know you better than that, and killing children? They deserved what they got. It's just... That Crimson Roses trash, he said you took out one of their witches. And then the witches wouldn't even deal with the Roses because she'd died on their watch. They cut off a solid avenue of cannon fodder—of insulation, of muscle—for an emotional reason. They altered their business, they quieted down, and yet, we have this."

She gestured to the destruction—or rather the lack of it. The pirates had killed someone not even of my pack, and I'd still gone after them. If this was retaliation for the witch's death, it was too late, too small, and too quiet.

"You think a storm's coming."

The wind stilled, even as Styx's thunder rumbled in the distance. Birds that had been so loud days ago were silent as the grave. Even the river itself seemed like it was waiting, watching, anticipating.

"If I were a betting woman, the storm is already here." Slowly, she pulled a single metal stick from her hair, her gaze searching the river as if it was speaking to her. "Move your people out. Now. There's someone on the water. Spying."

But I didn't need to tell anyone. Knox's golden eyes found mine, his harpy ears hearing every word she'd said. He let out a chittering call, low enough that my lieutenants heard it but not enough that it would carry to the river.

Penny and Jude froze for a split second before moving inland while Aster and Diana seemed to be ignoring his call altogether, the pair staring at something I couldn't see.

"Something's wrong," I murmured, trying to walk across the dock without alerting anyone to the fact that we knew shit was about to go down. Now that she'd said something, it was as if I could feel it on my skin, those eyes hidden by too much magic.

Styx nodded, skirting around the debris as she motioned to Jude and Knox to get back.

"Tripped a ward, I'd bet," she murmured, the calmness of her voice and demeanor at odds from the raging storm hiding underneath her skin. "We've sprung their trap."

Thunder rolled in with clouds that seemed to spring up from nowhere, the tiny crescent of a moon hiding from her wrath as lightning struck the water in great arches of electricity. Styx hadn't just claimed me in our bond, she'd claimed my pack, too.

And whoever was threatening it had just pissed her off.

"Shift if you can," I ordered under my breath, heading for Aster and Diana. "Get these people out of here."

Jude and Penny peeled off, but Knox stayed right where he was, his gaze pinned on my targets.

"Look at their feet," he murmured, not moving

an inch as the bones of his back snapped and cracked, his wings sprouting from his back as his face lengthened into a sharp beak, his harpy form ready to do damage.

Black tendrils of magic looped around their ankles, the watery wisps of power trailing up their calves, tethering them to the very wood they stood upon. Darkness overtook Aster's irises, clouding her sight. She whimpered, tears falling down her cheeks, even though she was frozen to the spot, the inky magic crawling up her leg.

But Diana was a whole different story. Gold glowed in her eyes as her jaw clenched, her hands in fists at her sides as the magic latched onto her feet, her legs, curling around her hips.

Styx was right.

This was a trap built just for us.

CHAPTER 22

STYX

The air almost froze for a long moment before everything seemed to happen at once.

Golden light exploded across the sky, lighting up the night with magic. The dock Aster and Diana were tethered to swelled, contracted, and then swelled again, detonating in a flash fire of debris, bodies, magic, and water.

Aster and Diana flew back, knocking into the wall of something called a "crab shack" as pieces of dock rained down on us all. A stone balustrade nearly took my head off before Corvin wrenched me out of the way, tossing me to the side as he knocked the stone from the air as if he were swatting a fly. Leathery wings erupted from his back, his top half turning to stone before my eyes as he ripped a metal pole from the dock and shot it like a javelin across the water.

The pole disappeared in the mirage that was the water, and that's when we knew we were well and truly fucked. And not in the good way. We looked at each other for a second before the pair of us sprang into action, grabbing Diana and Aster and ducking the golden magic rocketing toward us from the river.

I didn't have a problem with witches in general. As a rule, they were typically decent people with a good mind to balance. Right then, though, I wanted to rip them apart with my teeth.

Their magic seemed to come from nowhere and everywhere at once, until the white-robed women appeared out of thin air, the swirling magic from their illusion releasing them as if from a dream.

They strode over the water like they were made of it, as if it cradled their very feet as they converged on the ruined dock. Rage took the place of logic for a split second, and I rained lightning down on them, realizing just a touch too late that they were likely protected from it.

A golden trident was embroidered in the breast of their cloaks and yet I didn't give a shit. I wanted their master to know that I was alive and kicking.

One way or another they would feel my wrath, whether they were protected from it or not.

That golden trident was the insignia of the daughter, her weapon of choice what had sliced through my parents on that awful day, cutting them to pieces, their blood running into the river as if they were feeding it.

Xyla and Idall had too many followers for gods supposedly struck from history. It made me wonder how they got so many to blindly follow them, so many to die for them, so many to thoughtlessly walk into battle with me, without a shadow of doubt in their minds that they would survive.

They wouldn't—none had so far—but they still fought as if their victory was a given.

Corvin caught me around the waist, hauling me and Diana behind a thick piece of debris that likely used to be a wall of some kind.

"Fuck those fucking gods," he growled, checking on Aster as she tried to sit up. Blood ran from her nose, her dark hair wet with it as she tried to focus her gaze on me. "You with me?"

But Aster wasn't looking at him, her gaze was on me. "They aren't here for us," she gasped, her hand reaching for her bloody scalp. "They're—"

"Here for me," I growled. "I know. How did they even know I'd be here? *I* didn't know I'd be here."

But I knew the answer without her saying a word. They'd been watching. Them coming off the water like that? There wasn't a glamour in the world that could have hidden them that way—not that I couldn't see through.

They'd been getting help.

Celestial help.

Godly help.

No wonder Corvin had to stake them out.

They'd been protected.

Sheltered.

Stealing offerings to their goddess as they robbed the river blind.

Golden magic laced with death streaked over our heads, slamming into the crumbling dock under our feet, threatening to collapse us into the water.

Blind fury made me hang onto Diana a little tighter than I should have, and she squeaked, reminding me that it wasn't just me and Corvin on this dock. She'd fared much better than Aster had, with no injuries to show for being blown sky high. But that didn't mean I would be letting any of those bitches off the hook.

They were on my hook because they'd hurt my

people. People I cared about, innocent people, people who were in danger because I simply existed.

I let Diana go and latched onto Corvin's jacket, pulling him to me.

"Get them out of here," I hissed before pressing a swift kiss to his mouth and then shoving him away.

Eyes wide, he tried to reach me, but a wall of lightning barred his way, keeping him safe, keeping all of them safe. It didn't matter if I was hit with their magic—I'd survive. One way or another, I'd keep breathing because I had to.

I wouldn't if something happened to him—to them.

"Godsdammit, Styx," he roared. "Don't do this."

Didn't he know?

Couldn't he realize?

Then again, the truth had just hit me, so why had it not hit him yet?

I loved him. It didn't matter how much I'd fought it, it still happened. It didn't matter that I'd never been in love before or couldn't quite fathom exactly what it meant. The truth was I'd fallen for Corvin all those weeks ago when he'd begged me to just wait.

For months he'd been in my head—in my heart—and I couldn't let him go.

Not ever.

I loved him so much that I wouldn't let him get hurt for me.

Closing my eyes, I reached out to that power I hated so much. The power that leaked out of me anytime I was angry, anytime I was aroused, tied to my emotions tighter than the hangman's noose. I hated it more now with the reminder of what had been taken so fresh in my mind.

The reminder of what could be taken.

The reminder of how fragile my happiness was.

The sky above opened up, drenching us all in a gale of freezing rain as the fire of my anger struck the water, struck the ground around me, caging us in, protecting us from the vilest of spells.

I ripped the other stick from my hair, the rods warming against my palms as that power reached down to the heating metal. A sword of lightning formed in each hand, radiating the sheer power that I kept beneath my skin. Just like the men at the river all those days ago, these women were likely protected from the electricity I wielded.

But how much could they really be?

A cage of energy protected me as I raced—much to Corvin's protest—from our tenuous safety, launching myself at the closest witch unlucky enough to be my guinea pig.

The electricity didn't so much as faze her on the first pass, not until the second and third and fourth did her protections crumble, and I relished her screams as my power burned her from the inside out.

But I couldn't get in five hits by myself and keep everyone else breathing. I needed something else, something better, something I could use on all of them at once.

Ripping my jacket off, I ran across the last vestiges of the crumbling dock, diving into the water as the change took me. On land, my kelpie form looked like any other horse, only with a mane that reached the ground, the darkness of my hair blending into the night.

In the water, though, I looked vastly different.

Gills erupted from my neck as my back legs formed into a long tail, spikes grew on my spine, and those fangs that I kept so tightly leashed, grew in my mouth.

And when I was in the water, I could lure them in for a little swim.

The siren call of the water pulled at their very minds, beckoning them closer and closer to my clutches. Nearly all of the witches stopped their onslaught, the magic dying down as their arms fell to their sides. They turned as one to the river, but unlike on their approach, they seemed to want to dive beneath it, breathe it, taste it, taking in the muddy waters for themselves.

I drowned more people than I could count in my lifetime, some to eat, some to not, some just because they needed a lesson, and some because they were too stupid to back the wrong side and they had gotten too close to my river.

These acolytes, they were of the latter.

All too late, a few woke up, thrashing beneath the surface as they tried to swim to safety. But there was no safety in this water, not for them, not for anyone that would hurt those that I called mine.

That silly goddess had only thought to protect her acolytes from her father's power, thinking it was the only offensive weapon I had. She'd forgotten that I was just as deadly all on my own. One would think a sea goddess would understand just how dangerous the river could be, just how much destruction I could accomplish with just a bit of water.

My hunger grew as their thrashings stopped, and just this once, I suspended my "no women" rule, glutting myself on their blood, on their flesh. I ate my fill, their poor lives nourishing me, each one making me more powerful, more wrathful.

When I surfaced, the dock was quiet, but I refused to worry about what I had done. I had protected Corvin's pack, my pack, my herd, and I refused to apologize for how I chose to safeguard them.

The change snapped and cracked my bones, and yet after all this time, it didn't hurt one bit. Water puddled around me on the ruined wood, as I snatched my shirt from the dock, pulling it over my head, the silence stretching like taffy.

Corvin stood on the edge of the dock where the concrete met the wood, the rest a crumbling mess of debris, snapped supports, and twisted metal. His face was like one of my thunder clouds, foreboding and full of wrath, and through the bond, all I could feel was the fury of what I'd done.

Snatching up what clothes I could, I picked over the dock, ready to face whatever he had in store.

"Tell me why I shouldn't be pissed. Tell me why I shouldn't lose my shit right now, because baby, I'm struggling. You didn't give me so much as a hint of a chance to help you. What if you'd gotten hit? What if that magic had poisoned you just like before? What if—"

I covered his mouth with my fingers, but he swung me off my feet, clutching me to his chest as if I'd be ripped from him any second.

The truth of it bubbled up my throat, begging to be set free. "I love you," I whispered, trying to make him understand. "I protect those that I love."

Corvin pulled back as his gaze heated, the flames of his gargoyle so close to the surface that his eyes danced with them. Those fiery eyes searched my face, looking for any hint of a lie. He'd been denied so many times, it was no wonder he was scarcely able to believe the truth.

I let the love I kept under lock and key flood the bond, and the sweetness of it making his eyes close. His brow smoothed, something like relief hitting him square in the chest.

"As excuses go, that's a good one, Storm Cloud," he murmured, reeling me in again before pressing a kiss to my forehead, my cheek, my lips. "I love you, too. I love you so fucking much."

Corvin's love had reached me through the bond as soon as we'd cemented it. I'd known he loved me every second of every day since the second his fangs had sliced into my skin.

Still, hearing it was a balm to my soul.

"But just like you, I also protect those that I love. You can't do that to me again. You can't make it so I can't protect you just as much as you protect me."

This wasn't an argument that would get solved right away, so I gave him a noncommittal hum of an answer.

"Don't think I don't know what you're doing," he said, giving my ass a gentle smack before fetching my jeans from the dock. "I'll make you promise me one way or the other, Storm Cloud. Even if I have to resort to nefarious means to get the job done."

My sex clenched as I remembered all the ways he'd made me beg just last night.

"That's not fair. You're too good at that thing you do with your tongue."

"I haven't even got out the good restraints yet. Don't push me."

Was it wrong that I kind of really did want to push him? Then again, we'd just been lured into a trap, and we had bigger problems than what he was going to do to me later.

Job now, naked time later.

"How is Aster? The rest of the pack? The civilians? Did everybody make it out?"

Corvin pulled me to his side as we turned away

from the water. "She's healing but slowly. Penny's with her. She should be as good as new after a shift."

I was about to ask how we should handle a situation like this if something ever arose again, when a bedraggled woman covered in blood appeared from the wreckage. In her hand was a golden trident and in the other were her discarded bloody robes that had been white once upon a time.

I'd missed one.

I couldn't even so much as open my mouth to scream before she launched that trident our way. But it wasn't *our* way, it was *his* way. The trajectory made it clear who her target was, and as fast as I moved, as old as I was, there wasn't a damn thing I could do to stop it.

In horror, I watched as that golden weapon streaked toward him.

I was about to lose everything. His light, his smile, his heart, his touches, his kisses, the joy he brought to everyone and everything. All my dreams, all my happiness, everything would be lost, dead, gone.

Before that awful weapon could hit his skin, it seemed to freeze a foot away from Corvin's chest. And then Diana appeared out of thin air, that trident embedded in her shoulder, golden blood pouring from the wound as her form flickered and flashed.

Pure, unadulterated fury crossed her features that changed from Diana's, morphing into the face of Nadia, into a being of pure light, and back. Diana's crimson hair floated about her head as golden light poured from her eyes as she watched the witch tremble and shake, falling to her knees.

"My goddess, please forgive me," the witch begged, bowing in earnest. "I didn't know. Please, I would never hurt you, please forgive me."

Diana's body flickered and flashed, her glamours changing every second as she slowly strode toward the witch.

"You chose the wrong side. Mercy is too good for you."

Then Diana snapped her fingers, and the woman exploded in a cloud of ash.

Diana wasn't a Fae. Nadia wasn't a lamia. She wasn't anything of this world.

Whoever she was, she was a god, and she was pissed off.

Funny, so was I.

Betrayal flooded my veins as I watched Diana grasp the golden trident and yank it from her shoulder. Her knees went weak and Corvin caught her before she could pass out, easing her to the ground and propping her up against a mound of debris.

"What the fuck?" I growled, thunder rumbling the ruined dock under my feet, threatening to crumble it all into the river.

Diana's smile was weak, but it was there, and though it wasn't taunting, it pissed me off.

"You don't get to smile at me. Who the fuck are you?" I hissed, taking a bold step closer to a goddess I didn't know, who had been hiding in plain sight.

Who had lied to me from day one.

Corvin caught me around the waist as if he were holding me back from doing something stupid. And as accurate as that was, it pissed me off, too.

"I can do whatever I want," she croaked, trying to sit up, "but you already know who I am. I am Nadia. I am Diana. I am a goddess with no name, struck from history as I always should have been. Don't worry, I struck my children from history, too. You won't find them in those books."

The books Nadia had given me. That *she* had given me.

If she had gut-punched me, it would have hurt less. Then I focused on the correct portion of that statement.

"Your children?"

Her chuckle was mirthless. "I hear they've been looking for you. They keep finding you, too, but all their followers seemed to die. I have to say, I'm quite fine with that. Almost proud even."

I almost died and she had the nerve to chuckle?

"Are you fucking kidding me?" Corvin growled, pulling me away from the goddess I most definitely wanted to punch in the face. "I gave you a home. I gave you friends. I gave you family, and you've been lying to me the whole time?"

"Not so much as a lie as an omission of the

truth," she admitted, leaning her head against the debris, her eyes closed. She swallowed hard, pressing a hand to the wound, pouring golden blood.

But she knew a lie, was a lie, was a lie, and Nadia was a straight-up fallacy. I had half a mind to kick her.

"Just because I am both people doesn't mean I lied. Everything but my name was the truth, and even that wasn't a complete one. I have been Nadia and Diana and a million other names. A million other people. Just like your mate, I have been alive for a very long time."

Her lids cracked as she looked Corvin in the face. "When I came to join your pack, I knew who you were to her. I'd seen it in the stars ages ago. I needed to be close to you to know if I made the right decision, if you were right for her, if she was right for you. So, I waited and allowed you to believe whatever you wanted about me."

Diana snorted, shaking her head. "You thought I'd pissed off a father. I didn't. I pissed off my children, and they were looking for me. So, I hid in a place they wouldn't think to search and made sure that I was in the right place for when she came to you."

"So what? You can see the future? You can change your face at will, you can snap your fingers and explode people? Who the fuck are you?" I demanded, needing answers more than anything else.

"Before you walked through the portal to the gods all those years ago, I was married to one," she began. "He was spiteful and mean and didn't necessarily care that we had children and a life together. He wanted to do whatever he wished. He wanted power. He wanted to gain status—wanted to be more than he was. And then one day, he saw a beautiful woman walking through a portal and decided to follow her."

As it turned out, I didn't want to hear this story.

I didn't want anything to do with it at all.

Too bad she didn't stop telling it.

"I watched him pursue you, watched you deny him at every turn, telling him exactly why you wouldn't accept him. It didn't matter how much he tried, or why he wished to have you, you still told him no. Part of me admired that you didn't care that he was a god. You didn't care about his power. You just knew he wasn't for you, and so you denied him." She swallowed before letting out a pained groan. "Makes me wish I would have done the same."

Tasting bile at the back of my throat, I looked away, not wanting to hear the rest, wishing that trident would have actually killed her. But I was better than that, so I took a strip off her flannel shirt and started dressing her wound, my rage maybe making my movements rougher than they should have been, but at least I was helping.

"And then he stopped asking," she whispered, her hot gaze on my cheek. "So many would have just taken it because of who he was, but you fought him at every turn, every way that you possibly could have."

Hot tears hit my eyes, but I held them back. She didn't deserve my sadness, and she couldn't fucking have it. "You could have stepped in. You could have saved me. That was your husband. You could have stopped him."

I remembered begging the heavens for help, of wishing that someone—anyone would intervene. But no one did. She just sat right there, watching the horrors that I'd endured and did nothing.

"No, I didn't, and that's my burden to bear—a regret I will go to my grave with. I was too scared of him then, but I watched his fury as he tried to kill you and your strength because you just wouldn't die. And so, when you took that power, I sealed it inside of you so he couldn't take it back. He was finally mortal as he always should have been, too weak-minded to have power, and too stupid to wield what he already had. He'd lost it, his comeuppance just and swift, and in a split second, I was finally free."

A part of me wished I could have killed her right at that moment. Wished that she was as mortal as her husband was all those years ago.

"Glad I could do your dirty work for you," I spat, standing on my own two feet. "You are a goddess. You would have lived had you endured his wrath, instead you made me do it. Did you watch your children murder my family, too? Did you watch them slaughter them and take everything away from me? Did you watch them kill innocent people? *Children.* They killed fucking children, and you stood there and did nothing. Fuck you, lady. Fuck you sideways."

Tears filled her eyes, but she didn't get to do that, either. She didn't get to cry now. "I deserve that."

"That's not all you deserve. I'd say you deserved to have your family stripped from you, but you and I both know you hate those children. Because if you didn't, you would have raised them appropriately. I'd say you deserve to be tossed into Tartarus, but you and I both know it isn't the Hell your children thought it was. That place saved me more than it punished me, but I was still stuck. My skin holding on to this power that I didn't want, and you were the one to lock me in my prison. Sealed it inside me all because you wanted your husband to get his due, something you should have given him instead of me."

A lone tear fell down her cheek, and it made me want to scream.

"And I guess they're looking for you, aren't they? Because they want more power, and I'd venture a guess that they haven't had the life that they thought they would have after dear old daddy died. I bet they don't just want *your* power, they want the power that you sealed inside my skin, too. Which is why they're hunting for my fucking head. Do I have that right?"

"I thought you were smart five thousand years ago, and it turns out I wasn't wrong. You seem to be putting it all together." Her tone was snide, which I did not appreciate. Not one bit.

"Well, I'm sorry I don't have foresight in my

repertoire. Why don't you hit me with some of your power, and I'll take it from you, too, bitch."

Corvin caught me around the waist once again, whispering calming words in my ear, none of which I heard. I was sure some of them went along the lines of "Don't piss off the bleeding goddess," but I really couldn't give a fuck.

"Do you think I like the role I played?" she asked, her eyes sharp on my face as she tried and failed to sit up.

"I think I couldn't give that first fuck what you feel. This is not the 'Sympathize with Diana' show. This is where you explain what the fuck you did and how we're going to stop it, or I'm going to toss you in that river and never look back again. You think I don't have friends that are stronger than you? That could snap their fingers and break you in half? You're lucky you're dealing with me and not them."

Just the thought of what Legion or Caius would do to her made me smile just a little.

"Another wife would have blamed you for tempting their husband," she whispered, her tone almost accusatory, and I damn near lost it.

"If you can look at me," I whispered, my whole body shaking with the fury I held tightly under my skin, "and honestly say you thought I gave that man even the slightest hint of a chance, you are lying to yourself."

And then the truth of it hit me for maybe the very first time.

"It's not my fault what he did. He took advantage of a weaker woman, someone he knew he could use his power on, and when he couldn't cajole me to his side, he took what he wanted, anyway."

It wasn't my fault. None of it was. It was his. Never mine.

"I'd like to think what happened next was his punishment—instant and swift. You might have sealed his power inside my body, but you gave me a five-thousand-year reminder of exactly what he did. Every time I hear that thunder, I see my parents dying in front of me. I watch my sisters turn to ash. I feel him in every single cell of my body."

"But you still use his power."

"You think I shouldn't? You think I didn't earn it? You think I shouldn't have every single weapon in my arsenal at my disposal? I use it because I have no choice, because every single shred of me is dialed toward survival. I will not be ashamed of how I choose to stay breathing."

Diana's smile was almost smug. "See, I knew you were smart. Not smart enough to fully accept it, though, now, are you? You think this thunder and lightning, these parlor tricks, are all that Odaar was? All he could do? He might have been a little full of himself, but he wasn't delusional."

Her words echoed Broca's prophecy what seemed like years ago. Had it only been days?

"The only way you're going to make it through this is if you accept that power. If you decide that it was a gift given to you and not something you stole. If you finally realize that it was yours longer than he'd ever had it, that it belongs to you and only you. It's the only way they're not going to be able to take it from you. It's the only way you're going to survive."

"Is that your official premonition, Diana?" Corvin asked, his jaw clenched as he held me close to his chest, his disgust for his pack member clear as day through the bond.

I couldn't see a way to forgive her for what she had done to me, for her lack of action, for her spine-lessness.

"You think your father gave you that book all on his own?" she asked, tilting her head to the side. You think I didn't make sure that the Crimson Roses weren't a threat to you anymore? I've been eating them for a year, picking them off one by one to keep you and yours safe. You think I didn't direct you to this very dock so you could get your vengeance for the shifter killed? You think I haven't pulled every single string I could to make sure that you two got together? To make up for what I'd done to her? To make sure that you stayed breathing? To make sure that the mate Fate had chosen was everything she deserved?"

She scoffed as she shook her head, resting her skull on the debris as her mirthless chuckle turned into a cough.

"You think I haven't made sure that my children never got the power that they sought? That the only way to make sure you would deserve it was to allow you to be sent to Tartarus, was to make sure that you were nothing like them. I had to make sure that his power wouldn't corrupt you. It's been five thousand years of weaving the web, of tying everything tight so the fabric of what should be would stay together. Fate chose him for you. I'm the one who made sure Fate wasn't a fucking liar."

"Doesn't make it right," I whispered, latching on to Corvin's shirt as he hugged me tight. "You can think that you had a hand in it all you want. You can even take credit for how you orchestrated it all, but the only reason you felt you had to do something was because you had already failed. You did it all out of guilt, out of shame, and I won't take that from you. That's your burden. Not mine."

I backed away, not willing to talk to Diana a second more than I had to. Corvin parked me with Knox and Jude who were helping the civilians look for survivors. I shoved my legs into my pants and boots and helped them search, not willing to even turn in her direction. Penny took Diana and Aster back to the pack house for reasons I will probably never understand.

Diana had never been pack—not really. Everything she'd ever said was a lie. And yet, it was not my job to reject her. That was up to Corvin, though if she stayed, I couldn't figure out if I could, too. But that was a decision for another time.

Now, we had work to do.

Hours later, the dock had been cleared of survivors, and Corvin and I trudged back to the house. A part of me didn't want to go anywhere near it, but checking on Aster was higher up on my list than my own comfort when it came to Diana.

"I know you don't want her here," Corvin murmured in my ear as we stared at the house. I was hesitating going in, and it had been noticed.

"I can't ask you to kick out a member of your

pack," I grumbled. *No matter how much I might want you to.* "I don't have a say in the matter."

"Can't you? You're my mate. This is your pack, too. You may not have the crest tattooed into your shoulder, but you have my mating mark on your neck. Why would you think you wouldn't have a say?"

I hadn't really thought about it like that, but his words made sense. "Part of me feels like I'm being too sensitive, and the other part wants to rip her limb from limb. I'm having a tough time deciding which parts of myself to listen to."

"The second one," he growled, lacing his fingers with mine. "Always the second one. No part of you can possibly ever be too sensitive about what was done to you. The only reason I let her go back to the house at all was so she could be healthy enough when she stood trial for her crimes against you."

I stared at him like he'd grown another head.

"You plan on punishing a goddess?"

"If I fucking have to, but no. I planned on going to your family and letting them know who exactly to blame. And when they interrogate her, hopefully they'll find her shitty-ass children so I can rip their fucking throats out."

"She didn't... She wasn't the one who hurt me," I

countered, finally feeling every ounce of rage he'd had banked over the last few hours. It was immense and visceral and vast.

Corvin was practically radiating with it. "No, but she could have stopped it, and that makes her just as guilty."

He wasn't wrong.

"Don't go to Caius. If it comes down to it, I'll go myself. I have a feeling I'm going to need his help with Xyla and Idall anyway, especially with Diana in the mix. How did it all come to this?" I muttered, resting my head on his shoulder.

"No idea, Storm Cloud. I'm just glad I have you in my life, however that had to happen. It's fucked up that part of me wants to be thankful, and the other part wants to drop her right in a pit."

"You can always have both, you know. You can be thankful for her intervention and still think she needs to be dropped in a fiery pit to be spit-roasted by hellhounds for eternity."

Okay, so I'd given it some thought.

"I say we sleep on it. What do you think?"

Then he swung me up into his arms, hugging me close to his chest as I wrapped my legs around his back. It wasn't sexual. It was finding comfort in each other after a very long day. Maybe when we were rested, we would attack each other again. Right then, it just wasn't time.

"That sounds wonderful," I said into his neck, knowing I needed a shower and not even contemplating the energy for it.

We hadn't even made it in the door before Knox and Jude we're filing out of it.

"Oh, fuck. What now?" I griped because I needed sleep and or at the very least a mental break.

"I checked with the rest of the pack," Knox barked, "nobody has seen Penny or Aster or Diana. They never made it home."

I unwrapped my legs from Corvin's hips, slid down his body, and as soon as my feet touched the ground, my rage was firmly clicked into place.

I didn't particularly give two shits about Diana, but Aster and Penny I did.

Whoever took them was going to die.

CHAPTER 24

CORVIN

I wished I could say I was more worried about Aster and Penny than I was about Styx. Considering the storm brewing in the sky and the lightning strikes that got ever closer, that was not the case.

Still, I had a pack to run, and my mate would hate that I was focusing on her instead of the problem at hand.

"Anyone that can't fight needs to stay," I ordered, the Alpha in my tone brooking no argument. "Otherwise, everyone needs to be out looking for Penny and Aster."

That brought Jude up short. "What about Diana?"

Considering what she had done to Styx, the

crimes weighing on her shoulders, the absolute lack of action she'd taken, I would not devote a single vital resource to go look for her. She might be a member of my pack for the time being, but if I had my way, she'd be locked up with the worst of the worst in Tartarus.

"Diana is a goddess. She can take care of herself. Aster and Penny are not. And considering the crimes on her head, I don't particularly give a fuck what happens to her."

Jude paled, the bear of a man backing up a step. He'd been there on the docks with us, but since he was helping pull civilians from the wreckage, I doubted he knew the details. And though she'd saved my life by taking that trident for me, I still couldn't deign to grant her an ounce of mercy.

We were not square. We'd likely never be.

Styx put a calming hand to my chest but didn't say a word. Closing my eyes, I dropped a kiss to her forehead, breathing in her scent to settle the raging desire to rip apart whoever intended to hurt her.

"She's likely with Penny and Aster. If we find them, we'll find her," Styx said, easing my rage just a bit.

I swallowed, trying to calm myself. It wasn't Jude's fault that Diana had lied and betrayed and...

"Knox, please take an aerial look to see if they were held up on the way here, yeah?"

The way shit was going down lately, I seriously doubted they'd been held up anywhere, but covering our bases was a good idea.

My second nodded, his wings sprouting from his back in an instant as he took to the sky. Jude seemed abashed, but he still latched onto my shoulder. His large paw of a hand kept me still when I wanted to move.

"I'm sorry. I didn't know." He swallowed hard, his eyes beseeching. "I knew she might not be who she said she was, but..."

We'd go over that in detail later, but for now, it wasn't the time. "No need for apologies. Take a group with you and head for the dock. Send others to the train lines and sweep those. We'll backtrack until we get their scent."

Relief hit Jude's features, and he rounded up most of the pack. Half headed south and the other half headed north.

Styx watched him go, concern in her eyes and apprehension flooding the bond. "He had a thing for her. Or still does."

I nodded at her assessment. "Doesn't matter, she's not his mate. If I'd just watched you get stabbed in the chest, I guarantee there wouldn't be a person on that dock left alive. It wouldn't have mattered if my Alpha was right in front of you making sure you were okay, he'd have been tossed in that water for even breathing in your direction. I would have torn everyone apart. He doesn't know it yet, but whatever he feels for her is not nearly what he'll feel for his own mate."

Styx narrowed her eyes at me. "It's really tough to be pissed off when you're getting all mushy on me. Could you quit it? I need to focus."

"This isn't mushy, Storm Cloud. This is straight fact. Anyone who touches you dies. Friend or foe, god or goddess. No one hurts you and lives."

Styx's eyes went heavy-lidded, her heart beating so hard I could feel it through the bond. But it was nothing but the truth. Jude had no idea what a mate really meant to him because he didn't have one.

I did, and I knew that there was nothing I wouldn't sacrifice, nothing I wouldn't do, no one I wouldn't kill to keep her breathing.

A few moments later, Knox returned, landing not a yard from me, his face like Styx's thunder. "I didn't see them on this side of the river, but there's *something* on the east side. It's like a glamour, only it's over the whole area. Acres wide and following the river, it flickers every few seconds. I don't know where they are exactly, but if I had to guess, it wasn't on the side of the river."

Styx's thunder cracked so hard, the ground shook under our feet.

"Show us where the glamour flickers," she ordered. "That's likely an edge of the spell. We can start there."

Knox took off, launching into the sky, and in an instant, I remembered how old and how fast Styx was. She kept up with him, watching the east side of the river and my second dart through the air until the glamour that shielded their domain flickered in the night.

Knox landed, his eyes glowing as he tried to calm himself down. Penny was like his little sister, and she'd been hurt more in the last week than she'd been in her entire life under his care.

"There is where the glamour starts," he huffed, catching his breath.

"I'm done fucking with these idiots," she growled, and not a second later, the river itself seemed to move out of her way. "They want to play on the other side of the river? *Fine.*"

Styx's hand didn't so much as wave before a whole section of the river rose up into the air, still flowing, still moving, it just lifted from the riverbed, allowing her to walk underneath it. She marched across the muddy silt, reaching the end before either Knox or I moved at all.

It had taken Jude and Diana weeks to reroute the water so it was close to the property. Granted, Diana was hiding the majority of her power, but still. Styx had just lifted millions of gallons of swiftly flowing river as if it were a plastic toy, and she was rather put out that no one was following her.

"I'm not lifting up this water for my fucking health. Let's go."

I chose to keep my life and not remind her that Knox was not the only one who could fly. It seemed like the wisest choice. Knox and I followed her, the energy on the east side nothing like the west.

Even with a portal to Tartarus, there was an air of darkness, of death. And the scent was unreal, the decay stinging my nostrils so bad I coughed.

"This feels like the worst parts of Tartarus. This feels like the prison," Styx murmured, eyeing the shimmering glamour as if it could jump up and bite her.

She moved to go first, but I caught her around the waist, my glare hot enough to peel paint. We'd discuss later about her jumping into the fray and leaving me behind, a conversation I didn't think we would need to have again after I tanned her ass. However, a single raised eyebrow told her that there was no way on this earth I was budging.

"You're cute and all," she growled under her breath, "but if I get hit by a spell, I take it. If you get hit by a spell, you can die. You see the dilemma I'm having here. I kind of just got you and I don't plan on losing you so soon. So you can give me that raised eyebrow all you want to, I'm still going first."

Fuck, I loved this woman. "Gargoyles are immune to most spells, Storm Cloud. And the day you go ahead of me into the unknown is the day I'm no longer breathing, you got me?"

Her expression softened before she gave me those sparking eyes.

"What did I say about the mushy shit?"

"Yeah, yeah," I muttered, undressing as quickly as I could, handing Knox my shirt and pants as he rolled them into a ball and stuffed them into his travel pack. I had a feeling I'd need those later.

My bones snapped and cracked, reforming into the shape of my gargoyle, my skin solidifying into stone. If there was a spell to be had, I would take it first. Huffing, I shook out my wings, their comforting weight resting on my back as I lowered myself to the ground.

Styx looked at me like I was crazy. "I have two legs that work just fine."

I shot a look at Knox, and he rolled his eyes. "You do realize he's not going to move until you get on his back, right? He's just as stubborn as you are." He tilted his head. "Maybe more. You did break first."

Oh, those were fighting words for Styx, but she let it slide.

"This is ridiculous," Styx huffed, before climbing on my back, encircling her arms around my neck.

Now I knew she was safe. With this uncertainty, I just needed her within my reach. Because I knew as soon as we crossed that barrier, as soon as we moved forward, things were going to change.

I took point, shoving through the shimmering glamour as I waited for more magic to reach us. When nothing happened, my nerves grew tenfold. This had to be where they were, but nothing was different. The east side of the river was exactly as it had been before the portal opened in Portland, before humanity fell. Here, humanity had abandoned it long before the supernatural world took over.

Small run-down dwellings dotted the streets,

their boarded-up windows and cracked sidewalks barely visible as the vegetation tried to reclaim them. Beyond the small rowhouses were the rubble of taller tenements, the bricks crumbling, the façade barely winning the fight against gravity.

There was one intact building close to the water, and we headed in that direction, but as we picked through the debris, I heard a faint whimper.

All three of us turned at once, following the sound to a soft lump hiding under a piece of steel sheeting.

Styx leapt from my back, sprinting across the open space as Knox and I desperately tried to chase her. She didn't seem to care that it could be a trap. Didn't care that this had been just a touch too easy.

But as soon as she ripped that sheeting off, I knew exactly who we'd found.

The gray of Penny's fur was stained with blood, but worse were the burns. Knox yanked off his shirt, kneeling at Penny's feet. As he reached to touch her, she shied away, cowering to Styx's side as if she were the only safety.

Styx dropped a hand to her matted fur, her eyes flashing with wrath.

"I need you to shift, kiddo. I know it hurts. I know you don't want to, but you have to do it."

Penny whined again, either unable to do as she asked or refusing. Styx was having none of it.

"*Shift*," she ordered, the Alpha in her tone giving Penny no other option but to obey.

Her bones snapped and cracked, the healing of the shift taking over as her body reformed. Styx covered her in Knox's shirt, helping Penny put her limp arms in the sleeves.

"I gotcha, sweetheart. You're going to be okay," Styx cooed, her gentleness making my heart swell as the closing wounds on Penny's legs nearly drove me out of my mind.

Penny's tears clogged her throat until she let out an unholy gasp, and then she was sobbing, clinging to Styx as if she were the only thing keeping her tethered to the ground.

"Come on, take a breath for me. Focus your mind. Tell me what happened."

Penny shook her head, until Styx sent a gentle zap, knocking her out of her panic. "Easy. Breathe for me."

Penny's eyes flashed gold for a second before bleeding back to blue, her calm returning as she gave Styx a nod.

"Th-there was a man waiting for us before we even got on the train. He looked like Knox at first, but Diana told us to get back. She tried to warn us, but he was too fast." She shuddered, crawling closer to Styx as if she wanted to merge with her.

"His touch burned. It felt like it was searing through my skin. He tried to carry all three of us over the river, but he couldn't. Aster struggled, she fought, and he nearly dropped all of us. I fell. I wanted to go after them, but I couldn't move. I couldn't shift. I—"

"Idall," Styx murmured, her outward calmness hiding her disgust. "He's a shapeshifter just like his mommy. You couldn't have known."

"It wasn't me, Penny," Knox swore, reaching for her again. "I was still at the dock with the pack."

Penny's eyes filled with tears. "But how do I know? How do I know this isn't another trick? Tell me something only you would know."

"Okay, um..." His eyes brightened. "You eat peanut butter and mayo sandwiches, which I maintain is the most disgusting thing I've ever heard of. You are a closet crystal hoarder with an entire armoire full of just the clear ones. Your favorite is the melon-sized one you got from that Spirit and Sapphire asshole who traded it for a sleeping draught, remember? You have this weird obsession with craft supplies. You collect them but don't use them. You don't drink coffee and think all forms of pickle are the most disgusting things on the planet."

She breathed a sigh of relief, her tears flowing freely as she relaxed from Styx's side. She launched across the space, hugging Knox as if he were a lifeline. Knox had saved her from a coven of death witches when she was a girl who'd wanted to sacrifice her to get more power. They'd practically grown up together.

Styx and I shared a glance. Penny needed to get out of here and fast.

"Take Penny home, Knox," Styx murmured, straightening from the ground. "Then get your ass back here and bring the pack with you."

Knox held Penny close to him, his relief at finding her likely mixed with his loyalty to the pack —to me. He didn't want to leave me to fight this fight alone.

But I wasn't alone.

"I'll watch his back, Knox," Styx reassured him, putting an awkward but soothing hand on his shoulder. She'd been better at calming Penny, but I figured it was a start.

He slipped off the travel pack, handing it to Styx before securing Penny to his chest and taking off, his wings shooting them into the sky as he spirited her to safety.

Styx watched them go, worry etched on her face before she returned her gaze to the matter at hand.

Aster was still out there.

Clenching her jaw, she rolled her head, cracking her neck as if she were gearing up for a fight. Silently, we shared a nod, and she climbed onto my back. If Penny was that bad off and she'd gotten away, I had no idea if Aster would even be alive.

My gut clenched as I moved, cutting across the open space as I prayed that the chameleonlike magic that made me difficult to see extended to Styx.

The hackles on my back rose in earnest the closer to the building we got, the lack of traps and wards sending all my alarm bells ringing.

This was supposed to be a witch stronghold, right? Full of river pirates ready and willing to tear us limb from limb. So where the fuck were they?

Styx slid off my back, ignoring my growl as she refused to stay behind me. With a dagger in one hand and a hair stick in the other, she put her back to the building's wall.

The doors on the side of the building were wide open, the entrance just big enough that I could squeeze through, so I went for it, knowing that if we hadn't been hit by a spell yet, we likely weren't going to. Considering how many of Xyla and Idall's followers we'd killed over the last week, it was completely possible that there were none left.

I hoped there were none left.

The building had been a car repair shop once upon a time back when cars were widely used and weren't run on magic.

Chains hung from the ceiling, rigged up to a pulley system, and on a hook wrapped in golden magic was the one person I did not come here to save.

Diana.

Alone and barely breathing, the goddess hung from the chains, her wrists bound above her head. Blood poured from the wound in her shoulder and fresh ones on her wrists and ankles, a basin positioned underneath her catching the metallic drops.

"I recognize that bullshit magic," Styx muttered, her jaw clenched hard enough she could crush rocks. "Idall used it trying to gather some from their father. Too bad his ass was burnt to a crisp."

She seemed almost smug about that, and I couldn't blame her.

With a flash of light, Styx sent a bolt of lightning toward the golden ropes, overloading the magic as the bonds disintegrated. Before Diana could hit the ground, Styx caught her and then set her away from her body as if her very touch made her skin crawl.

Diana's eyelids cracked, her ice-like eyes unerringly finding Styx in the dim.

"You came," she croaked.

"Not for you," Styx reminded her. Then she pressed a hand to her shoulder. "This will hurt. Be quiet or I'll let you bleed out on this shitty-ass floor."

Then that same lightning that had been used to kill her enemies, pulsed from Styx's hand, cauterizing Diana's wound. The goddess' eyes flashed as she gritted her teeth, her feeble fingers clawing at the cement floor as she did her best to hold still.

"Good," Styx growled, "now you won't die. Want to tell me where Aster is?"

Diana's eyes latched onto Styx's as she grabbed her wrist in an iron grip.

"F-follow t-the d-death."

Then she pointed at the trail of scarlet leading across the floor to a closed door.

And over the scent of death and decay, over the rancid odors of long-dead witches, was the perfume of Aster's blood.

CHAPTER 25

STYX

A pit of dread yawned wide in my belly as I stared at Aster's blood painting the stone floor red. There were very few creatures that could survive losing that much blood, and I didn't know if she was one of them.

And still, I couldn't move.

Abandoning Diana wasn't a hardship, but the potential of walking into a trap was. I flipped the dagger over in my hand, contemplating just what I was walking into—what we were walking into. I stared at Corvin, wondering if this would be the last good look I had of him, wondering if we even had enough strength between us to fight Diana's children.

"All these years and you're still so fucking stubborn," Diana croaked, her face drawn. "Accept the power. It's why I made sure you kept it. It's the only way you're both going to survive this."

What did she expect me to do, skip on over five thousand years' worth of anger and hate and disgust and just jump right into acceptance as if I hadn't lost everything once already?

"You don't have to forgive him to accept his power. You just have to realize that it's not his anymore. He was a god. If he could have lost it so easily, it never was his to begin with."

What was she, my therapist now? "Get out of my head."

"Stop making it so fucking difficult, and I will."

Growling, I sheathed the dagger at my back and pulled the lightning rods from my hair.

She wanted me to accept this awful fucking power?

She wanted me to realize that I was more than just clouds and sky?

That I was more than storms and lightning?

Fine.

Closing my eyes, I sensed the power that had once been Odaar's, the power I'd stolen all those years ago. It was golden just like the blood that fell from Diana's shoulder, pulsing and powerful. It ached to reach out, to break free from the confines I had so carefully crafted over the years.

And I fucking hated it. I hated it, but I needed it.

To save Aster.

To protect Corvin.

To finally avenge my family.

To...

But I couldn't. I'd survived thousands of years without accepting that power. I'd survived her children. I'd survived her husband. I'd survived the worst of the worst in Tartarus all on my own. I didn't need his power—I didn't want it. In fact, I'd been trying to get rid of it for more years than I'd care to count.

"I'm stronger than you think I am," I growled, staring at the trail of blood before me.

Twirling my lightning rods in my hands, I marched forward, leaving Diana behind. Corvin caught up with me, his big body nearly blocking the way. He was made to protect, made to defend his pack, made to be a good mate, which was why I didn't stop him when he ran at the door like a battering ram so I wouldn't go first, when he knocked through the wall without knowing what was on the other side.

But *didn't* he know? I knew what I would find

just as much as he did. We would find Aster—whether she was breathing or not. We would find Idall and Xyla in whatever forms they chose to take, and we would find the river.

I supposed I expected to also find a small throng of the acolytes left, the most devoted followers of their god and goddess, attempting to garner the power they so sought.

But the riverbank only held three people, and no matter how few there were, it was still the mother of all traps.

Idall had Aster by the throat, her feet dangling from the earth as he held her in front of him like a shield, his smug grin barely visible behind her dark hair. Xyla, though, was spinning her trident in her hands, her avarice plain as day.

Corvin roared, flames erupting from his mouth as his serpentlike tail thrashed.

"Well, look who has finally come out to play," Idall taunted, stage whispering in Aster's ear as she clawed at his hand with her half-shifted claws. And as sharp as they likely were, they did nothing to his skin.

The scent of her burning flesh had my stomach rolling, and I wished I could hit Idall without hurting Aster, but I didn't see a way.

The thief finally shows up," Xyla taunted, her grip on the trident sure and steady. "Funny, I thought I put you in a cage."

"Yes, yes. You threw me in Tartarus, I got out, I have your daddy's power, and you want it. The problem is, you can't have it. Now put the girl down before I spank you like your mommy should have all those years ago."

Xyla puffed up in affront.

"You dare speak to me with such insolence?" she growled, readying her weapon as if she actually planned on using it.

But I already knew the truth. I knew what they wanted. They just couldn't fucking have it.

"Cut the shit. You barely have any power left. You gave it all to your acolytes and what did they do? Oh, that's right. They died under my knives, under my teeth, under my river. You have no more followers. You have no more power. Even the history books don't remember you. How does that feel? They remember me killing your father, but as hard as you try, they don't remember you."

"You think that's the only power we have? You think their deaths didn't serve us just as much as their faith did?" Xyla jeered, tilting her head to the side as if she knew a secret I didn't.

Maybe she did.

Blood sacrifices were as common as potato chips in this world. Why wouldn't they lower themselves into the dirtiest form of magic?

"By the time we're done with you, you'll be begging to give that power up."

"Let me guess," I said, tapping my lip with one of my lightning rods. "You'll let the girl go if I give you your father's power. Do you honestly believe that I'll trust you after what you've done?"

"Who said we planned on giving the girl up?" Idall taunted. "I like her. She smells like death and destruction, two of my favorite things. I might just keep her in my pocket for after I kill you."

So what was the incentive to not attack them on the spot? Thunder shook the very earth itself as my rage seemed to come out of my pores. Lightning struck the ground over and over, getting closer to my targets with each passing second. Corvin's serpentlike tail whipped back and forth, his eagerness to strike held at bay because of the danger to his pack member.

The sound of sizzling skin hit my ears, and Aster screamed the last bit of air she had in her lungs. Then she met my gaze, tears in hers as her face purpled, and I could tell she was giving me permission to go ahead and kill him—even if I had to kill her, too.

But I wouldn't do that.

I would do what Diana should have done for me all those years ago.

I would save her.

"Okay! Okay. Let her go, and I'll give it to you," I pleaded, throwing down my lightning rods, knowing that this could all go sideways if I didn't play it right.

Corvin roared again, his tail wrapping around my waist as he yanked me behind him. All we had to do was stall long enough for the pack to get here. I put a quelling hand to his hind flank, trying to tell him all I couldn't say out loud.

Just a little longer.

I love you.

Please don't hate me for this.

"Put the girl down, Idall," Xyla huffed. "It's a small price to pay for what we're owed."

I rushed to Corvin's face, taking his large jowls in my hands.

"Don't. I have to do this," I said, meeting his betrayed gaze. I raked my palm over one of his fangs as I dropped a kiss to the bridge of his large nose, the stone warm under my lips.

His chimera venom filled me for a single second before I felt the ache of it in my own fangs, absorbing his power as my own, I gave him a subtle wink. "Love you. So much. Not long now."

Just a little longer.

Corvin vibrated with barely suppressed rage, the fear of losing me filling the bond as I took a step back. Then another. And when I was within Idall's reach, that terror hit its peak before his gaze shifted ever so slightly. Anyone who didn't know him wouldn't have noticed.

But I did.

Just a little longer.

Idall snatched me off my feet, letting Aster's limp body fall to the ground. His touch was the heat of a thousand suns, burning me with a power he didn't realize I was leeching from his very skin.

Just a little longer.

And then everything seemed to happen at once.

The faint flutter of Knox's wings hit my ears as I forced myself to shove the pain down. Knox dove, snatching Aster from the ground as I spun in Idall's arms. Without preamble, I took his power in earnest, allowing it to fill me as I sank my fangs into his shoulder, pumping him with venom as his protection filtered into my bones. Tearing him away from me, I left him for Corvin and set my sights on his sister.

Xyla's smug expression melted off her face as she touched her neck, her fingers coming away with golden blood, even though she shouldn't have a wound. Even though no one had touched her.

Blood right where I'd bitten her brother.

No wonder the two were still alive, even though they hated each other. Even though they were both hungry for the same power. Even though they would destroy each other in the end.

They were linked.

Xyla's shock morphed into rage as she spun that trident again, only this time, she brought the river with it, the flowing water rising into the air, forming into a wall so high it nearly blocked out the moon. That wall changed into the shape of a dagger, rocketing toward me like a missile.

The force of it nearly knocked me off my feet, but I fought the strength of it with power of my own, tossing it back in her face. The water split in two, submerging the shore as I launched myself at her.

She wanted to play in the water? Fine. We'd fucking play.

My shift hit me on the fly as my hooves connected with her chest, the force of my hit knocking her backward into the river. The water parted around her, but I didn't care, I just needed her to hit me once, and she'd be as done as her brother.

The river churned around us, forming into a whirlpool, threatening to pull me under. Or at least it would have been a threat if I couldn't wield the water just as well as she could. And better? I had her father's lightning at my disposal. Bolts crashed into the surface of the river, edging closer and closer to her as she tried to fight them off with spouts of her power.

I wished I could tell her she'd met her match. Maybe twist the knife a bit and taunt her as she had done to me once upon a time. But I was done playing with this bitch. As much as she held me back, I fought her at every turn, tiring her out as I caught sight of her brother fighting and failing against Corvin.

This family was done.

And that was no more true after I leapt through the drink, my fangs at the ready as I pulled her under. Corvin's venom pumped into her flesh, her scream of agony muffled by the very water she tried to use as a weapon. With glee, I thrashed, ripping the wound wide enough that it would never close, tossing her back to the shore like the trash she was.

Coughing and gasping for air, she crawled from the river, trying to reach her brother, but he paid no mind to his dying sister, ignoring his gaping wounds, determination and desperation stamped on every line of him.

Idall dodged Corvin's tail, his face pale as death as he allowed his golden wings to sprout from his back. Trying to flee, he shot into the sky, realizing all too late that Corvin could follow him.

I watched Corvin launch himself after the god, ready to finish this battle once and for all. Shifting back to my human form, I pressed my foot on Xyla's neck, cutting off her air as her brother had done to me all those years ago. Eyes widening, she tried to shove me off of her, but I would not be moved.

"Watch your brother die like I watched my sisters, my parents."

I turned to the battle in the sky, watching as Idall climbed higher and higher, trying to outrun Corvin. Then my mate slashed at his stomach, Idall's skin splitting as he lost his fight with gravity. Xyla let out a gurgling scream as Idall began to fall back to the earth, but unlike his sister, he wouldn't go without a fight.

As Idall fell, a golden bow formed in his hand, and he shot a single arrow into the sky. Unerringly, that arrow found the most devastating of targets, hitting Corvin directly in his heart.

I let out my own scream as he fell, his stone body hurtling toward the river at breakneck speed. In that split second, I had a choice to make.

I could ensure my enemies' deaths.

Or I could save my mate.

CHAPTER 26

STYX

orvin hit the water, his gargoyle body sinking like the rock he was, and I dove into the river without a second thought, my vengeance left behind as soon as that arrow hit his chest.

The current caught him, sweeping him downstream, but I was faster, pulling him to me by sheer force of will. My fingers reached him, and I yanked him into my arms, reality hitting me as I finally saw the awful wound.

Idall's arrow was still buried in his chest, the fiery weapon burning him from the inside out. My hands fluttered over it, not even beginning to know what to do. If I pulled it out, he would die within seconds, the barb shredding his heart.

If I left it in…

And he wasn't breathing.

He wasn't breathing.

Please. I just got him. Please don't take him now.

Broca's words echoed in my brain as I took Corvin into my arms, his stone body melting into his human one.

She twists the arrow, her soul torn in two,

Love or vengeance she must choose.

And then Diana's order, the truth of it hitting me as swift as Idall's arrow.

Accept the power.

It's why I made sure you kept it.

It's the only way you're both going to survive this.

I would have to do the one thing I never wanted, but if it meant he would live, I would do it a thousand times over.

Closing my eyes, I sensed the golden light of the power that had once been Odaar's. I latched onto it, yanking it from the confines of my will. And as much as it hurt, I took that power into me, consumed it, allowed it to spread through my body, my blood, my bones.

The force of it lifted us out of the water, the sky claiming me as its own. Twisting with what I already was, a death horse bound to the water, the darkness of my true form changed the power to fit me, molding to my will alone.

Gravity reclaimed us and we fell back to the river, the current swirling into a whirlpool as every ounce of that power filled me.

The thunder that merely rumbled the earth now shook it in earnest as the river swirled around us. I could feel every molecule of the air, every raindrop in the sky, every beat of electricity in my own beating heart, and the lack of it in Corvin's.

Gritting my teeth, I sliced my hand onto Idall's arrow, my blood mingling with his final power, stealing it, too.

And I *took.*

I took Idall's fiery energy into myself before yanking the weapon from Corvin's chest, and then...

I gave it back.

Only this time it wasn't an explosion.

No, this time it was life, it was breath, it was all that Idall was and all he would be, all his years and all his power. I gave it to Corvin, calling him back from the brink of death. Lightning struck us both, filling us with the power I'd been granted.

Corvin's eyes flashed open as he sucked in a breath, his gaze unerringly finding mine. Relief hit me and I hugged him to my chest, forcing the current to carry us to shore. Corvin pulled me from the water, hugging me back with all the strength and vigor I prayed I could give him.

"You..."

My hand brushed over where Idall's arrow had been, the healing flesh pink as if it had been healing for months, not seconds. Even I didn't quite understand what I did, and as long as Corvin was alive, I didn't care.

"You saved me. I was dying. I-I felt it. I felt my soul trying to leave my body, and you forced it back. You breathed life into me. I don't"—He shook his head as he cupped my face in his hands—"How did you do it?"

Tears—of relief, of sorrow—hit my eyes, and I let them fall freely, not scared anymore that he would see them. Corvin was alive, he was alive, and he was breathing, and he was warm in my arms, and that was the only thing that I cared about. Idall and Xyla could heal and walk this earth forever, and I wouldn't care as long as he was breathing.

"I don't know. I don't know what I did. I don't know how I saved you. I'm just glad I did."

Lifting me into his arms, his mouth crashed into mine, the heat and passion of his lips on mine stealing every thought, every worry, every doubt in my head.

When he broke the kiss, he rested his forehead against mine, breathing me in as I did him.

"I love you, Styx—more than anything."

"I love you, too," I croaked. "More than anything."

"I want to celebrate every second, every minute, every breath with you. But first you need your vengeance."

Corvin's transformation hit him in an instant, and even though the ride was destined to be uncomfortable, I climbed onto his back, allowing his wings to hug me close to him as we shot into the sky, eating up the distance the current had carried us.

Idall and Xyla were exactly where we'd left them, the shore drenched in their golden blood. The only difference was now the rest of the pack had joined them, surrounded them, made sure when they took their last breath it would be under their watchful eyes. At the center of it all was Jude, holding on to a barely alive Diana, her sad eyes watching her children slowly die.

Those sad eyes hit me as Corvin and I touched down.

Her smile was slight, but I could see a hint of

pride as she examined us. Corvin handed me a large shirt, and I pulled it over my head as I approached the goddess.

"I see you finally took my advice. I'm glad it worked. I'm glad all of this wasn't for nothing."

"Thank you for giving it, for giving me him, for keeping him safe. I don't know what I would do without him." I swallowed hard, tears hitting my eyes for the second time in as many minutes. "It doesn't fix everything between us. I don't think anything will do that, but it goes a long way."

Her smile widened before it fell into a despair that could only be described as a mother's grief. "Will you help me up? There are things I still need to do."

Nodding, I grabbed her hands, pulling her into my arms and out of Jude's, his sorrow so acute I could almost feel it in my own chest. Together, Diana and I walked to Xyla, her golden blood soaking the ground underneath her and running toward the water. Gently, Diana turned her so she was face-up.

"A long time ago, before you were corrupted, I wished of nothing but your happiness. It was as if I could give you everything I had ever been denied. But over the years, I gave in too much. I allowed too many wrongs to go unrighted. You had everything at your fingertips, and you squandered it. You took lives out of spite, you harmed innocents, and as much as I wished for you, I now must end you.”

Diana formed her hand into a knife blade and pressed it to her daughter's sternum, reaching inside her chest, she pulled out a glowing golden orb. Xyla, already mortally wounded, crumbled to ash almost immediately in her mother's arms.

A single golden tear fell down Diana's cheek as she held that golden orb in her hand.

“For the lives of your parents,” she said, before pressing that golden orb into my chest.

Pain like I'd never felt hit every single cell in my body, but I knew just like with Odaar's power, the only option was to accept it. I breathed it in, allowing the power of the waters and the sea to fill me.

When I could see again, Diana was cupping my cheeks, her forehead pressed to mine.

“One more,” she whispered.

We stood together, and I took her to her son. His eyes wide, hardly breathing, his gaze barely focused on his mother's face.

“I wished for you to be strong and smart, but that turned into ruthlessness too fast for me to stop it. Just like your sister, you've had everything, but instead of hurting out of spite, you hurt out of malice. You chose wrath instead of justice, taking too much in exchange for too little. You don't deserve the soul you have, and I pray that history continues to forget you."

And just like with Xyla, she reached inside his chest and pulled the remainder of his power from him. Idall's orb was much smaller, what I had taken already the majority, and once again Diana put that power in me.

The pain was considerably less, and it was over in moments.

When I opened my eyes, Diana's hand was poised at her own chest. Jude screamed out in protest, the big man clawing at the very earth to get to her, but Diana only gave him a soft smile.

"It was never to be, my sweet man. Your mate is coming soon enough, and when she finally sees you for who you are, you will know that I am right, and you will forgive this."

Then she plunged her fingers into her own chest, her ball of light the biggest of all. But this was the one I didn't want, and even though I tried to back away, she latched on to me as if she hadn't ripped her own soul out of her chest.

This isn't my soul, she said, her thoughts filling my mind. *This is my immortality. This is my power, and I am giving it all to you. This is my apology for all the wrongs I have done to you, for all of the neglect, for what my children have done to you and yours. For what I allowed my husband to do. This is my penance.*

But before I could dispute any of those points, she shoved that power into me, searing my soul with the enormity of it, with the knowledge it brought, with the sight it afforded me. I knew now that this had always been her plan from the very beginning. After she had seen what her husband had done, she had seen it all.

She allowed her children to drop me into Tartarus to make sure I was worthy, allowing my wrath to stay sealed for five thousand years.

She'd watched the stars, waiting for the portal to open, staying silent as she got closer to Corvin, making sure the Crimson Roses were never a threat. She'd orchestrated it all to make sure that I was worthy, that he was.

That the Syndicates would turn him out.

That he would come to Crossroads looking to build a home.

That we would find each other.

Every facet she had made so, and as much as it

was a betrayal, as much as every bit of that hurt the both of us, I couldn't find it in me to hate her for it.

My eyes opened and I watched as Diana deteriorated, her breaths labored, her blood flowing red instead of gold, her immortality gone.

This couldn't stand.

As much as I didn't trust her, as wrong as her actions were, the one thing she didn't deserve was to die.

"Not yet," I hissed, pulling her into my arms as Corvin knelt at my side.

"Storm Cloud, she's—"

"Dying? Yes, I'm aware. But she doesn't have to be. Hold on to me," I ordered.

After searching my gaze for a single moment, Corvin nodded, his strong grip latching onto my shoulder. Closing my eyes, I sought the power she'd given me, accepting it as I allowed it to pull us through space and time, aiming for the very portal that I had once detested.

The guard stumbled back in shock but stood aside as Corvin and I walked right through.

"Caius," I yelled, my voice taking on Diana's and Xyla's and Idall's power, echoing off the stone walls as I begged for my oldest friend to help me in this one task.

Caius appeared out of the shadows, his brow furrowed as he raced to me—to us.

"You've changed, old friend. What's happened to you?"

I shook my head. "I'll tell you everything, just stop her from dying for a little bit. You can decide in a minute whether you want to keep her that way or not."

Confusion lit his features, but he gave me a singular nod, his hand forming a fist. "She won't be going anywhere. Explain."

This one time, I told my oldest friend everything. By the time I was done, Caius was practically apoplectic.

"And you want to *save* her life?" he growled, still holding on to her death as requested. "Have you lost your fucking mind?"

It was a distinct possibility since I had almost lost my mate, thinking clearly probably wasn't happening for the time being, but this felt like the one thing I had to do.

"If you could see what I can see, you'd know. She had to pull threads just right or we would have never found each other. Either that, or I would never be worthy of the power I now hold. I can see it now, the web all laid out in front of me. How she had to move each string one by one so they would all connect together. I'm not saying what she did was right—it wasn't. She was absent at best and negligent at worst, but she can—"

"Atone," Corvin supplied, his hand and mine as I pleaded her case. "She can atone for the wrongs she's done, and she could do it here. You could remake her so she wouldn't be a goddess. She could be a shadow shifter like Styx was, and she could spend the rest of eternity in Tartarus. No more gifts, no more magic, just sharing her body with an animal as she learns what it means to be mortal again."

Caius' eyebrows rose to his hairline, and a slow smile curled his lips into a thoughtful grin.

"I knew I liked you," he muttered before giving me a singular nod.

"I will do as you ask, but only because you have pled her case. If I had my way, she'd be Nog's new chew toy."

Backing away, I left her on the onyx stone as Caius's shadows crept toward Diana, coating her body from head to toe. Her form jolted, her screams echoing off the walls as the snaps and cracks of bones breaking followed suit.

When the shadows faded, Diana's body was in

the form of a charcoal wolf, her fur as black as the Tartarus sky.

"She will start at the prison. When she wakes, she'll work her way up. She has five thousand years to answer for, and she will earn off every single one of them. She will know the meaning of *atonement*," Caius decreed, and I couldn't find it in me to argue.

He had saved her life, what he chose to do with it was now up to him.

"She may not appreciate the gift she's been given," I murmured, staring at the sleeping wolf, wondering if I did the right thing.

"She will. Eventually. Which is why she's going to the prison first. Once she realizes this was the only way, she'll calm down."

I winced, thinking about my own first years here. Hopefully, it wouldn't take her a century to get used to the place.

Caius summoned guards, and they retrieved Diana from the floor, carrying her limp body in the direction of the prison.

Corvin slid an arm around my shoulders, pulling me into his chest as he watched her go. "Come on, Storm Cloud. What do you say we go home?"

Caius snorted, but quickly sobered when I shot him a glare as a boom of thunder shook the entire castle. Yeah, the power had jumped up a notch. I'd need to get a handle on it.

"Sleep and food?" I asked, turning back to my mate, the hopefulness in my tone palpable.

"Not necessarily in that order. I'll even introduce you to pizza. What do you say?"

It sounded like absolute heaven.

Closing my eyes, the web of Diana's—of *my*—power showed me all the possibilities of what was to be.

In each one, was a fair amount of heaven.

CHAPTER 27

CORVIN

aving a primordial god sitting at my kitchen table was never a thing I thought was possible. Then again, a goddess graced my bed every night, so what did I know of possible?

A year ago, I'd thought I'd lost everything. I had no home.

No family.

No pack.

No nothing.

All I'd had was the currency I'd collected over the last two centuries and an amorphous plan that somehow included making a family for myself. Someplace without Syndicates, without the taint of my bloodline, without... my past and my horrible decisions coming back to haunt me every single day.

I'd never expected to find my mate—especially not the very same woman I had been in love with since I was a boy, reading the book of myths my father had gifted me. I had always dreamed of loving a woman like that, and yet, I'd always thought it was out of reach, a hint of a promise never to be.

I'd never expected to succeed in creating this growing pack.

I'd never expected to be happy.

And the sheer number of blessings that had been bestowed upon me continued to boggle my mind.

I refilled Caius' coffee mug, his plate abandoned in front of him as we stared out the window at my mate.

She stood next to the river with Aster and Penny at her side, pointing to where she wanted to create tributaries to help feed the property as she started the clean-up process that she deemed essential for her to continue living here. Bit by bit, the muddy river was becoming new again, changing with every second that she touched it.

But every few minutes, she stopped at whatever piece of junk or debris or new thing she found in the river, bitching to the heavens above about what had been done to her water.

And it *was* her water now.

The entirety of the Mississippi had been claimed by my mate, and as of yet, no one had really tried to fight her on it. Considering she had the power of four separate gods all teeming inside her skin, I hadn't yet found somebody with balls big enough to tell her she couldn't do whatever the fuck she wanted to do.

Granted, no one was dumb enough to do that *before* she'd absorbed their power, so...

The entirety of the river was within the bounds of No Man's Land, save for a few smaller offshoot waterways that she gladly allowed their Houses to keep on the express instruction that they were to be respected. Truth be told, I had a feeling she considered all the water in all the connecting rivers hers, but for political purposes, she was choosing to be flexible.

We were still getting used to Styx's new powers, and there had been some growing pains. For one, my mate was now pretty much immune to fire, Idall's sunlike ability making it difficult for her to discern temperature for the time being. This was why she was never allowed to serve anyone food or drink. A few days ago, Styx had given Penny a cup of tea so scorching, it had nearly scalded the poor girl's skin off, not knowing that the cup was far too hot for anyone else's skin but hers.

Or mine.

The other growing pains would ease as well, and eventually, she'd get a handle on them, but it would take some time—time that she had.

Time that we both had now that she had given me a second chance on life. I rubbed at my chest where Idall's arrow had pierced my heart. Of all the injuries I'd ever received, this was the only one that had left a scar. Every time Styx saw it, her face would get tight, and I knew she was remembering how I'd almost died.

And every time, I would remind her that she herself had saved me. That I was alive, and with her, and I wasn't going anywhere. Usually, that would lead to *other* things. If we kept going at this rate, it was a wonder we'd ever leave our bed.

Styx said something outside that I couldn't catch, and both Penny and Aster tossed their heads back and laughed. My mate turned to look at them, a pleased expression on her face as she watched them closely.

When she wasn't with me, she was spending

time with them, roping Jude in whenever she could. Penny had taken a few days to adjust, the compounding traumas of being assaulted by her mate and then a literal god, a bit too much. Just like all of us, she'd get there, it would just take some time.

Aster, on the other hand, was doing just fine. It had taken longer for her to heal from her wounds than it had for her to begin smiling again. I think she knew that we were always coming for her, and so when her assumption was proven correct, she knew she'd make it out.

Jude was just glad Styx had refused to let Diana die, his hope to be reunited with her one day probably the only thing that was keeping him together. Styx watched him closely, and I figured if there was a problem, I'd be the first person she told about it.

Jude said something to her back, and a bolt of lightning struck the ground not ten feet from him. He scrambled to his feet, his arms raised in surrender, but his smile was genuine.

"Do you think at any point in the next year she's going to stop complaining about that water?" I asked Caius, sitting down next to him with my own cup of coffee.

He rolled his eyes. "She still bitches about shit

that happened three thousand years ago, so no. No, you will be hearing about the monstrosity of that river for the rest of your lives. A mind like a steel-trap, that one."

Considering how filthy that fucking river was even after days of her ministrations, I supposed that was fair. I'd just have to give her new things to bitch about.

Still, Caius couldn't possibly want to watch his friend complain about her undertaking through the window while he ate my food. It was about time for him to get to the point.

"So you wanted to meet on my pack's land for *breakfast* of all things. I have to say, I am very curious as to what you could possibly have to meet with me about."

Caius gave me a speculative look, his black eyes always assessing in one way or another. This close, they almost looked like the cosmos, their glittering depths as frightening as they were interesting.

"I came to offer you a job. You and your pack."

Confused, I took a sip of my coffee as I sat back in my chair.

My pack had grown considerably after the news had spread about the battle at the river. How Styx and my pack had decimated the river pirates, how we'd had taken their leaders to task and killed them all, freeing the community at large from the fear of getting everything they'd ever worked for stolen from them. How we'd helped the survivors at the docks. How we'd taken over the trains, making them safer. How we'd ousted some of the Crimson Roses, too.

Any shifter with a brain in their heads wanted to be in a pack with Alphas like that.

We had new recruits every day coming to beg to be a member of the Blackwell Pack. There were plenty that we turned away, Styx's evaluation of them absolute. Considering the gifts Diana had bestowed upon my mate, Styx now saw all the threads of what the future could be, advising who I should take and who would bring about our ruin.

She never said how, the possibilities too great for her to enumerate, but I listened, grateful for everything she gave me. Grateful for the breath in my lungs. Grateful for every new member.

The pack was now over a hundred members deep and growing by the day. Luckily, we'd already started construction on the cabins to allow for families to stay close to the pack. So far there were very few empty ones with new ones going up as fast as we could get them.

"What job could you possibly have to offer me?" I asked, tilting my head back to the window, watching my mate weave the water in the air as she cleaned it.

"The portal," he began before pausing to take a sip of his coffee. "I require your assistance in guarding it on this side."

This had the air of when the father-in-law offered the new son-in-law a job in his company just to keep his daughter close. Nepotism at its finest, and I told him so. "No offense to you, and I'm not saying no, but this feels kind of like bullshit. I'm not taking her away from you, you know."

"It's not bullshit," he replied, a smile on his face, amused at my analogy. "And I don't think you're taking her away. Soon the Houses will descend on this area as the new portal becomes more widely known. I will need help in defending it by people I trust. I trust Styx, and I trust you. I trust that your pack is best suited for the job."

"Excuse me for pointing this out, but don't you have an entire army of people just waiting on the other side of that portal ready to fuck shit up?"

I'd fought in war games with plenty of them, and considering the lack of lethal force used, they were still the most formidable force I had ever seen in my life.

"Yes, but not all of them are fit to leave Tartarus. With the Houses coming, we would need this world's face on the portal instead of my own. In certain circles, I am still known as the 'Soulless One.' If people from Crossroads help guard the portal, then it looks less like we're about to engage in a full-blown invasion. It helps ease people's minds. People we don't want sniffing around my portal too hard, thinking they can pull a fast one."

And while he had a point... "Yeah, still feels like bullshit." I reminded myself that this was Styx's family, and keeping them close was not a bad idea. Especially if her powers got out of control. "But if you honestly believe that my pack can help, I'll think about it."

"Again, not bullshit. It's politics, which frequently resembles bullshit, so I understand the misconception."

I snorted into my coffee. "You got that right."

"And just so you know, I will be asking Styx to resume her advisory role in my court."

Freezing for a second, I contemplated what that could look like. A pit opened wide in my stomach, as

I feared Styx would be kept from me, feared he planned on taking her away.

I must have conveyed my displeasure at that thought, because he put a quelling hand on my shoulder.

"I just miss my friend. Tartarus isn't the same without her surly demeanor. When I offer her the job, I will request that she live here on this side with you, and only travel back and forth as needed."

That eased my hackles some before I finally got it.

"If you wanted her to be a spy, you could have just said that. With the pack being installed around the portal, and the Houses sniffing around, you want all the info, don't you?"

"Styx said you were smart. I'm glad to see she was right."

Huffing a laugh at the sideways compliment, I rose from my chair to refill my coffee.

It was an odd quiet time in the house where few pack members were awake, still sleeping off the night before. But Styx did love her sunrises. After five thousand years without them, I couldn't blame her.

Each morning, as soon as the sun crested the horizon, she was awake to watch it, the star seeming to call to her more now that she had absorbed so much of Idall's power. I didn't have the same compunction, figuring most of his abilities had burnt up inside me as we fought off death together.

After stirring a spoonful of sugar into the black liquid, I took another sip as I rested a hip against the counter.

"We'll take the job," I answered, knowing that Styx would agree.

Keeping her family close, tying the pack to Tartarus, would give her a sense of home, of unity.

It would make her happy.

And making her happy was my absolute favorite thing to do.

EPILOGUE: STYX

Over the last few months, I had grown used to the pack house being filled with a sea of people. Today, however, it was full to bursting, the mating ceremony set to start as soon as the moon reached its apex.

Guests from all over we're coming to the ceremony—both trusted friends and family from Tartarus, the whole pack, plus dignitaries from a few Houses whose waters fed into my river. But the ones I'd sought out were the Queen and Kings of Destiny and Dragomir.

Corvin had no idea that I'd invited them, and I wanted to intercept the group before there could be an unfortunate incident.

I had been greeting far too many people over the

last few hours, pasting a very fake smile on my face that was due to crack any minute now, until I saw a familiar blond head of hair slicked back into a knot at the base of his skull.

Isaac.

He was flanked by two men and a woman, everyone dressed to the nines as relayed by the invitation. The woman was otherworldly beautiful, with light-blonde hair piled on top of her head, her slitted pupils surveying everything with wonder.

The man to her left was the tallest of the bunch with dark hair and eyes, his gaze searching the crowd for threats. The man to her back was only slightly shorter, his long hair also pulled back, his golden eyes likely seeking out the one person I did not want him to find.

Ronan Rose was Corvin's half-brother, their mother an unfortunate woman I hoped would follow one of the many threads I saw for her to her inevitable miserable ending. None of the lives I saw for her were to her liking, and as someone who didn't enjoy life except for what she could get out of it, she would be unhappy no matter what path she chose.

His brother, though, was different.

As much as I wanted to seek vengeance on my

mate's behalf, his brother was actually a good man. Each thread I saw for him was long and fruitful, his happiness with his mates nearly guaranteed by the universe as a whole.

It just figured that the one person I wanted to punish was actually a stand-up guy.

Excusing myself, I approached the group, moving slowly so my power signature registered. I hadn't yet been able to figure out how to keep the waving red flag of my power under wraps. I had a feeling it was a skill I would need to use sooner rather than later.

Still, when it came to apex predators, it was best not to approach them too quickly.

The woman sensed me first, her nose fluttering as golden scales shimmered over her skin, her eyes glowing with an animal I was very familiar with. She was a dragon.

"You must be Styx," she said, reaching out for my hand with both of her own, her smile wide as she pulled me in for a hug.

Interesting way to take my measure, but I'd allow it.

"We're so happy we received your invitation. I'm glad that Corvin has found a home here."

I wondered what she must think of her brother-in-law, given his part in her near usurping, but she seemed genuine and open, the past not bothering her a bit.

"It's a surprise for him. I know how much he really wanted true family. With his father gone and everything, I just didn't want him to go through the whole day without at least someone from his bloodline."

A part of me still hurt that my family was gone, that they would miss finally seeing me happy. I didn't want that for Corvin.

My gaze found Ronan's. The gold color aside, the shape of his eyes, of his nose, of his chin was very familiar. It was obvious they were related, the resemblance astounding.

Ronan pulled the collar of his tuxedo, seeming unsure for a moment. "I figured he wouldn't be the one to invite me. We didn't exactly end things on good terms. I'm glad to see him find his feet."

I tilted my head, assessing the truth of that statement.

"I wanted to thank you personally," I said, my voice like the threat it most definitely was. "Had you not banished him, I likely would never have met him. We would have been searching for each other for a very long time."

His eyebrows rose to his hairline for a second, and then dropped immediately once thunder rumbled the ground underneath us. Lightning cracked in the air, striking the river three times before the clouds rolled away and the moonlight shined in earnest. Sweat dotted his brow as Isaac let out a snort of laughter.

I gave Isaac a beaming smile, this one not fake for the first time all day. "We need to renegotiate. Your cloaking didn't hide shit. No favor for you."

He seemed offended, pressing a hand to his chest, his smile lingering on his lips, he pointed to the sky where I'd so recently displayed my power. "It's not my fault that you basically signal to the world where you are every time you're pissed off. There's not a cloaking in the universe that can control that."

I narrowed my eyes at him, holding up my thumb and forefinger held barely apart. "A little favor. With conditions. And I get to say no. Deal?"

He pretended to think it over, but he and I both knew that he had no intention of actually asking me for anything.

"I guess, but only because you're family." He elbowed Ronan in the side. "A goddess owes me a favor," he said under his breath, making Ronan roll his eyes. "And luckily, she actually likes me. Unlike *you.*"

"Don't push it," I groused, making the tall man at Cira's side bust out laughing.

Only then did I feel the warmth of Corvin's approach. Turning, I gave him an assessing glance, wondering what he thought of his brother being at his mating ceremony.

I could tell a part of him was pleased. He had always wanted a relationship with Ronan. Now there was a chance that he could have one. The other part of him was conflicted. New York and the Syndicates had rejected him, and it took him a long time to bring himself back from that.

I wrapped an arm around his waist, looking up at those beautiful steel-blue eyes, ones that I would stare at forever.

Ones that had once haunted me.

Ones that I never wanted to live without.

"You scaring our guests, Storm Cloud?"

My smile was devious as I faked innocence. "Who me? *Never.* Just making a point is all."

He dropped a kiss to my lips, not giving that single first shit that he was likely smearing my lipstick. "Sure you are."

I rubbed my thumb against his lips, my skin coming away red.

Yep, I would definitely need to fix my lipstick, but I couldn't find it in me to care even a little.

Because today, I was getting everything I never knew I'd always wanted, breaking every rule I had, every barrier I'd ever made for myself.

And with every thread, with every possibility, with every future, I knew this was the very best one.

The End.

Thank you for reading SHADOW ME! I hope you enjoyed Styx and Corvin's love story. To read a special extended epilogue of Styx and Corvin, join my newsletter HERE.

The following is a list of characters we saw in Shadow Me and their books.

Isaac is BURY ME.
Reagan & Caius is MATE ME.
Legion is HUNT ME.
Oberon is SPURN ME.

I'm thrilled to offer a sneak peek of one of my favorite paranormal romances: BURY ME.

The world ended the night I was born. Coincidence? *I think not.*

Stuck living in the catacombs underneath what used to be NYC, I've managed to stay hidden... and alive... and safe... *ish.*

But when my guardian fails to return from a supply run, I'm forced to contemplate life on the surface.

Worse? Three warriors have infiltrated my home, insisting that I am the last gold dragon they've been searching for. That everything I know–everything I've believed–is a lie. And more?

They each think they're mated... to me.

Bury Me is a spicy standalone paranormal romance in the IV&V universe. You can expect 'touch her and I'll unalive you' vibes and three sinfully hot, super growly mates who will do anything to keep her. Mature themes will be present. Reader discretion is advised.

Sneak Peek of Bury Me

ISAAC

Fate was a cruel bitch, wasn't she?

I should have known at the first taste of the pig's blood who Cira was to me—should have sensed that she was different—but I'd ignored that pull like a dumbass. Now that we were in the middle of this tunnel underneath the city, with her scent in my nose and her fear yanking at my heart...

With Ronan's flame lighting the way, I knew it for certain.

I was a goner.

Her golden eyes were what hit me first. Over the scent of her blood and fear, it was those gorgeous eyes that reached into my chest, ripped out my heart, and stuffed it into her nonexistent pocket. Because I probably should have noticed she was buck-ass naked first.

I didn't.

I should have noticed the unhealing claw marks at her middle that were spilling more blood than she could heal, the useless leg she was dragging behind her as she tried to get away from us. But no, it was those damned eyes shining from a face covered in soot, dirt, filth, and blood. Those eyes that nearly rooted me to the ground and scrambled my brain.

And then her fear finally registered—her need to escape even though she was so close to dying. Everything I thought I knew just fell away. Before I thought better of it, I removed my jacket. I was sure I said something first—trying to calm the situation —but I couldn't remember whatever nonsense had fallen out of my mouth. I just wanted her safe, in my arms, and on our way to a healer. Because death was coming if we didn't get her out of here and pronto.

Slowly I approached, holding out my coat like I was waving the white flag of surrender. As soon as she was covered, I had her in my arms, pulling her from the dirt, letting the brilliant heat of her body filter into me.

Cira latched onto my shirt, clinging to it like I was offering some form of protection. And then the look on Alex's face finally fucking registered. I didn't know what was going on behind those dark eyes or why they were flashing the gold of his animal, but I could smell the rage.

I knew a blood rage when I saw one, and he was millimeters away from doing something stupid.

"Give her to me," he ordered, the thread of Alpha

in his tone like he was the big man and not the youngest among us.

Cira sucked in a frightened gasp as she clung to me, fisting her hand in my shirt like she was afraid I'd let her go. He moved to take her, and I had to fight every instinct inside me to not kill one of my closest friends right where he stood.

As gently as I could, I hugged her closer to me, telling her it would be all right. Only once she'd settled did I look him in the eye. "You try and take her away from me, and I will beat you to death with your own arms. You're scaring the shit out of her. Knock it the fuck off."

Because I knew the truth of the matter just like he did, or maybe he was finally realizing just how fucked this situation was.

Cira didn't have *one* mate. If the way Alex was acting were any indication, she had *two*.

I'd gotten the gist of what Cira's life had been like in these tunnels from that small taste of Vaspir's blood. She was brand new to this world and had no idea who we were or what we wanted. I'd been alone like she had once upon a time, and I wouldn't let my mate feel that way for one second longer than she had to.

Centuries ago, when I was far younger than she

was now, I had been left, too. Granted, my parents hadn't tried to sell me to the highest bidder like her fuck stick of a guardian had. They'd been taken by force, ripped from this life. From me. At present, I was doing my level best to bring down the mother-fucker who'd done it. I'd even infiltrated his clan, posed as an enforcer, and brick by brick, I was going to dismantle him.

Six years ago, I would have sold out both of my closest friends to get revenge.

Three months ago, I would have used this dragon as a bargaining chip to take Clan Tepes down.

Five minutes ago, I had a plan.

But as of thirty seconds ago, there was no chance of me using Cira—not ever.

Well, not unless she asked me to.

Alex—thankfully—took a small step backward, seeming to swallow down the reality of the situation. Cira was hurt. I wasn't even sure we'd make it to a healer in time.

"We're going to help you, sweetheart. Don't you worry," I murmured, clutching her close to my chest, like I could keep her alive with my touch alone.

"I'll call Amala," Ronan offered, pulling a phone from his pocket, his conjured flame following him as he headed back the way we'd come. "She can meet me at one of my properties. It's not far."

But the scent of death clung to her, telling me we didn't have that kind of time. "I don't know if she'll make it," I muttered, tightening my hold on her body as I followed, the coldness seeming to seep from her very bones.

Cira shivered as a pained moan slipped from her lips.

"Fuck," Alex growled, his nose sucking in the scent of death that had nothing to do with the men we passed on our way out—the same ones she'd killed to stay free. "You have to help her."

Rushing to Ronan's SUV, Alex and I helped Cira get in the back while Ronan took the wheel, barely letting us close the doors before he was peeling away from the curb and hauling ass across the bridge.

Given the dead we'd left behind—something that would need to be taken care of at some point—I was glad we weren't staying in Manhattan. Plus, the farther away we were from Clan Tepes, the better.

As we moved, Cira's golden eyes fluttered closed, her fight for consciousness a losing battle as her breathing went from ragged to labored.

"I swear to the gods if you let my mate die in

your arms, I'll fucking kill you," Alex growled, his hands becoming nothing more than the birdlike talons of his griffin as they bit into my shoulder.

"What?" Ronan barked from the front, weaving through cars and obstacles like we had a tail on our asses.

I shook him off. "In case it wasn't clear to you, Cira doesn't have just one mate. You'd think having a sister with three mates you'd clue in, but *nooooo*... And I'm not letting *my* mate die on my watch."

Without further ado, I ripped into my forearm with my fangs, making sure the wound was big enough to not close too quickly. Alex peeled the jacket away from Cira's middle, letting the blood drip on the worst of the injuries. To a lesser shifter or Fae, this wound could have easily caused more blood loss than their weaker bodies could handle. Even younger vampires could lose consciousness at the amount of blood pouring out of her.

She was strong.

Strong enough to live, dammit.

She might not accept the mate bond—she could easily reject me if she had a mind to. But I wasn't going to lose her—not like this. I knew this was the magic of the mate bond, Fate's cruel hand dealing me another blow, making me prioritize a woman I hadn't even known about an hour ago over a centuries-long blood feud. But I couldn't deny I'd longed for a connection like this—something tethering me to something bigger than my own hate.

Cira just had to live long enough.

The worst of the wounds started knitting back together, the blood from the both of us slowing to nothing. The tightness in her body eased a little, and she melted into me, her eyes fluttering open as golden scales shimmered across her skin. Those eyes carried a slit pupil for a moment before going round again.

Alex broke our stare, putting my jacket back over her middle, adding his own to the mix. Cira flinched at his hand on her ankle, but it wasn't in fear. No, I'd finally figured out why the limb had been useless as she'd dragged it behind her in the tunnel.

There had been a Man of War shifter in the pile of dead bodies in the antechamber. He'd been the one with a battle-ax embedded in his chest. We—Ronan, Alex, and I—used Man of War venom to hinder healing and paralyze people when we needed information from them. There was only one Man of War shifter I knew of in Syndicate territory, and he was probably dead in that tunnel. And he just so happened to run with a faction of shifters trying to take over Manhattan.

Fabulous.

"We're taking you to a healer," Alex growled, his dark gaze locked on Cira like he'd love to rip her out of my arms. "Nod if you understand."

Cira gripped my shirt tighter, but nodded all the same.

"No one is going to hurt you again, sweetheart," I added, trying to soften whatever the fuck was going on with Alex. "Promise."

Cira's eyes nailed me to the seat, her expression telling me that she didn't believe that for a second.

"You did good defending yourself. I take it you're the one doing the handiwork with the axe?" I asked, trying to make conversation. "Six on one. I know seasoned fighters who couldn't handle that."

Her gaze shuttered as she pulled my jacket closer to her chest.

"He means it," Ronan said from the driver's seat. "Taking out six fighters by yourself—especially those ones—is no small task."

Cira blushed a bit—hard to do with so much blood loss, but she did it.

"The healer will fix you all up," Alex murmured, patting her uninjured foot, his hand human-shaped now that she was out of the woods."

Three minutes—which seemed like an eternity—and we were at one of the Rose properties, the dainty healer with her medicine bag waiting for us at the entrance. Amala was ancient—not that she looked it—knowledgeable, and the best healer money could buy. Granted, her talents leaned toward the necromancy bent, but she'd diversified a bit out of necessity. She'd saved our asses more times than I could count, and she was great on privacy.

Well, that, and she'd made a deal with Ronan. He'd never tell us what she'd asked for, but Amala had always been there for us when we'd needed her. We didn't typically deal with the Outcast Coven, but Amala was different.

"Are you fucking kidding me with this shit?" Amala griped as Alex exited the SUV, helping Cira and I out. She huffed into the building, eyeing Cira with contempt as all five of us piled into the elevator. "You bring me a naked girl covered in blood who seems *not* near death like you told me she was, Ronan."

Ronan simply shrugged, letting his head fall back to rest on the elevator wall. "She *was* dying.

Isaac gave her blood so she didn't die in the car, but she has a Man of War tentacle embedded in her leg and gods know what else. How about you do your job and quit bitching about it?"

By the time we'd made it to the penthouse, Alex was practically vibrating with rage, I still hadn't let Cira go, and Ronan was clearly tired of all of us. Amala procured the first bedroom on the left, instructing me to set Cira down on the bed so she could get to work.

That, I was having trouble with. I wanted her to be seen. I wanted Cira to be all fixed up, but...

Letting her go was becoming more and more of a problem.

"Is it okay with you if I leave you with Amala?" I asked, hoping Cira would say no.

Slowly, she nodded, her eyes darting around the room. But the scent of fear was absent, so reluctantly, I placed her on the bed.

"We'll be right outside if you need anything, okay?" I couldn't say why I wanted to reassure her, but I did. Eventually, I let her go, leaving her with Amala like I was ripping out my own heart and serving it up on a platter.

By the time Amala shoved me out the door, I had

to stave off the urge three times not to fight my way back in that room.

And as soon as the door closed, I got a little dose of reality.

Cira had two mates, and her other one was pissed the fuck off.

His chosen method of expressing that fact?

A fist right to my face.

START READING BURY ME NOW

BOOKS BY ANNIE ANDERSON

IMMORTAL VICES & VIRTUES

HER MONSTROUS MATES

Bury Me

SHADOW SHIFTER BONDS

Shadow Me

THE ARCANE SOULS WORLD

GRAVE TALKER SERIES

Dead to Me

Dead & Gone

Dead Calm

Dead Shift

Dead Ahead

Dead Wrong

Dead & Buried

SOUL READER SERIES

Night Watch

Death Watch

Grave Watch

THE WRONG WITCH SERIES

Spells & Slip-ups

Magic & Mayhem

Errors & Exorcisms

THE LOST WITCH SERIES

Curses & Chaos

Hexes & Hijinx

THE ETHEREAL WORLD

PHOENIX RISING SERIES

(Formerly the Ashes to Ashes Series)

Flame Kissed

Death Kissed

Fate Kissed

Shade Kissed

Sight Kissed

ROGUE ETHEREAL SERIES

Woman of Blood & Bone

Daughter of Souls & Silence

Lady of Madness & Moonlight

Sister of Embers & Echoes

Priestess of Storms & Stone

Queen of Fate & Fire

ACKNOWLEDGMENTS

A huge, honking thank you to the crew that holds me together (it's with duct tape, but together...) Shawn, Barb, Jade, Angela, Kelly, Erin, and Heather.

You know what you did.

Every single one of you rock and I couldn't have done it without you.

Also, I have to give a special thank you to Jade B. from The Legion reader group for naming Nadia's/Diana's bookshop.

ABOUT THE AUTHOR

Annie Anderson is the author of the international bestselling Rogue Ethereal series. A United States Air Force veteran, Annie pens fast-paced Paranormal Romance and Urban Fantasy novels filled with strong, snarky heroines and a boatload of magic. When she takes a break from writing, she can be found binge-watching The Magicians, flirting with her husband, wrangling children, or bribing her cantankerous dogs to go on a walk.

To find out more about Annie and her books, visit www.annieande.com

facebook.com/AuthorAnnieAnderson

instagram.com/AnnieAnde

amazon.com/author/annieande

bookbub.com/authors/annie-anderson

goodreads.com/AnnieAnde

pinterest.com/annieande

tiktok.com/@authorannieanderson

patreon.com/annieanderson